Praise for Noelle Mack

"A sexy romp on the wild side . . . compelling characters. Mack does an excellent job. A true page-turner."
—*Romantic Times*, a Top Pick! 4 ½-star review on *Nights in Black Satin*

"Dangerously delicious!"
—Shannon McKenna on *Nights in Black Satin*

"Sizzling and innovative . . . this is a winner."
—*Romantic Times* on *Juicy*, a Top Pick! 4 ½-star review

"Incredibly sensual and well-done."
—*Romantic Times* on Noelle Mack's novella in *The Harem*

"Mack does a great job of blending sensuality, sexuality, and humor . . . to create memorable characters and stories that are romantically satisfying."
—*Romantic Times* on *Red Velvet*, four-star review

"A truly sensual story that will titillate and captivate readers."
—*Romantic Times* on *Three*, four-star review

"The queen of seduction meets the king of rakes. Sensual, sexual, stupendous."
—Harriet Klausner Reviews on *Three*

One Wicked Night

NOELLE MACK

APHRODISIA
KENSINGTON BOOKS
http://www.kensingtonbooks.com

APHRODISIA BOOKS are published by

Kensington Publishing Corp.
850 Third Avenue
New York, NY 10022

Copyright © 2008 by Noelle Mack

All Kensington Titles, Imprints, and Distributed Lines are available at special quantity discounts for bulk purchases for sales promotions, premiums, fund-raising, and educational or institutional use.

Special book excerpts or customized printings can also be created to fit spe-cific needs. For details, write or phone the office of the Kensington special sales manager: Kensington Publishing Corp., 850 Third Avenue, New York, NY 10022, attn: Special Sales Department, Phone: 1-800-221-2647.

Aphrodisia and the A logo Reg. U.S. Pat & TM Off.

ISBN-13: 978-0-7582-1773-8
ISBN-10: 0-7582-1773-0

First Kensington Trade Paperback Printing: January 2008

10 9 8 7 6 5 4 3 2 1

Printed in the United States of America

For JWR, and why not?

AUTHOR'S NOTE

Meet Lord Edward Delamar, who first appeared in THREE, having a very good time with Lady Fiona. This story happened before he met her—but if you look closely, you will find her in ONE WICKED NIGHT.

1

It began with one night. But what man would stop there? Not I, not then, for I was just twenty and not yet schooled in the infinite variety of pleasure. My sensual education began upon the stroke of twelve during that long-ago encounter. The lady and I loved each other well in that one wicked night. My beautiful tutor was someone I cannot name, wanton in all her ways but necessarily discreet, as she taught me to be.

In six hours with her I learned more than most men learn in six years of vigorous whoring, or during the sort of fashionable *affaires de coeur* that so seldom involve that most vulnerable of human organs, the heart. She was somewhat older than I and far more experienced, and she taught me well, pleased to have such an eager student who wanted to learn everything at once. My dear love—she was my first love—did her best in the brief time that we had.

Of course, we had known each other, although not intimately, for a while before she acted upon her secret passion, having guessed my feelings for her. Until our first kiss, I had never experienced such ardent tenderness. A decade later, I remember it well.

I am straightforward as a rule, but only the most romantic words serve to describe her, such were her charms. Where to begin? She had eyes the sweet brown of meadow honey, and unruly hair like afternoon sunshine, golden and long. My hand was lost in her tresses when she let her hair down and allowed me to touch her for the first time. But it was her open-hearted nature that captivated me most of all, expressed to perfection by a voice so soft and mellow that . . . ah, a man never forgets his first love, it is said. If he is given to writing, as I am, she will appear again and again, in many different guises.

She is in this book. But no—I cannot very well bestow the name of Book upon the heap of miscellaneous paper presently upon my desk, at my right hand. A casual look through it reveals pages and pages of my private musings upon my affair with a very different woman: Lady X. There are also rough drafts of erotic tales I wrote to please *that* insatiable female, penning the finished versions in a little volume of which there is only one copy. And, of course, many amorous missives from me, read attentively and promptly returned—my darling X was not the sort of female who bound such things in silk ribbon and sighed over them.

All were written in secret. My crest does not appear upon the cream-colored paper that makes up so much of the pile, mingled with torn pages from lewd chapbooks that she sent her maid to buy. I often wondered what the girl thought of those. She could not read but the illustrations made the subject quite clear.

A faint scent of perfume still clings to the note-sheets on which my darling scribbled sexual fantasies of her own that aroused me to the point of fever, a fever that only she could cure. Many of her notes bear only a swiftly penned message. *Come to me.* Words that I kissed each time I received them.

We are all doomed to remember our greatest joy, the mingling of our soul with that of another, when we are utterly alone, as I am now. Perhaps solitude has led me to attempt to make sense of it all. Certainly several of the stories I wrote were inspired by the Lady X, although other lovely creatures appear in them now and again.

It has been whispered that only I am privileged to know the intimate desires of the most sensual and daring women in London. Perhaps it is so. Some of these wantons are entirely fictional, but many are real, masquerading under different names and costumes. They, and the pages on which they appear in promiscuous array, crowd my mind as well as my desk.

I would be rid of them all. When I am done, I shall consign every page, every memento of her and the others, to the fire. Erotica created by a sensual imagination may well make the hottest blaze of all.

Ah, the myriad sources of my inspiration might not be pleased if they knew of their ultimate end in a drawing-room grate. But they will never know. It is not masculine boasting to say that I bedded many women in the ten years that passed since the night of my initiation. My heart, however, had remained untouched. It could be argued that my dear Lady X thought me, a rake with a deservedly wicked reputation, essentially naïve and easy to deceive. She was a highly intelligent woman.

Once our affair was over, I could scarcely comprehend what had happened between us. And so I collected these papers and began to reread them, adding to them here and there for my own edification and for no other reason. Certainly not for publication—do I repeat myself? I am a man of honor, and every lady's secrets are safe with me.

Some minutes later . . .

I have returned with a glass of brandy that will fortify me to look more closely through my odd collection. I especially treasure the stories that Lady X set down in a fine, light hand that brings back the memory of her touch, something I would like very much to forget. But I find I cannot. Not yet.

Damnation! I have knocked over the glass—

The fumes ignited, owing to the shortness of the candle, which had burned low. The hour is late. For a few seconds, a blue fire danced over the surface of my desk but I pushed the hodgepodge of paper to the floor in time. However, I will take the mishap as a sign of sorts: I must be careful.

In any event, a trustworthy friend, Richard Whiston, who is also my secretary, has instructions to destroy my personal ephemera upon my death, if I have not done so first. Only he and I have keys to the safe hiding place to which I return the collection when I am done leafing through it and scribbling. Having rescued it this very night from untimely destruction, I suppose I should pick it all up and sort it as best I can . . . my contributions in one pile, Xavi's in another . . .

There, I have done so—got it back upon the desk, if not sorted it—and finished the brandy in the decanter. After some moments of reflection I find I have not the heart to separate my things from hers. The task could be accomplished quickly. The writings of Lady X—she did beg me to destroy them, which I will in due time—are easy enough to distinguish from mine, owing to the different paper and the delightful small sketches that sometimes enlivened them. Here is one of hers—it has jumped to the top of the pile!—a drawing of a fetching little whore in black stockings and nothing else. She very much resembles X, who told her stories from a feminine point of view, of course, providing a highly stimulating counterpoint to mine. She had a rare talent for becoming anyone she pleased.

My naughty inamorata was *the* Lady X, of course. Notorious. Uncommonly lovely. And for a while, the talk of London.

The scandal sheets never printed her full first names, Xaviera Innocencia, let alone her last.

Don Diego Mendez y Cartegna was her husband, a grandee in his own land, a person of great influence in ours as the Peninsular Wars dragged on.

Don Diego prided himself on his jealous supervision of his young wife. Nonetheless, Xavi assured me that after he had taken her virginity—adding that it was without a doubt the most unpleasant five minutes of her life—she never went again to his great gilt bed, knowing that her side of it was sure to be occupied by a housemaid or some other unfortunate female who did not have the power to refuse the lord and master of the household.

So perhaps her infidelity was justified—she thought so and I was not inclined to argue the point. My feelings for her had been sparked in an instant and the fire between us leaped high for many months. Yet our passion was unequal and it was clear from the beginning that I loved her rather more than she loved me. At least she was truthful about that.

Her desire for sex was more than a match for mine. Hence the little blank book in which I wrote, at her request and for her amusement, of amorous adventures. Rescued, it sits on the other side of my desk, holding down a ream of my preferred paper: foolscap. The word is appropriate. Love is a fool's game, no matter one's skill at it.

In that arena, I would call myself simply lucky, although there were women who told me—their fervent words, not mine—that my magnificent build and remarkable height and handsomeness and so forth and so on were enough to make them swoon. Romantic flattery, nothing more. Some females need a reason to be overcome, and if my appearance met with their approval, then well and good.

I myself do not set much store by physical perfection, being attracted just as much by intelligence and high spirits—the quality the French call *joie de vivre*—and the way a woman carried herself. If, underneath her frills and furbelows, a female of new acquaintance seemed quite at home in her own skin, as lithe as a healthy animal and as bold, then I marked her as mine.

Xavi had all those qualities and a sultry beauty of her own that set her apart from English women. She was outwardly demure; inwardly, not at all. She called to mind the most outrageous erotic fantasies.

Naked from the waist down, straddling a chair . . . her full breasts bared and held up high by her tight stays, her nipples turned deep pink from the light tugging and rolling between my fingers . . . her soft lips, parted to tell me what she wanted . . . ah, I envisioned her just in that way at the moment I saw her.

I happened to be visiting the studio of my good friend, Everett Quinn, a portrait painter of note. Men who had risen far above their humble beginnings, millionaire brewers and the like, came to him for gilt-framed ancestors to hang on the walls of their new country houses. Any ancestors would do, so long as their painted faces suggested a distinguished pedigree.

Bewigged, ruffed, clad in courtly velvet or sober Jacobean black, the subjects were entirely imaginary but they bore an unmistakable resemblance to whoever had commissioned them in the first place. Quinn's skill at reinventing a given set of features through the centuries was unrivaled and he commanded high fees.

He also did the portraits of actresses lucky enough to bag a peer or wealthy lover. These men paid well to have their women immortalized at the height of their beauty and fame. Quinn had a knack for making them look altogether respectable at the same time, to everyone's amusement.

It was at his studio that I first glimpsed Xavi. Quinn was seldom alone there, and various people came and went at all hours. There was an older woman, a Miss Reynaud, who did the drawings for the engraved reproductions of his paintings, which were peddled in the print shops; and Rob Hutchenson, the apprentice who mixed his colors and did the other dirty work; and his models, human and otherwise. For a while Quinn had kept two small spotted pigs he'd needed for a rustic landscape. They clattered about on the bare wood floors and stuck their snouts into everything and he'd had to give them away.

But on that day only the apprentice was there, a lad of nineteen or so who showed me in without taking my hat or my greatcoat. He didn't bother to introduce me to a pretty girl, neatly dressed, who I took to be a ladies' maid. Not of the more fashionable French type, to be sure, and new to her calling— the girl had an air of the Surrey countryside about her and seemed English to the bone. She sat quietly in a straight-backed chair and did not look up as I passed by. I assumed she had been brought along to give the appearance of propriety.

No doubt the subject of Quinn's latest commission was in the next room. I wondered idly who it might be this time as I pushed aside the heavy curtain that blocked the door.

Quinn was always working and there were many paintings propped against the walls, some framed and some not. He liked to fiddle with them and add improvements: dabbing rosy cheeks on the plainer females and painting breasts upon females not thus blessed by Mother Nature, who had not thought to buy a pair of artificial ones in the shops to fill out their bodices.

But the woman I glimpsed in the center of the room needed no help of that kind with her complexion or her figure. Calling a halloo, I entered without further ado—Quinn cared nothing for social niceties—and then stopped and stared.

She was sitting on a raised platform in perfect stillness, her exquisite profile turned into the light that flooded the room from the high, north-facing windows, so that she did not see me looking at her. I was thunderstruck. She was remarkably beautiful, almost exotic, and her body, even clothed, was utterly graceful in seated repose.

Motionless and silent, she scarcely seemed to breathe, but I perceived the slight rise and fall of her bosom when I came back to my senses. I turned my back to her and mouthed a question to Quinn. *Who is she?*

He winked at me, noticing my obvious interest, and put down his brush and palette to answer, thinking for a moment before he raced through the syllables of a very long Spanish name, the sort of name which included ancestors and in-laws and several Catholic saints. She had just come to England, he explained. They had exchanged only a few words—sit here, look there—and he did not think she spoke or understood much English.

I looked over his shoulder at the woman whose outline was sketched upon the canvas supported by Quinn's easel. Her gaze rested now upon two finished, nearly life-size portraits hanging on a wall of the studio, a matched set meant to convey the appearance of happy matrimony between the earl and the countess depicted. I had to smile. I knew both of them, though not well. In any case, their names—or the first letters of their names, followed by unsubtle dashes—frequently popped up in the press, which gleefully chronicled their affairs with others and their noisy public squabbling.

Xavi studied the portraits thoughtfully. Something about her deliberate consideration of the two, as if she were assessing everything from the sitters' clothes to their character, suggested a considerable intelligence and made me think that she did understand us. But I could not stop Quinn from continuing blithely on, although he kept his voice low.

The lady who sat so patiently upon his platform was the wife of the Spanish ambassador, he explained. The man was descended from an ancient family of Castile and was a disgusting old goat—

"Have you met him, Quinn?"

"No. He sends payment through an intermediary."

"What is his name?"

"The intermediary? He is called Vendela, I think—"

"Not him, her husband."

"Oh—"

I barely heard my talkative friend say her husband's name because Xavi had turned to look at me at last. Quinn chattered on, but she spoke not a word, observing me calmly with large dark eyes. Her lustrous black hair was swept up in a thick coil that left the nape of her neck adorned with a curl or two that I suddenly, passionately, longed to kiss. I had never seen so beautiful a woman, yet even a passing flirtation with this one was entirely out of the question.

Even if her husband's name had barely registered—I did know I had never met the man—Don Diego's position at court had. Although I did not spend time there, my own interests were at stake in those important circles, having to do with the manufacture of munitions—but I will say no more on that subject. My business affairs are recorded elsewhere and those papers will not be burnt. Suffice it to say that my plans were likely to make me a wealthy man. Or so I hoped. Like many a nobleman, I had inherited a distinguished title but little more.

I considered the matter for a moment, while I wondered where she lived. Dallying with the wives of powerful men was best done at some distance from London if it was to be done at all. Most of us took our pleasure with women who were not received in polite society in any case.

But someone like Lady X would be welcomed in the highest circles. Her looks alone ensured that she would be a sought-after guest at elegant soirees and balls, and surely she was about to burst upon the social scene. Being the wife of Don Diego might keep predatory males at a respectable distance, if he was as passionate and vengeful as Spaniards were reputed to be. But what had Quinn just called him? A disgusting old goat? I felt pity for her.

Gazing at Xaviera Innocencia, drinking her in, it occurred to me then that even had she not been married, she was very different from the brave little butterflies of London who flitted from one dance partner to the next, their fragile wings growing more tattered with each season, until at last they vanished into the brothels or married some poor but dashing officer past his prime as well.

She seemed to possess an inner strength that puzzled me not a little. I noted her air of reserve, attributing it to her youth and the strictures of the convent in which she had undoubtedly been shut away for her schooling, in the custom of her country. Married young, I mused, she'd had no time to invite the admiration of men.

That she was accompanied by a young and pretty ladies' maid and not a hideous duenna of mature years was also something that puzzled me. Virtuous Spanish ladies were well-guarded. The modicum of freedom that we Englishmen permitted our women, single or married, was not her lot in life. But the girl I had seen on my way in seemed too naïve for the task.

Lady X might easily give a chit like that the slip. Don Diego's beautiful wife had a sensual look in her eyes that mesmerized me. Her dark gaze held mine until Quinn took me by the arm and broke the spell.

Never one to stand on ceremony, he introduced me, talking loudly as if that would help her understand. She listened to him with polite indifference and looked me over so thoroughly that I grew erect and was forced to hold my hat over the front of my breeches so as not to give offense.

A faint, very faint, smile appeared on her curving lips.

I straightened my spine and fought to compose myself as she turned her face away, resuming her study of the paintings on the wall. Miss Reynaud came and went in silence, taking Quinn's preliminary drawings for the portrait with her. She seldom spoke. In fact, she was so nondescript that she seemed to possess the power of invisibility, a standing joke of Quinn's when the copyist was out of earshot.

To keep from staring at Lady X, I too studied the portraits of the earl and his countess, hoping to dampen the amorous fire within me. They had once loved each other wildly, had been so ardent, in fact, that they seldom came down to dinner at country house parties and were sometimes seen disporting themselves in the shrubbery. But, done in oils for posterity, their bland countenances betrayed nothing of their passionate past or their famously unpleasant quarrels in the present.

All love affairs were variations on that theme, I told myself, stealing another long look at Lady X. She ignored my conversation with Quinn, which was just as well. My few words to him were neither witty nor wise, addled as I was by her unexpected presence.

Perhaps Quinn understood. Waving a brush whose bristles were stiff and prickly with dried paint, he told her to step down and walk about to keep from tiring. Inwardly I gasped as she rose from her seat and arranged the folds of her gown about herself. The stuff of which it was made was not sheer, but neither was it impervious to the strong light that flooded the room. Her body was outlined beneath it, curving and strong. My hands tingled, alive with my instantaneous desire to caress her all over and give her the ultimate pleasure . . . I nearly dropped my hat.

Quinn, damn him, offered at that moment to take it and my coat, saying he would send his lad out for some tea for the lady and heartier refreshments for me, if I wished. I hesitated, then said yes. If I were to see the Lady X again, it was likely to be in circumstances that were far less intimate and easy. The idea of bowing and scraping to her and her distinguished husband at a ball, observing the necessary courtesies and making awkward conversation, was not at all to my liking.

By great good fortune, I had happened to meet her here first. No one but my friend Quinn could observe what I said and did—well, there was her maid, but I supposed the girl could be bribed and did not like her Spanish master in any case.

And perhaps the apprentice could be bribed as well to take the maid for a walk in the park—and if Quinn should happen to go out for ale and cheese at the pub on the corner, the Lady X and I might contrive to—I reminded myself that she spoke very little English.

As it happened, matters proceeded in precisely that way, and I soon found out that Xavi knew far more than she let on . . .

A month later, we became lovers, meeting first at Quinn's studio by his invitation but when he was out. He was pursuing an affair of his own with a badly behaved duchess who had sat for her portrait and taken a fancy to him. She, a former artist's model who flung off her clothes at the slightest opportunity, did not seem to mind the smell of turpentine and the splashes of paint everywhere.

But Xaviera did, expressing her displeasure in excellent if charmingly accented English. The nuns—I write the word with a smile—had taught her well, or so she said. All to the good, as I spoke no Spanish. As I wished only to please her in every way, I made a few discreet inquiries and another friend offered the use of his house in town, an anonymous three-story building on a quiet street. He asked no questions before providing me with a double set of keys, understanding without my saying so that my request must remain a private matter and no more was said. Xaviera assured me that her husband was preoccupied with intrigues of his own, both political and amorous. He would never know. I chose to believe her.

Once she had proposed that I write a book just for her—the small volume that I mentioned—we devised our method of exchanging it quickly enough. Xavi liked to read such tales at her leisure, preferring those I penned to all others. Thus she was always prepared for me, fully aroused, rosy with lust and eager for my caresses when at last I could steal away to the secluded house to which we had the keys. The place was impeccably furnished but otherwise empty, as my friend never came there, preferring his mistress's apartments in Soho.

From time to time, we made solo visits, heading straight for the locked cabinet in the library where we would leave sealed letters for each other, billets-doux with practical postscripts that set the times of our meetings in advance. The arrangement required no assistance from servants who might or might not be trustworthy, and it proved to be mutually—and highly—satisfying.

As did the tales of lust and love that slowly filled the pages of the little book. As the months went on, I penned many stories for her private amusement, some too long to fit in the book as they were written. Once edited, they were added, but I kept the longer versions as well, splotched with ink and crossed-out words—ah, here is the first of those—and the thirty-first, thrown together by chance. I will read them later.

Xavi begged not to appear in any, by name or by description, should she be caught while reading them and her illicit pastime revealed. If that had happened, Don Diego would be sure to express his wrath in the traditional way, tying my poor Xavi face down upon the seat of a chair that she might study the design of his carpet while he rolled up his sleeves to prepare for the necessary punishment. Of course the old brute would ignore her feminine protests, caring nothing for her dignity. Up would go her skirts and down would come his hand upon the sensitive skin of her bare bottom, chastising her in a way that would not be at all to her liking. The lady preferred such attentions to come from me, of course, and to be given with love and subtle consideration for her pleasure, never in anger.

She loved to lie naked over my lap and I loved to serve as her chair, whether I was clothed or not. She pronounced herself comforted by the tight hold of my arm and warmed by my thighs, to say nothing of the immense erection trapped between them. It often took all my self-control to keep from ejaculating against her soft belly, as she bucked with the pleasure she took in a properly administered spanking.

Xavi very much enjoyed them, and that was but one of many outré scenarios in which she delighted. For myself, reddening her pretty bottom as she commanded me to do was an intense satisfaction as well. I endeavored to explore each one of her sexual fantasies to her satisfaction, in writing and in the flesh.

She vowed that my stories brought her to a pitch of excitement that had her lifting her gown the moment I entered the house for a rendezvous. When I had tempted her well and truly, she endeavored to return the favor by tempting me with the sight of her pretty cunny and the tiny red ribbon she sometimes tied in her short curls to expose her clitoris. I loved to see its tender tip peeping out, swollen with need, as she held her skirts high and begged for me to suckle it.

Kneeling before her, I did just that while she clutched my head and moaned with soft joy. Burying my face between her legs to savor every drop of her juice, licking and sucking with all the skill I possessed, I held and caressed her beautiful arse, squeezing her shapely buttocks. With my hands, I encouraged her to push freely against my loving mouth so that I could suck her to climax even before I fondled her breasts and nipples.

My darling Xavi was shameless to a fault, wanting more and more—sometimes more than an ordinary man could give. Is it boastful to say that I always rose to the occasion? Then I will boast. I often gave her a swift orgasm to start, so that her next would be that much stronger when I thrust into her, while she lay on her back or rocked on all fours, whichever she preferred. An aroused woman is both snug and juicy, the best and most stimulating sheath for a long, thick cock like mine.

I liked to fuck Xavi slowly at first, especially from behind, until tears of pleasure ran down her lovely face. Gently, always gently, I pulled her long black hair away from her face so I could see her cry, see the streaks upon her flushed cheeks, and how she licked them away from her panting mouth.

It aroused me beyond belief to see her well-fleshed arse shake as her hungry cunny took me deeper, and when she began to push back, moaning like an animal, I would go faster, clasping her hips to pull her tightly against my groin, and ram hard. Her breasts bounced freely and I dropped over her back to slap them with one hand, pulling on a nipple when I could catch one, nipping her ear.

Wanton as a cat in heat, she kept her face in a pillow to muffle her cries when I rose up and began again. She knew what I wanted then: for her to reach round and spread her buttocks for me as I swived on. The sight of her arsehole, pulsing and tightening in rhythm with the cunny filled up and banged hard by my unbearably stiff cock, spurred me to a dominating intensity that excited her to new heights. She came first, brought to ecstasy by my teasing fingers, and then I did, pounding with frantic haste, my balls no longer swinging, drawn tight between my thighs.

Still, my hands craved the feel of her skin and I caressed her trembling buttocks over and over, grateful that she knew just how to brace herself against my body, crying out as each hot jet of cum spurted forth inside her. At such moments, I lost all sense of the boundaries between us . . . we were truly one.

Is it any wonder I was so devoted to Lady X? She, in turn, craved my full attention. Was she devoted to me? Yes, in her way, when free time and our mutual desire coincided. In the meantime, she had the book, so small that she could keep it in a pocket concealed within each of her gowns. Since my numerous letters had to be returned with dispatch, it pleased me to know that its fine leather bindings were warmed by her body when she retained it, the little book swinging near her most intimate flesh.

When I had it in my keeping, I fancied that the very pages gave off her scent, a mixture of delicate female sweat and the smell of her cunny, the French soap she used, and even the starch that stiffened the fine linen of her petticoats.

I envied those petticoats. Her round-cheeked arse brushed against them, sat firmly upon them, all day. When not fucking her, it was my delight to have her sit just as firmly upon my face and take my tongue deep inside for a good session of cunnilingus, which is every lady's delight. Xavi wiggled her behind while I did so, and I brought her down to enfold my face in bountiful flesh while I squeezed and caressed it—her skin was most sensitive there.

Shyly, she sometimes asked that I slip a fingertip just inside the snug puckers of her tempting little arsehole . . . then go deeper . . . then begged to have the whole length of my finger moving in and out. Thus probed, my tongue thrusting away, she reached a strong climax within seconds, strong enough to make her cunny squeeze my tongue just as it had done to my cock.

The sensation intrigued her and one day she requested that I stimulate only her arse and her arsehole, curious to see if she could have an orgasm in that way alone. As it turned out, she could not, but we enjoyed very great pleasure in the attempt, beginning with the softest of caresses and progressing to tingling slaps with one hand while the longest finger of the other probed her tender anus as deeply as she wished. My slaps had to be light enough to leave no mark. I took no chances on our being discovered. Still, I wanted to satisfy her, and well she knew it.

How quickly Xavi learned to tease me! Employing my technique upon herself at another time, she twisted round to give me a wanton look over her shoulder and licked her slender finger, pulling it in and out of her mouth. Then she set her knees far apart to help spread the rosy buttocks I had just spanked . . . and reached to touch the little hole between them with her wetted fingertip. Her action sufficed to make my cock spring up to full attention. I was wild with lust, compelled to hold my rod with painful tightness and even dig my fingernails into its skin to keep from ejaculating freely at that second.

Xavi glanced down at my cock and only shrugged, playing the role of bitch to her heart's content. But her indifference excited me. Still holding my cock, I squeezed my balls hard until they ached unpleasantly, lest I shoot too soon. She only laughed, again looking at me over her shoulder.

I looked back but only for a second. She wanted me to stare at her hot arse and what she was doing to herself, and I did. Then—oh, I was nearly undone—then Xavi pushed her slick finger well inside the snug hole, up to the second knuckle, and asked me how I liked seeing her do that.

I made her pull her finger out and I believe she enjoyed what came next. I fucked her cunny for a full hour, my gaze focused upon her stimulated, pulsing arsehole, and my hands clasping and squeezing her womanly buttocks nearly hard enough to bruise them. Such pretty peaches—I dropped down over her back and supported myself on my hands so that her body would appear untouched to other eyes when we were done rutting like animals. I came again and again, three times to her four. Spent at last, I cradled her for as long as I dared.

But I did not always have my cock in her cunny or my head between her legs or my finger up her naughty arse. When our mutual desire for each other was fully satisfied, when we had the precious gift of time, we walked and talked like all lovers, grateful for our borrowed hideaway. We preferred the overgrown garden where we could not be seen from nearby houses, or the spacious rooms downstairs if the weather was inclement. She would play the piano and sing for me—her voice was a balm to me, melodic and merry. Xavi delighted in the gossip of London, and I was rather good at representing the conversations I had overheard, leaving out not a scrap of scandal.

Some served as bawdy inspiration for the stories I penned. I marveled at how mere words could work such wonders—but then, the sensual imagination of a woman is easily stimulated by one who knows how. After each rendezvous, Xavi would sometimes ask for a particular scenario. I would write another tale or two, and leave the book or loose pages in the locked cabinet at the house where we met, allowing her to peruse it when she could get away, and think about the fantasy until we met again.

Imagining her slender hand slipping down to stimulate herself while she read was a favorite fantasy of mine. I loved to think of her blushing, and then, overcome, pressing immodestly against a sofa pillow or rubbing herself through her dress, too aroused to wait for me. Should she feel the pangs of lust too keenly, Xavi would employ an ivory rod to enjoy complete penetration while she read. I had presented her with the thing myself, an indecent but thoughtful gift, as I was sometimes away and did not want my love to yearn too long for the sexual satisfaction she craved so . . .

I had left the book in the locked cabinet, our usual place, adding a few more lascivious details to a scenario that I thought we both might find highly entertaining, should it be her pleasure to indulge me. The next day, I entered the house alone to see that the book was gone, and found a note to tell me that she would be waiting at the appointed time. When I entered the bedchamber, Xavi sat upon the chair exactly as I had requested, her back to me. Her thick black hair cascaded down in waves, left unbound and concealing for the most part the abbreviated stays she had left on at my request. Her magnificent arse was completely spread, as I had asked that she show her little hole, which I always liked to see. Her legs, clad in silk stockings that were gartered with ribbons above her knees, were set wide apart on either side of the chair. Her cunny was nestled against the cushion, as I had specified.

Xavi glanced over her shoulder, giving me a heavy-lidded look that made it clear how aroused she already was. Not uncomfortably, she moved upon the chair and I caught a glimpse of white between her spread buttocks. She had the ivory rod in her cunny. All the way in, so deeply that I had not seen it at first.

"Lift up," I said. "But not all the way."

She obeyed, rising a few inches with one hand on the back of the chair and one hand on the base of the dildo so as to hold the head of the thing inside. The thick rod gleamed as it slid partly out, and I knew it would be hot to the touch, and slick.

"I want you to pleasure yourself," I whispered, "just as you do when you are all alone, with no man to satisfy you."

"Oh, Edward . . ."

She hesitated for a second but only a second. Then Xavi slid up and down on it—never all the way down and never up enough to let it fall. I crossed the room and stood behind her, instantly erect at the sight of the big dildo in her juicy cunny, amused by how skillful she was at using it in this unusual way.

"I would rather ride you," she said softly, resting her cheek on the back of the chair, her voice wistful but suffused with sexual longing.

Her words made me smile, but I went down on one knee behind her and encircled the dildo's base with my fingers, holding it in a fist. "Not yet." The thing was indeed hot, and so slippery it was difficult to hold onto. I wanted her to slide up and down again, pound her arse and cunny against my fist, moving at the precise tempo that excited her to a frenzy. And I wanted to watch from this vantage point, nearly as close as if I were actually doing the fucking. "Show me how you ride, my love. Go as hard and as fast as you like."

I pressed kisses upon her buttocks, nipping her here and there. Xavi sighed with renewed pleasure and slid down again. And again. And again. She seemed to very much enjoy the sensual pressure of my large fist against her nether regions as she came down. I held on to the ivory rod that was privileged to enter her cunny, relishing the sweet softness of her buttocks as they touched my hand upon each downward stroke. My fingers were wet from her flowing juices and I grasped the dildo harder, enjoying the odd illusion of jerking off inside her—I sometimes liked to bring myself to a punishing orgasm in this way—yet my stiff cock was still trapped within my breeches.

She began to cry out and her downward thrusts upon the dildo were faster . . . and faster still. Taking it as deeply as she was, there was no longer need for her to hold its base. Oblivious to everything but her onrushing orgasm, Xavi lightly pulled and pinched at her clitoris to stimulate herself. I had seen her do this many times and my arousal always matched her own, understanding that her little rod experienced the same intense sensations as my much larger organ.

Pulling on her clitoris harder now, she breathed raggedly. I knew she liked to do this in a mirror where she could observe her arousal, see the bit of flesh rolled between her fingertips and imagine herself ejaculating like me. I could just feel her busy fingertips touch my fist with every little tug and I steadied her, slipping my free hand under the short corset and holding her hip as she rode on. As always, I saw her pretty little arsehole tighten and pulse as the waves of pleasure coursed through her cunny.

I pressed my cheek on her bare buttocks, rubbing my face on her behind as she rocked upon the soft cushion, drenching it with her juice. Lucky cushion, lucky chair. Lucky me, to be witness once again to her moment of satisfaction, and be able to enjoy the animal quality of her moans. I soothed her through it, stroking her hair and her back, allowing the feeling to echo and die away little by little.

Then I stood up and let her turn around. Her lips were slightly parted and I freed my cock with haste, thrusting it inside her willing mouth, telling her to suck and suck hard. Playfully obedient, she did, sliding her tongue over the sensitive front of my rod and holding the bottom two inches clasped in her fingers, pumping assiduously. I was at the point of climax when I pulled out, surprising her. She opened her eyes and gave me a dreamy look.

"On your knees, my girl."

Again she obeyed, scrambling off the chair to the thick carpet on the floor. Her black hair tumbled over her shoulders and breasts as she settled down but only partway, so that her mouth was level with my cock and balls. She looked up expectantly, not sure of what I wanted, but trusting me all the same.

"Open your mouth again."

She did and I came a little closer, holding my cock fully in my grasp to keep it away from her eager tongue. It was my balls that needed a good licking. She began at once, instinctively knowing what I wanted, doing the honors with her silky tongue, giving me a warmly sensual bath. The sensation, once I forced my cock to wait, was most pleasurable. I wanted it to go on for a while longer. As she had spread her body for me, I wanted to spread for her. But over her. Above her. Dominant and fully male, with my hugely swollen cock brushing her face, until my balls filled her mouth and the sensual bath from her expert tongue began again.

"Get on the bed, Xavi."

She wiped her wet lips with the back of her hand and grinned at me. Certainly ball worship was more easily done when the one who licked could lie beneath the recipient of the licking. Bare and beautiful, she clambered onto the bed and lay on her back, reaching out her arms to me as I joined her. We shared an embrace and kissed lightly, then turned head to foot. On all fours, I parted my thighs and let her wriggle up until her head was between them. I no longer held onto my cock. It excited me deeply to know that she could see nothing at the moment besides my cock and balls over her face, about to descend, and that she wanted to give me as much oral satisfaction as I craved. With a deft fingertip, she took a clear drop of hot fluid from the head of my cock, popping it into her mouth and tasting me with a satisfied sigh.

My dear Xavi reached up to play with my balls as my shoulders dropped down and I rested my head upon her thigh, aroused by the fragrance of her still-excited pussy and wanting to look at it as she licked me. I eased down and felt her take the heavy sac fully into her mouth. It felt deeply satisfying to be tongued so well, and once I was wet, she applied her sensual ingenuity to increase my pleasure, tightening her lips around one ball and letting the other slip out, then reversing it.

Lost in the feeling, I suddenly lost the sense of being dominant, even though I was still on top. And I lost the sense of being male, realizing to my unspoken surprise, that my mind was capable of encompassing both sexes. I allowed myself to imagine—I was not so overcome as to say so out loud and certainly I was not in a position that encouraged conversation—that this was what it was like to be a woman with a woman. No penetration. No rough handling. Nothing but a soft, wet mouth upon one's private parts, making the sort of love that left not the slightest trace of the delight it provided, one lover truly drinking in the other with the utmost tenderness. Had I been born with a cunny I would have wanted this more than anything.

Murmuring incoherently against Xavi's thigh, I let the fantasy of Sapphic sex take hold of my imagination. As if she could read my mind, she brought her hands up to my arse, kneading my buttocks in much the way I liked to do hers at times. She continued to tongue-tease my balls. The muscularity of my body did not allow for the voluptuous pleasure I always took in the softness of her flesh, but what ran through my mind as she stroked and caressed me more than made up for it.

Fully male as my body was, my thoughts at that moment were indeed those of a woman. I wanted only to yield for a little while, to be passive, to lie upon the bed and receive whatever my lover would give.

As it happened, my balls were out of her mouth—she was fondling them gently now, playing with me somewhat absently. I lifted up and turned around to stretch out beside her for a few minutes, cupping her breasts, arousing her again, whispering that I wanted her to keep her cunny on my face while she sucked and stroked me to orgasm.

Xavi only nodded.

I lay back and watched her swing her fine big arse around so I could see her cunny snugged between her thighs. Well, I was a man, after all, and a strong one, able to lift her and position her over my face even when I was lying down. And I did.

With her sex only inches away from my lips, the female scent of her intoxicating me, my unusual fantasy took hold of my mind once more. As she took my cock into her mouth, fellating me with uncommon skill, I imagined it as a clitoris, tiny but exquisitely sensitive. A woman making love to a woman would never choke on such a dainty morsel. That thought made my poor cock grow longer and stiffer, but Xavi moved back just enough to keep control.

Indeed, she was completely in control. Without telling her I had completely surrendered. Perhaps she chalked it up to a sensual languor on my part, perhaps she enjoyed the change from my usual vigorous performance. Xavi's hands reached around and underneath my body and clasped my buttocks, squeezing rhythmically. A soul-deep sigh escaped me.

Lying on my back instead of on my hands and knees over her prone body, my buttocks were no longer tensed and hard. Blissfully, I allowed her to manipulate my arse, her hands between me and the bed, rolling just a little as she did so, taking with silent joy the subtle pleasure I had given her so often.

She continued to suck my cock and I knew I was very near climax. As tenderly as she, I spread my hands over the feminine arse so near my face, pulling her hips to me, pushing my face between her soft buttocks.

Xavi shifted position so that my tongue could explore her delicious cunny and tease her clitoris as well. No two female friends were ever so amorous as we were that day, and no ladies ever enjoyed their secret pleasure as we did. If she guessed what I was thinking as I came in her mouth and she in mine, my darling did not say. But I had not dreamed such dreams until Xaviera Innocencia became my lover, and I have not since. She awakened my deepest sexuality and I am grateful to her for that. So much of what we did ended up in the little book—it is an unbearably poignant reminder of our time together. It shall be the very last thing I throw into the purifying flames.

Did I mention that she was a storyteller in her own right? Yes . . . yes, looking back over these hastily scribbled pages, I see that I did. Drinking brandy in the hours after midnight is unwise. I find that the pen grows heavy in my hand. I would rather read . . . and let memory speak for me . . .

2

My sexual awakening . . .

Since I swore never to reveal hers, I will assign a name to the lady who taught me of love: Anne Leonard. She was the older sister of a boyhood friend of mine, whom I will call Thomas, who was away at the time.

A third son with no prospects, he had been sent suddenly to the West Indies at the age of twenty, which was my age at that time. All the other expendable Leonard males had perished there of yellow fever, leaving the family's interests and property in rack and ruin. Thomas had been instructed to rebuild and reinvest, or marry an heiress with a plantation. Neither seemed likely. As a preventative against disease, or so his letters said, he downed a half-pint of rum daily and stayed away from the whores, dallying instead with a French planter's rich young widow.

His family had asked me to come for my every-other-year visit all the same. I missed my friend but not overmuch. To my utter astonishment, I was soon invited by Anne to keep her company as she went about her ladylike pursuits. No one thought anything of it. I had been a friend of her brother's for so long.

Unchaperoned, we were free to wander, and while away the long days of a Devonshire summer together. I was happy to carry her hat and her sketchbook and watercolors to whatever far field she wished to paint. But being alone so often changed the nature of our relationship. I had loved her long, but in the way of a shy boy, yearning and hoping, that sort of thing.

In our weeks together during that pleasant sojourn in the country, I came to know her much better. Her wit, her intelligence, her sunny temperament and golden beauty captivated me anew. I was besotted. But inexperienced as I was at twenty, I did not dream she could think of me as a lover.

Yet it began to dawn upon me that Anne looked often in my direction when she thought I did not see. True, I had grown taller since she had last seen me at the age of eighteen, a transformation she seemed to appreciate, although she did not comment upon it. But her gaze lingered upon my face, and a smile, upon her lips, as if having to look up at me now amused her a great deal.

She had scarcely seemed to notice me in the years before, dismissing her brother and me with an affectionate comment and a flick of her skirts should she encounter us in the halls of the manor house where the family spent the halcyon months of summer. Of course, she had much to do and took great pleasure in managing the household, her parents being long dead, when not pursuing her creative interests. Anne was capable as well as charming, and the staff instantly obeyed her every command.

Being politely ignored is an excellent stimulus to love, especially for an imaginative boy who was prone to silent but whole-hearted admiration of the female sex (I blame my mother, who was lovely and kind, and died far too young). Anne was the first woman who aroused me, before I knew what the word meant. How would I have known? I was years younger.

By the time I turned eighteen, matters were not much better. I remained essentially innocent and yet . . . not. I was extremely aware, as a male of that age will be, of all the women around me. In my fumbling, foolish way, I still adored Anne, not openly—I never mentioned it to Thomas. Her brother would have thrashed me thoroughly had I confided my fondness for the older sister he pretended to dislike.

No, two years before he sailed away to the palm-fringed shores of Jamaica and the welcoming arms of the French widow. He and I satisfied our sexual curiosity by following the prettier female servants about and playing pranks, until the butler intervened and threatened to tell Lord So-and-so, Thomas's guardian. We had no wish to attract the notice of his lordship, a strapping man with a volatile temper. At the manor and in London, miscreants got what he thought they deserved: a good birching.

Thomas and I avoided him by staying out-of-doors, preferring the meadows where we could ride and the brooks where we swam naked, throwing our clothes upon the bushes. And then we found a better hunting ground for female flesh: the lawns where the household linens were spread upon the grass to dry and whiten in the sun. We climbed the trees at the edge, the laundrymaids quite unaware of our hidden presence. It was the work of a moment for us to select a leafy branch that would bear our weight and straddle it to spy upon them.

They often stripped down to their shifts as they toiled, happy enough to work in the fresh air and get away from the house—most had grown up on the surrounding farms—where they could gossip freely. They laughed like hoydens when they discussed the male visitors to the manor, comparing the size and might of individual cocks. Their strong, shapely bodies meant they were considered fair game by men down from London. If one were to believe all that they said, it was understood that they had their pick of the pricks and took their pleasure accordingly.

One broiling day the laundrymaids wore less than usual and so did we, having left our shirts down by the brook, and our socks and shoes as well. At eighteen we were no longer boys and more than old enough to be uncomfortably stirred by the least glimpse of feminine skin. We rode upon our individual branches and swung our bare feet as we struggled to see. Despite the heat of the day, the laundrymaids had brought out a demijohn of ale and were livelier than ever, and their chatter was spirited. Thomas, on a lower branch, had a better vantage point than I. "Look at her," he whispered.

The laundrymaid in question had high, full breasts and pert nipples that showed pink under her chemise, damp and clinging with the moisture of the linens she had carried out to lay upon the grass. I think her name was Lucy—well, the name will do for my purposes if it was not. She wore a tattered petticoat that revealed her bare arse now and again as she bent over. Thomas craned his neck trying to see more.

Feeling playful—and, I supposed, emboldened by the ale—a new laundrymaid grabbed the hem and lifted the petticoat to Lucy's waist, displaying her gloriously naked behind, which was as round and firm as the rest of her. Lucy only laughed. "Kiss it then," she said to the other girl.

My boyhood friend gasped and nearly fell off his branch as the other maid dropped to her knees and pressed lusty kisses on both of Lucy's bare buttocks and added a few stinging slaps for good measure.

The other three or four who were watching screamed with merriment. It was all in play, but extremely stimulating for two untried youths. Still, we could not let go of the branches we clung to in order to soothe the unbearable ache of lust. The two women, giddy from the heat and the ale and who knew what else, wrestled each other down to the grass and rolled about in mock battle. They were laughing, but gripping each other's arse cheeks hard as they pretended to fuck, forcing thighs between thighs and pressing excited pussies together, leaving wet stains upon shift and tattered petticoat alike.

Then I caught a glimpse of an approaching figure at some distance, a young woman in a hat and full-skirted gown and re-alized it was Anne. She was too far away to see what was happening, but her steps were brisk and there was not much time.

"Make them stop!" I whispered to Thomas. "Your sister is coming!"

He looked frantically to where I pointed and swore under his breath, then dropped from the tree, advancing upon the laundrymaids. As he was clad only in breeches, a manly fire in his eyes, they stopped what they were doing at once. The two clasped in playful lust, rolled apart and scrambled to their feet, shrieking with the others as they all ran off, leaving the sheets and pillowcases neatly spread upon the grass. As Anne came closer, she spied her brother, half-naked and barefoot, and her eyebrows drew together in a puzzled frown.

"Where is your shirt, Thomas? And your shoes?" she asked him, looking about as if expecting to find a female similarly un-clothed.

"Down by the brook," Thomas said. "Edward and I were swimming." He glanced upward unthinkingly to where I sat, still straddling the branch, wishing there were some way I could vanish.

Anne looked up at me and smiled. Her hat fell off her head as she did so, taking the hatpins with it. Thick tresses of dark blond tumbled down her back.

"What are you doing up there?"

"Ah—picking plums," I replied hastily.

She laughed lightly. "In an oak tree?"

"No wonder there were none." The gravity I tried to instill in my youthful voice only made her laugh more.

"Come down, Edward."

I obeyed and landed on the grass not too far from Thomas. Anne had put on her hat again, for which I was grateful. To appear thus undressed before a woman I secretly worshipped was embarrassing indeed. My smooth chest, my lean body, which was just on the verge of growing tall, would not impress her in any way. I wanted desperately to seem a man in her eyes at that moment and not a youth.

But she was not paying attention and the brim of her hat concealed her gaze. She spoke softly to Thomas about some trivial matter, and I listened in silence, enjoying the sound of her voice. My groin tensed as I imagined her speaking to me in so intimate a tone.

Visions of the buxom laundrymaids and their wanton play swam in my mind. The two who had entwined their thighs and grabbed each other's bums were a stimulating contrast to the demure Anne. Yet her much more modest attire was no less stimulating. It was as if I could see underneath . . .

Then—damn my overheated brain!—I entertained a wicked fantasy of Anne chastising Lucy with her guardian's birch, meting out punishment upon quivering buttocks with measured patience. Yes—the second girl would hold up the tattered petticoat again and the others would hold Lucy still, watching with avid eyes—I forced the exciting thoughts away. We English find too much enjoyment in whipping, perhaps, but done right and lightly, it provides considerable pleasure to the giver and recipient.

I waited for Anne and Thomas to finish talking, and finally she turned in my direction, head lifted so I could see her eyes at last. Swiftly she took me in from head to toe, and the intensity of her gaze made me feel positively hot all over. The midday sun had moved lower in the sky, behind the tall trees Thomas and I had climbed, so there was no reason for the sensation of warmth that afflicted me.

My eighteen-year-old cock, ever alert if seldom satisfied, stiffened to its full length, restrained by the old breeches I wore that were somewhat too small for me. Anne immediately looked away. I noted the deep blush that tinted her cheeks, and my humiliation knew no bounds. I told my unruly member to soften and it eventually obeyed.

Not soon enough, Thomas and his sister finished their conversation, and she turned to bid me adieu. She kept her eyes firmly fixed upon my face. My only response was a nod. If she had been able to read my mind . . . ah, what would she have thought?

Two years later, during the summer of my initiation at her gentle hands, she seemed to have forgotten all about our encounter on the lawn. From her point of view there would have been very little to remember, of course. The fantasy that had come unbidden to my mind soon faded away, to be replaced by a thousand more—I learned to masturbate often but always with her in mind, no matter where I was.

Even though Thomas was away in Jamaica, it was a rare gift to return at twenty to the house where I had spent so many happy days with him, for I now had Anne. I very much enjoyed playing the part of her devoted servant during our rambles.

The manor house, built of golden stone, glowed in the afternoon light as we made our way back through the fields, watched only by drowsy cattle. There was no one looking out from the windows of the house and the world seemed to belong to us alone—and then I remembered that most of the household had decamped to Bath for a fashionable wedding.

"Thank you, Edward, for your company today," she said as we began to walk down the allee of arching trees that led to the front of the house. Her words were formal but something in her tone was not. "I did enjoy myself."

"As did I," I answered.

She paused and looked at me tenderly. I was aware of a subtle shift in her mood, as if she had come to a decision on some matter that had long been on her mind. She seemed about to speak—then thought better of it and continued on, walking faster.

I kept pace with her, still holding her things, tall enough to look down her dress and no longer the awkward youth I had been. Her round breasts rose and fell with each breath, barely concealed by the bodice of her light gown. It was all I could do not to put my arms around her and stop her somehow. I longed suddenly to kiss her, to make my feelings known, to caress her—then Anne turned suddenly and planted herself in my path.

My hands went around her waist as her face turned upward to mine. Pushing against mine, her body vibrated with an eagerness that caused my cock to swell. Our lips met in an ardent kiss that went on and on—her mouth was hot and silky wet.

I was dizzy with delight when she broke it off, still pressing her body to mine. Under the material of her skirts, I felt something delicious: she was rubbing the soft little mound between her legs upon one of my thighs. "Come to me tonight," she whispered. "No one will know. The only servants left are in the kitchen."

"A good mile from your bedchamber," I whispered back, pressing a kiss to her ear. Not believing my good fortune, I felt compelled to mention the risk we ran. "But should your guardian find out, I will be as good as dead. I will have to fight a duel—or marry you—"

"He has pledged me to another. I did not tell you."

Too surprised to speak for a moment, I brushed my thumb against her cheek. I could reply only with platitudes. "You should have. A woman's wedding day is the happiest of her life, is it not?" I could not fathom why she had kept such important information from me during our days together.

She was silent for a little while. "Not always. My guardian chose the man."

The man. Not *my love* or even *my fiancé.* Just *the man.* It was as if she had been given away to a stranger—and I was to find out later that she had.

"No one can know of this, Edward." Anne's troubled eyes searched mine.

"Of what?"

"That I have kissed you. And that I want you—desperately."

Her words took me aback. I was not able to think. Only much later did it occur to me how odd it was that so lovely a woman had been on the shelf so long, as if her guardian had kept her there for himself for some unknown reason. I had given the matter no thought at all before that moment, naïve as I was.

"Of course not. No one will know." My reply was meant to be soothing but perhaps it sounded automatic. She put her hands on my arms as if to push me away. I had no idea what to do or say.

Perhaps she wanted me to come to her rescue. But claiming her as my own had been the farthest thing from my mind, despite my love for her. There was the difference in our age, and—and perhaps I knew even then that romantic fantasy is rather better than the cold realities of married life.

An odd silence came between us. What did I not know about Anne? She could not be a virgin, I suddenly thought. Her knowing air and the speed with which she had issued such a wanton invitation to me made that suddenly clear. But I was. I wanted her. And she had said she wanted me.

* * *

How often had I stripped off my clothes and tossed them upon a chair, never giving a second thought to my nakedness? I felt different now, undressing by candlelight before a woman who was still clothed, obeying her soft commands, desiring only to please her in every way for this, my first time. Unlike my friends, I had yet to go a-whoring in the brothels of London or slake my lust with a willing servant girl. I was protected from such temptation by my boyhood love for Anne. Once she had decided to seduce me, I wanted to be totally and completely hers.

Not knowing quite what to do, hoping she would explain what it was she wanted before I made a fool of myself, I stood before her as she sat in an armchair, my cock so hard and standing up so stiffly from the soft curls at its base that it could not jut out unless I held it and forced it down. She would not let me clasp myself.

"Stand with your legs apart. I would see all of you, Edward."

Again I obeyed. Her hand slid between my thighs and touched my balls, stroking with a teasing touch. Expertly she drew down my foreskin and put her sweet lips around the head of my cock, tasting the clear drop of fluid that sprang from the small hole with just the tip of her tongue. I could feel her fingers play upon my balls, which tightened. A strong rush of sensation—too soon, too soon—made me push her hands away and pull my cock from her mouth.

I closed my eyes and drew in long breaths, willing myself to wait. Anne murmured something I could not quite hear. I opened my eyes and looked down at her. She had unlaced her bodice and was fondling her breasts while staring at my cock. Stiff as a soldier but more of a gentleman than I, the damned thing bobbed its head.

"So you know that you must not come too soon—very good. My pleasure takes longer. Ah, you are truly a man at last. I love to look at you."

The mirror opposite reflected us both. She was a picture of erotic delicacy, pulling her nipples with slender fingers, poised upon the chair in a light summer dress that was coming apart little by little as she undid this and opened that. In contrast to her femininity, I had filled out by that summer and was indeed a man, far more muscular than I had been as a youth of eighteen. If the sight of me naked aroused her so readily, then she might feast her eyes upon me as long as she liked.

"Turn around," she said. "Ah. Even better. Now bend over. Like that—yes."

I braced my hands upon my knees and did as she bade me. Again a soft hand reached between my legs to stroke my balls. The curious subservience of the position did not trouble me—I have thought since that if men love to study women's private parts in every possible way, it is only fitting that we should allow them the same privilege.

Her hand reached further to stroke my member with subtle motions. Anne ran her fingertips along the engorged veins in a way that made me tremble with renewed lust.

She stopped and ran her hands over my arse, soothing me until I straightened, then stroking the backs of my thighs until I turned around. Her touch was highly sensual and obviously skilled—I knew then that my lovely lady found her greatest pleasure in teaching young men the arts of sexual love.

Desiring to be initiated with all my heart, on fire with erotic sensation, it mattered not at all to me if I was not the first who had submitted to her gentle will. Indeed, in my present state the thought of the others aroused me even more. It was as if I could see them in her dreamy eyes, displaying the same impossibly high erection I had.

Her dress had slipped off her shoulders and lay in folds about her waist. Then, knowing I was watching her every move, Anne lifted and pushed aside the flowing material to display her cunny. I had seen other such but none so pretty. There were the servants that Thomas and I spied on, an occasional slut who hoisted her bedraggled skirts to display her wares in London lanes, and only once, a tight, shaved slit belonging to a noblewoman in a carriage who took a peculiar pleasure in exhibiting herself to men, then riding on.

But Anne's was irresistible, with deep-pink folds inside blond curls, a honeypot dripping with sweetness. I dropped to my knees, eager to taste her. I was clumsy at first but I soon understood what excited her most. She spread her thighs far apart and leaned back upon the accommodating armchair, pushing her hips forward. Then she ran her fingers through my hair, drawing my head down so my mouth was on her cunny and firmly keeping it there.

I began to lick eagerly, exploring the succulent flesh with my tongue, flicking it over the little bit at the top—ah, that was best of all. Anne writhed and held my head more closely to her private parts. Small but highly sensitive under the hood of skin, the bit of flesh felt like a little rod. Sucking it seemed only natural. And so I took it between my lips and sucked it with gentle emphasis, aware of her ever-increasing pleasure from her moans.

Two might tease. Novice that I was, I let go and sat back on my haunches, resting my hands on her thighs to hold them open and look at what I had been tasting. Anne opened her eyes and tried to sit up, but I prevented her and made her slide her arse down instead.

Then I lifted her legs up nearly to her shoulders and told her to hold them there, guessing that her cunny would be nicely squeezed between her thighs. She obeyed me this time, clasping her legs behind her knees and hiding her face behind them. I liked seeing her this way, legs, arse, and cunny, presented for my pleasure. Her labia were swollen, flushed with sexual excitement, and dripping with a warm juice that I lapped up, slowly at first, then faster.

In this position I could also see her arsehole, and touched it tentatively, not sure if women enjoyed the sort of sport in which stableboys indulged, bending each other over bales of hay to fuck and be fucked.

I was growing bolder and bolder, my status as an initiate soon to be over. Anne had given up the secrets of her body one by one, and the pulsing spot under my fingertip was the last. The juice from her cunny trickled down and wet my finger liberally. Without further ado, I thrust it in.

Anne cried out with pleasure. Her arsehole was quite tight at first, but she seemed to welcome my exploring finger in that place, and I enjoyed her shamelessness.

My cock was ready to explode. I got up, and handled her somewhat roughly and ripped the dress off. I cared nothing for who might see it on the morrow.

She kissed and caressed me with wild abandon as I carried her to the bed and tossed her down as she laughed with anticipation. Anne got on all fours and begged me to enter her. I refused. Standing behind her, I spread and spanked her buttocks until they turned bright pink. She moaned her satisfaction with my firm treatment of her flesh, whispering of her taste for the birch, taking and giving. Ah—my early fantasy of her whipping Lucy had been real enough. Had I a bundle of slender twigs at hand, I would have done that to Anne too.

It seemed no surprise to her that a relative innocent could suddenly seem so sure of himself. For my part, I found out that one could learn many things very quickly when nature had its wild way. With my finger and thumb, I stretched her cunny lips apart and looked within. The glistening folds opened slightly, so swollen that only a thick and extraordinarily stiff cock could penetrate them.

I grasped mine and came closer, pushing just the head into the soft heat of her cunny. I told her not to move—the delicate sensation of her ever-swelling flesh enfolding my knob was a thrill like nothing I had ever experienced. I rested my hands upon her back at her waist, the heat from her thoroughly spanked arse perceptible on my skin, and simply waited.

To have my love in this way, poised and still, her ragged breathing the only motion she allowed herself, in deference to my wishes, was a very great pleasure and one I wished to savor.

But the involuntary tightening of my groin and balls made me enter her with one powerful thrust. Anne cried out and rocked back, banging her hot arse against me. I clasped her waist and gave myself over to the sensations flooding through me, not wanting to come, unwilling to stop. She seemed strong enough to carry my weight and so I dropped down over her to hold her bouncing tits in my hands. The feel of her erect nipples in the center of my palms was all it took. I rammed her with all my strength as the first scorching jet pulsed through my cock—then another, and another, until it seemed that my very soul desired release.

Together we found it . . . and as the hours went by, much more. I was well-schooled in her loving arms and taught everything I needed to know about how to please a woman. Young as I was, I thought at the time that the only one I would ever want was her. It was not to be.

After that night, we were parted forever. From all reports she was soon married and a dutiful wife in the end, safe and secure as women must be, since they cannot make their own way in the world, but must needs rely upon the strength and support of men.

But I wondered during the ensuing years if I had been her last young lover. Certainly it was not a subject that I would ever discuss with Thomas. My correspondence with him never even mentioned Anne—he knew nothing of my affair with his older sister and I wanted to keep it that way.

But I have heard that Thomas has returned from the West Indies just this year. If I should see him on the street, I will enquire after her.

3

Several weeks later . . .

So much for my past. One's youth passes swiftly and I have no regrets (but then I am only thirty—give me time).

To return to Xavi or rather, my memories of Xavi, it is necessary to sort through the collection of papers at last. It will not take long and I am feeling more level-headed than usual where that lady is concerned. But then, I have had time to think.

The weather has been dreadful and I have been too much in the house, watching the rain streak down the tall windows and the wind lash the trees. When it eases, which is not often, I take to the streets, but the ebb and flow of London humanity is as dispiriting as the brimming river that threatens daily to overflow its banks.

One look at the sweet-faced girls and the eager youths who pursue them, one look more at the older women whose eyes tell of their disappointment in life and the careworn men who hurry along the cobblestones, and the sadness at my heart overwhelms me.

But sequestering myself within these walls is not the answer. Albermarle Street is pleasant enough and this house, which belonged to my late father, serves my purposes. I can write undisturbed, sleep alone if I wish, my everyday needs seen to by capable servants ... but I often find the rooms unbearably lonely. For that reason, I am out and about more often than I am here.

The past is a trap. Perhaps it was a mistake to set down my memories of Anne a month ago. I did love her. My subsequent affairs were about physical pleasure and little more. Easily obtainable from lovers who were easily replaceable.

Xavi, the wife of a jealous brute who had no real use for her, was unique. And she was taken. Perhaps I fell in love with her because I knew I could not have her all to myself. Ah, our stolen hours were infinitely precious to me—damnation! Remembering her when I am alone is unwise. What happened is all in the past and I ought not to brood as I do. But there is no one I can tell of my real feelings. A pragmatist like Quinn would only laugh at me. Besides, it is easy enough to distract myself. I frequent coffeehouses and inns and places like that, where the hubbub drowns out the echo of memory.

Lately all the talk is of the great storm off the coast of Portugal, which sent a fleet of merchantmen straight to the bottom and sank the fortunes of the fleet's backers and insurers as well. By the grace of God, many were saved. But the cargo was not and I so I find myself without the brandy I prefer.

Perhaps the Almighty took it for Himself, along with the drowned sailors. Such rough fellows will make odd angels, I suspect, but it is said that our Heavenly Father loves us all. I would venture to present myself as an exception.

Does that sound cynical? I am not a religious man, although I do not mind the practice of it in others.

My dear Xavi had been raised according to the rites of Rome—

penance and confession and such—in fact, Quinn painted her
with a rosary of fine pearls wound around her fingers. All the
same, my talented friend could not make her look pious.

Ah. I have found the etching I was looking for, reproducing
that very portrait. It is a handsome one, as crisp as the day it
was pressed and pulled from the engraver's plate. Unsigned,
though.

Miss Reynaud swore it was not her handiwork, though she
excelled at drawing from Quinn's lively art, and also supervised
the engraver who worked from her drawings, or from his scandalous sketches—she sniffed at these.

Inexpensive reproductions were displayed by the dozen in
printshops and popular subjects—adorable children, virtuous
daughters, country cottages—were quite profitable. Risqué
subjects made even more money. At two guineas for six etchings, in print runs of, oh, two thousand at a time, Quinn did
very well indeed. Of course, he spent the guineas nearly as fast
as they came in, taking pride in being dissipated and wild, like
most artists.

It was a good thing that Miss Reynaud put up with him. She
insisted on skillful engraving, disgusted by the look of prints
pulled from plates that had been used too many times. The better the quality, the happier the customer. She also excelled at ex-
tracting payment from printsellers, thus ensuring her meager
wages would be promptly paid.

But Quinn did not sell cheap versions of his commissioned
portraits. His wealthy patrons would have abandoned him in
droves.

They abhorred the crowds that gathered outside the display
in the printseller's, exclaiming and pointing—and sometimes
going in to rent an entire portfolio for a night's amusement.
Such private viewings had less to do with the appreciation of art
than with seeing the nude female body in all its splendor.

Quinn had little interest in producing male nudes, but other artists supplied the demand.

My secretary, Richard Whiston, collected these by the dozen, favoring Grecian themes: young athletes, mighty wrestlers, satyrs, and so forth. To each his own.

He lived—and still does—with another man in perfect harmony. They have long been together, a fact that Richard attributes to the open nature of their relationship. Their love endured; their passions were fleeting. The arrangement is not uncommon within his milieu—I often heard outré tales of this world from him, but I will not repeat them upon these pages.

Richard is discreet, necessarily so. And highly intelligent. But he had his own life and much to do besides the employment I provided, and could not always be with me when I needed him most.

If only I had listened to him concerning my affair with Xavi . . .

Her beautiful face was worthy of immortality. That was why her formal portrait was redone in elegant mezzotint and displayed in a Piccadilly shop, before Don Diego had paid for the original done in oils. Quinn was horrified. He had not authorized the reproduction but there it was. At least she was not identified by name—the engraving bore the title *A Portrait of a Lady* and nothing more.

But the indignation of Don Diego Mendez y Cartegna knew no bounds. According to Spanish custom, women, whether married or not, were rarely seen outside their homes and here was his wife, gazing out serenely through a shop window.

He communicated his wrath in a letter to Quinn, who wrote back that the mezzotint was not his doing. Such things happened all the time to famous artists, and he had no idea who had copied Xavi's portrait.

Don Diego was not satisfied with this explanation. Fiercely

proud, he was furious that the image of his young wife could be sold to anyone with the money to buy. It mattered not to him that the portrait was decorous. In his mind, Xaviera was his and his alone. Yet she persuaded him to control his anger and let well enough alone. The reproduction showed only her face, after all, and not the lissome body beneath. But that face captivated many a man who stopped to look.

Not since the young wife of the Persian ambassador had come to London had there been such a stir. Everyone knew *her* name: Laila. The papers printed many images of her lounging on velvet-draped divans and invented vignettes of harem life— bare-breasted, bejeweled slaves dancing for the caliph, scimitar-wielding soldiers at the gates of this forbidden paradise, eunuchs in splendid robes and so forth.

The trade in such tawdry fantasies was brisk.

Have I mentioned that I have an extensive collection of Quinn's erotic work? I had even attended a few of the soirees that inspired the best of it. As models he hired shopgirls down on their luck and strumpets who had not yet gone to ruin— these drove a hard bargain and charged by the piece for each part of the body he wished them to reveal. Genteel women and noblewomen posed for free, delighted with their decadent immortality so long as he concealed their identity.

In the positions they chose—on their backs with legs spread, on all fours, arses up—it would have been difficult to determine this in any case. Above all, Quinn drew Woman, not individual females.

It could be argued that a certain man portrayed taking his pleasure among his models resembles me. I do not deny it—but then, it is only a resemblance. And that happened before I met Xavi and fell in love for the second time in my life.

She wanted to hear all about those soirees. Having been in Quinn's studio off and on for weeks, she enjoyed a peek behind the curtain, so to speak, that separated one aspect of his life from another.

Quinn made his reputation as a society portrait painter whose clients wished to be remembered for all eternity and maintained suitably solemn expressions while he did so. But he was also a free spirit who saw nothing wrong with naked bacchanals.

Highborn ladies flocked to him for their portraits. Just to be looked over and sized up by him brought a becoming blush to their cheeks. And elsewhere. His models were no better.

And what I told Xavi of him became the first story in the little book. Here it is.

The woman on the dais was a perfect nymph. But her origins were more St. Giles's than Grecian, although she was lovely indeed. Corinne Perry was a milliner's assistant in need of an extra shilling now and then who would rather not whore for it—well, not right away. She had seen Quinn's notice requesting models on a Soho notice board and applied at once. Her pure white skin and delicate features guaranteed her employment by him, but he had no time for dalliance, as the painting she sat for was to go to the king's private collection.

Corinne sighed and willed herself to stay absolutely still. The material that Rob had soaked in watery clay and draped around her lower half had dried upon her legs, leaving every fold of the fabric set in place for Quinn to sketch.

"May I scratch?" she asked after a while.

"Indeed not." The porte-crayon in his hand continued to move swiftly over the primed canvas. "Goddesses never scratch."

Corinne frowned and looked down at her classical drapery. "But this damned cloth itches unbearably."

"Great art requires sacrifices. Please do not move."

She scowled.

"There must be easier ways to earn a shilling," she said at last.

"Yes, I suppose there are," Quinn said absently. He stepped back to inspect his preliminary sketch, seeming satisfied. The convoluted shadows of classical drapery were his specialty—admirers of ancient art liked them as much as the bare breasts and flowing hair of the goddesses he produced in quantity. "I am done, I think. I can work from this drawing. Help her down," he said to his apprentice.

The lad peeled away the stiff material with care, too absorbed in his task to see Corinne flinch as it came off. Eventually she was entirely bare, if muddy. She stepped down from the dais and walked to a tub of water set nearby in readiness, stepping in to wash herself standing up, shivering from the cold.

She picked up the sponge that floated in the water, and squeezed it over her skin. Trickles of water dissolved the mud and made it run down her legs and over her buttocks. The painter and his apprentice stood rooted to the spot—there was something deeply sensual about her bath, even to their jaded eyes. Models posed in stiff drapery had to bathe afterwards; they had seen it before.

But she was a marvel of femininity. Dipping into the water had made her long hair curl into fetching ringlets that bobbed over her breasts, one little spiral even encircling a pink nipple as the men stared, fascinated.

Little by little Corinne got herself clean, dawdling at the task. She slid the dripping sponge over her breasts and belly, then twisted round to get her buttocks clean, scrubbing them until her white skin was glossy and faintly pink. She stepped from the bath and stood dripping upon the floor, shivering again.

"I need fresh water," she said imperiously.

"Of course." Quinn propelled his apprentice toward the

door. "Get it warm this time, Rob. Whatever milady wants." Rob came to his senses and left the room to shout downstairs for more, which two scullery maids lugged up in pails, trying not to look at Corinne. Once the tub had been emptied and filled, Corinne kneeled down in it. She looked more than ever like a nymph gazing down into a reflecting pool. The two men pulled up chairs and sat together.

She glanced up at them. "And what must I do to earn more money?"

"Anything you like, my girl," Quinn answered. His voice was rough, and his cock was up, straining against his breeches. The younger man shifted uncomfortably in his seat, unable to calm the erection that threatened to burst forth.

Corinne settled down into the water, laughing a little as her breasts floated up. "Come closer then."

Quinn and his apprentice looked at each other.

Did she mean to be shared by them? There was no telling but they did as she commanded, dragging their chairs to the side of the tub.

She continued to tease them, letting them look and only look at her body shimmering under the water. She tugged at her nipples and fondled her breasts, pushing away the first hand that reached for them. Then she slipped a hand beneath the water to play with her cunny and pleasured herself as they watched closely, the fire in their eyes giving away their agitation, as if the increasing length of their cocks were not proof of that.

Corinne sighed. She extended one wet leg and then the other out of the water, resting her calves on the rim of the tub. Quinn and Rob had an even better view between her legs. She concealed herself primly with both hands. "Get to work. Folded towels, please. The metal edge presses into my skin."

Quinn shoved Rob's shoulder, and the younger man got up, searching through the painter's rags for some that were cleaner.

He dragged two from a pile in the corner and folded them carefully before he knelt by the tub.

"Ah, I should have done the honors," Quinn said regretfully, realizing that his apprentice would have the pleasure of lifting the model's legs and making her comfortable.

Rob clasped one slender ankle and lifted her leg, resting it on his shoulder. He positioned the folded cloth over the rim of the tub with care. Then he set down her leg where it had been.

"Taking your sweet time about it, you are," Quinn grumbled.

"Be still," Corinne said. "He is very gentle and I do like him. He may take as much time as he likes."

Rob turned crimson and kept his eyes averted from the painter—but not from Corinne. She patted and played with her cunny while he put her other leg on his shoulder and arranged the cloth. He was still kneeling, looking almost worshipfully— at her face, for a wonder.

Her cheeks were rosy and her eyes shone with impudence. The apprentice's lovemaking agreed with her. Toiling in a hat shop or posing in clay-caked drapery was a far cry from lounging in a bath, enjoying the ardent attentions of two men.

"You are a sweet fellow," she murmured to him. "So you shall have me first."

He nodded but made no other reply, sitting back on his haunches. Corinne's foot slipped off his shoulder and she rested it against his chest, wiggling her toes. Her feet were slender and pretty, and she used them like a dancer, lifting the one on his chest to the side of his face. Rob turned and pressed a kiss against the high arch of her instep. Whatever she would give him, he wanted. It was almost as if Quinn were not there. The older man kept quiet, his arms folded across his chest, watching intently.

Corinne laughed in a low voice. "Go on then. Do as you will."

Rob clasped her foot in one hand, rubbing the sole gently and deeply with the other.

"How good that feels," she said with satisfaction.

He pressed his thumb against the ball of her foot, rubbing that in slow circles that made her arch with pleasure as far as the confines of the tub would let her. Then Rob moved to her toes, caressing each one in turn. Corinne sighed. He kissed her foot again and again, then applied his mouth to those pretty toes, sucking them one by one.

"Ahh." The exclamation was almost involuntary.

Quinn stood up. "Two can play at that game, Miss Perry."

She glanced up at him. "Then have at, Mr. Quinn."

The older man took his place by the younger, taking her other foot and treating it to rubs, kisses, and tender sucking. Corinne behaved as if such treatment were entirely her due, picking up the rags and refolding them to make a pillow for her neck. She wriggled around a bit to get it into position, then leaned her head back, letting her ringlets fall outside the tub. Dreamily, she watched the two men play with her feet and move on to stroking her calves. In silent agreement, they spread her legs farther apart. Corinne understood her cue. Her hands pulled apart the lips of her cunny and she let them have a good, long look at it.

When Quinn finally spoke, his voice was once again rough with lust. "Let us continue this on dry land, my dear. Come—we shall help you out." He extended a hand to her, and Rob followed his lead.

A little awkwardly, they pulled Corinne up and out. Quinn had the superior strength, having apprenticed as a housepainter in his youth. Hauling himself up a scaffold had built powerful shoulders and arms that he had never lost. She stood by the tub for only a moment before Quinn whipped off his linen shirt and began to dry her thoroughly. "My apologies—it is the only clean thing about—but it will do—"

She wriggled, enjoying the light texture of the linen upon her damp skin, turning this way and that to let him get at every inch of her. Then she put one foot upon a chair and took the shirt from him, wrapping her hair in an improvised turban that let a few wet ringlets escape.

The arms-up position showed her breasts to best advantage and put her bum on display as well. Rob reached out to stroke her buttocks.

Corinne looked over her shoulder, smiling at him. "Your hands are nicely warm. Keep on," she said.

Quinn cupped her full breasts. "And I shall warm these for you." He rubbed and squeezed the white flesh, trapping each of her nipples between his fingers, bending down to suck each one in turn as he had sucked her toes.

"Mmm," Corinne murmured. She placed a hand upon his bare, lightly furred chest, playing with Quinn's flat nipples in return, pinching one delicately and making him flinch. But his cock inside his breeches grew more stiff. She trailed her hand over his well-defined muscles, scratching him lightly with her fingernails and pinching his nipples again. Quinn relinquished her breasts and his head came up. He kissed her very roughly indeed, holding the back of her head and keeping her mouth where he wanted it, tonguing her and nipping at her lips. All the while, Rob stroked and fondled her arse, ceding the dominant role to his master.

Quinn broke it off, his breaths coming faster now. "Do you like her arse, then?" he asked Rob.

The apprentice nodded but stopped what he was doing.

"Then kneel and spread her cheeks. We shall tease her as she teased us. Apply your tongue to that nice, clean little arsehole and then push in the tip. It will not go far, but that will be all the more pleasurable for her. Lick and push, lick and push. We shall see how she likes it."

Corinne's eyes widened but she made no protest.

Rob dropped to his knees behind her and separated her buttocks. Quinn held Corinne where she was, looking over her shoulder and down at the apprentice. "Yes. That's the way, lad."

The younger man buried his face where he had been directed to do so, applying his tongue to the well-scrubbed hole. Held fast by Quinn, Corinne began to moan. She reached down a hand to stimulate her cunny, but Quinn grabbed her wrist before she could.

"No. Play with your tits, my girl. Both hands now. Give me a good show."

Steadied by Rob's hands upon her spread-open arse, Corinne kept her foot up on the chair, and caressed her breasts as Quinn watched. She took her erect nipples in her fingers and tugged at them, pulling her breasts into points.

"I would not have handled you so roughly," Quinn muttered. "But I like to see you do that."

"Kiss me again," she begged.

He bent down to oblige her, capturing her moans with his mouth. Rob stayed on his knees, providing tender stimulation to her arsehole, stopping now and then to nip her bum cheeks and kiss them too.

"Now then," Quinn said at last, his voice ragged. "Which of us shall go first?"

Corinne shook her head. "Neither."

He drew back as if he would slap her and Rob scrambled to his feet. "What?" Quinn asked angrily.

She patted his face. "I want both of you at once."

The older man relaxed. "Well, then. Decide what goes where."

Corinne whispered in Quinn's ear, as Rob stood sentinel, waiting with eager anticipation, as if he knew he would like whatever he would get.

"Very good," Quinn said, breaking into a smile. He let her

go and went to a cabinet to take out a rolled rug, a prop for his paintings, of Oriental design, thick, soft, and new, unrolling it on the floor. "One to suck and one to fuck. On all fours, my dear Miss Perry."

She inclined her head as elegantly as any duchess and the turban unwound, letting her hair spill over her shoulders. Corrine stepped upon the rug and kneeled down. Quinn was close enough for her to lay a hand upon the huge bulge in his breeches. He let her squeeze his rod several times, then set his legs wide apart so she could fondle his balls as well.

"Fair is fair," Quinn said in a minute. "You must do Rob as well. But take his cock out. Let's see how long he lasts, skin to skin."

With an indrawn breath, the apprentice hastily undid his breeches, pushing up the shirt he still wore. He had a fine, long rod that sprang forth, then stood up smack against his belly.

"Handle yourself, lad," Quinn said. "Don't mind me. Give the lady a mouthful if you want."

Looking down at Corinne on her knees before both of them, Rob began to masturbate with slow strokes that quickly became faster. His youthful balls, not so large as Quinn's, rose so high that the base of his cock swelled with them. She clasped his wrist and made him stop.

"You will come too soon," she said softly.

"Ah—don't—I want to—"

He let go and, without him touching himself at all, strong jets of cum shot from his rod, spraying freely all over her breasts. Corinne laughed for joy and rubbed the hot fluid into her skin. Rob struggled to catch his breath, unable to speak.

"Never mind. Rest a few minutes and it will happen again," Quinn said. "There are many advantages to being twenty-one."

The apprentice collapsed into a chair, the front flap of his breeches down, still holding up his shirt. His cock had not lost an iota of its stiffness.

"*Young Man In Repose*. A fine title. I ought to paint you," Quinn said thoughtfully.

"Not now, for God's sake," Rob muttered. He wrapped his member in a fold of his shirt and squeezed hard, taking away some of the sensitivity. A few extra drops of cum appeared at the hole in his knob and Corinne came forward on her knees to lick them up, polite as you please.

Rob moaned and closed his eyes.

"You licked my arsehole very nicely," she said. "I must return the favor—"

"You must see to my pleasure now," Quinn interrupted. He had shed his breeches, hose and shoes, and stood naked, towering over her.

"Very well." She stayed facing Rob, and wiggled her arse to indicate that the older man could come behind her if he wished to fuck her on all fours. Quinn walked around her as if he were at a Tattersalls horse show. Then he stepped over her body, his back to Rob, who watched them both through half-closed eyes, recovering. Quinn bent over to part Corinne's buttocks again, looking at the folds of flesh snugged between them. He squeezed her buttocks together, then separated them quickly, repeating the action several times, enjoying the juicy noise her cunny made, ignoring her faint protests at his rough play.

"I should like to stick a dildo up you," he mused lewdly. "And if you would be so good as to hold it half in and half out—I want to see you like that, Corinne. Enjoying a fine big cock that is neither mine nor Rob's."

"I don't mind." She looked over her shoulder at Quinn but only saw his arse. He had not turned around.

Quinn stepped off the rug and went to a different cabinet, his thick rod bobbing in front of him, stiff and strong. Rob sighed and got up, taking the opportunity to remove his clothes. His master returned.

Corinne's eyes shone with pleasure when she saw what Quinn held. A rod of smooth leather around a hard core, thicker in the middle than at either end, with a huge knob at the tip.

"Sit up," he commanded. "Play with this and see if you will like it."

She sat on her haunches and considered the possibilities of the thing, running her hand over it and squeezing the end.

"I like the softness of the big knob," she said. "With the hard rod driving it in, it will feel very good deep in my cunny."

"Oh? And have you such a device by your bed, my girl?"

Corinne blushed but only a little. "No. But if I had to invent something for women's pleasure, it would look like this."

Rob sat down again, his back as straight and stiff as his rested cock.

"Come around behind her," Quinn said. "The wench loves to be wanton."

The apprentice shook his head. "I would rather see her face. And I shall play with her tits while you fuck her with that."

"As you wish, lad. But you are missing the moment of penetration. And Corinne is extremely hot. She needs this rammed in, with all due respect to her person, as far as it will go. Do you not want to see that?"

Rob laughed and got up again. "Yes, I do."

Corinne handed over the dildo to Quinn and dropped her head down between her arms, eager to experience this new sensation. With two men watching her from behind, she seemed more excited than ever. A delicate flush crept over the skin of her neck and upper back.

Quinn's fingers separated cunny lips that were almost too swollen to be separated. He gently pushed the huge knob in between them, showing Rob how—after all, the young man was an apprentice in lovemaking too. Corinne pushed her bottom back, hungry for more, but Quinn's big hand stilled her. He rotated the knob just inside her tight cunny, then began to push it in, back and forth, but less than a fraction of an inch.

"She is tight, lad. And she has not lain often with men," he explained. "I can tell."

Her face covered by her abundant ringlets, Corinne nodded. The rosy flush upon her skin grew darker as embarrassment mingled with naughty delight.

"Are you ready?" Quinn asked. "Do you wish to be fucked now, love?"

She nodded again.

The older man thrust the dildo in, deeply but not hard, until it would go no further. Then he began to plunge it in and out, in and out. Corinne gasped with excitement, rocking on hands and knees to make the most of each stroke.

"There, Rob, you have seen that. Now you may look at her face."

The apprentice nodded and went around to the front of the rug, pushing her hair, now damp with sweat, away from her face. He stroked her back, soothing her, talking to her softly and telling her how beautiful she was.

"Like a young mare, eh?" Quinn said jovially. "All she needs is a pretty little saddle on her back and a silver bit in her mouth."

Rob made no reply as his master slid the dildo in and out, continuing to talk. "I have seen a mare take a big horse-cock for the first time, my lad. The animal was not so willing or so well-behaved."

The apprentice nodded absently, concentrating on Corinne, who was trembling. Quinn stopped and held the dildo in as far as it would go for several moments. "There, there, love," Quinn said. "It is deep inside, the way you like it best. I shall not stop again."

His voice was as soothing as Rob's caresses. Quinn resumed the steady thrusting. He looked down when the retreating knob made her cunny lips swell but never let it pop out, and alternated thrusting with delicious screwing. Corinne gave herself over completely to intense sensations that made her cunny drip upon the rug she kneeled on. The precious drops sank into the design without a trace until Quinn reached under to catch one in his palm, licking it up like the connoisseur of female flesh he was.

Quinn, an experienced rake, knew well that she could not reach orgasm unless her tiny bud was touched. He, however, was getting close to release. He stopped, leaving the rod half in and amused himself by making the half that was outside her body bounce, slapping it lightly. This new motion caused Corinne to cry out with frustrated pleasure. Rob craned his neck to see what his master was doing, and caught a glimpse of the dildo's rise and fall.

"Do you want to taste her, lad?" Quinn asked.

"No . . . no," Corinne moaned. "Do not take it out."

Quinn patted her behind. "Of course not. I meant for him to slide underneath you now and attend to your cunny. I shall push this big thing in and out and spin the knob, and he will suckle your clitoris all the while, as tenderly as female friends give each other pleasant relief when men will not."

Rob shook his head, not to say no, but in wonder at the erotic ease of his master's talk.

"First . . ." Corinne's voice was the merest whisper. "First let me have his cock in my mouth while that one is in me."

"Yes," Rob said to her. "Dear God, yes."

He positioned himself swiftly and she rose up, swallowing his erection halfway and fellating him with skill. He threw his head back and let her do it, not pushing so he would not choke her. Rob thrust his hands into her hair, though, so he could see. Quinn kept the dildo moving as he eyed the younger man's groin. When the muscles there tensed repeatedly, he withdrew the thing in an instant.

"Enough," Quinn said to Rob. "I want to fuck her and I want you to watch. I suspect that you like to."

A shudder ran through Rob's body, as if his seed, about to spray out harder than before, had been forcibly withdrawn inside him as well. "I do," was all he said.

The older man turned Corinne onto her back at last, letting her relax into a sprawl with her creamy thighs far apart. He picked up the dildo and put the knob to her lips, watching with a half-smile as she licked it absent-mindedly.

"Mmm. Now you are lazy. How lovely you are," he said, putting the thing to one side. "I shall take you first. Legs up to your shoulders, if you please. Rob, hold her feet."

Corinne raised her legs and rocked on her arse, kicking her feet for Rob to catch. Once more he sucked her toes, then stopped when his master came over the woman they shared, holding himself up with his strong arms while his apprentice kept her in position. In a second Quinn plunged his thick cock into her cunny, pounding down in a perfect frenzy of lust. His balls hit her upraised bottom with each stroke, and the sensation made her wilder than before. It was all Rob could do to hang on, so vigorously did his master swive the girl. But it was not long before Quinn pulled out, roaring in anticipation of climax.

He pumped his slick, throbbing member with one strong hand until he ejaculated, aiming a fountain's spray at Corinne's rounded thighs. In another minute Rob let go of her feet, but she kept her legs up, rubbing Quinn's cum into the skin there as she had first rubbed Rob's into her breasts.

The older man dropped onto the rug next to her, throwing his arm over his head and panting. "You next, lad. I shall be the cunny man and not you. Up you get," he said to Corinne.

She rolled about and got on all fours once more, shoving her breasts into Quinn's face. Exhausted as he was, he sucked and fondled them, making sounds of satisfaction. When he saw Rob's feet walk around them both, Quinn let go and edged backward, resting his head between Corinne's knees.

"Excellent view," he murmured. "Come on, Rob. I don't bite. But I might give you a lick too. Can't be helped."

The apprentice's thighs appeared behind Corinne, pressing in as his long cock dangled between her thighs. Rob put the head of his cock at her cunny, then thrust—and slipped. Quinn sighed. He grabbed the younger man's cock, and positioned it properly.

"There. Go!"

The excitement that all three were experiencing made inhibition vanish. Rob pushed in, Corinne slammed back, and Quinn brought his head up to give her cunny what it craved. His expert stimulation had her to the point of orgasm a second after Rob's thighs began to shake. The apprentice howled with his final thrust, buried far inside her. Sucking away, his forehead wet from rubbing her cunny, Quinn barely heard Corinne cry out too. It was Rob's name she was calling, he realized. Oh, well . . . but seeing a huge cock and balls pushing hard into a cunny had got him excited all over again.

The trio came apart, looking at each other with bewildered but happy eyes. Quinn wiped his mouth.

"One more time," he said. "For me, that is."

"But . . ." Rob threw his master a surprised look.

Corinne only laughed and rolled over onto her belly. "Coming twice is not only for young men, Rob."

"Really? And how would you know that?" he asked indignantly. She did not bother to reply, but twirled a ringlet around her finger and looked at the ceiling.

"Watch me," said Quinn. "Corinne, put your feet together."

She obliged, kicking a little in a flirtatious way, as satisfied as a well-fucked woman could be.

"This requires oil." The older man got up, his erection a

proud contrast to the now limp Rob, who looked somewhat abashed.

He found a small bottle and uncorked it, dripping a little on Corinne's feet, then rubbing them again, taking and giving even more pleasure in doing so this time. She sighed with pleasure and rested her head on her arms. Quinn stood as Rob watched, interested despite his momentary flash of jealousy. The artist put one big hand around Corinne's ankles, holding her feet in such a way that her pretty arches made a hole.

Into which Quinn's cock slid. She aided him by pressing her feet together, smiling all the while. His knob, flushed dark purple-red, thrust repeatedly through the snug opening she provided for him. Looking down at her bouncing behind and the sinuous curves of her back, Quinn began to groan as he fucked harder. He held her ankles tighter, thoroughly enjoying the well-lubricated friction that reddened the soles of her feet. With one last prodigious roar, Quinn came again.

Quickly written but written well enough. It was, as I said, the first story in the book. Watching Xavi read it was quite amusing—her eyes widened and she sighed appreciatively in all the right places. Of course, I had to ask if she liked it. Literary vanity can never be underestimated.

"Very much, Edward. But is it true?"

I shrugged. "Most stories have a grain or two of truth. What does it matter?"

She raised an eyebrow and launched into a tale of her own, about her two stalwart footmen and how they had serviced her. I assumed she was merely trying to make me jealous and that all of it was invented, but I could not be positive. Xavi's behavior in the bedroom gave the lie to her innocent appearance, and it was not as if we were always together. What she did in the other hours of the day—and with whom—was a secret known to her alone, and I tried not to think about it overmuch.

4

By the end of the month . . .

I begin again. I am getting nowhere. Mrs. Mayhew, a capable housekeeper who sees to every detail so that I may write undisturbed far into the night, gave me three tall candles hours ago, smooth and straight. They are but stubs now, the last of the molten wax dripping from the candelabra in delicate curlicues. The flames are sputtering. I ought to stop.

My attempts to organize the papers are half-hearted and I am no further along than I was two weeks ago. As no one will ever read this but me, perhaps it makes no difference if my account moves back and forth in time, and does not follow the rules of conventional narrative. I only confuse myself.

Nonetheless, at times I find my Sisyphean labor quite entertaining. Unlike the unfortunate Sisyphus and the monstrous rock he was doomed to roll uphill for all eternity, I find that paper is somewhat lighter.

Memories and thoughts, of course, are less substantial than air. But they matter. A careful examination of one's past is a worthwhile endeavor for a man who wishes not to repeat past mistakes. And I have made many. It is my nature to act first and think later.

As to other aspects of my personality, I see that I have provided a description that is accurate and not altogether flattering.

I am both sentimental and rational, with a marked ambivalence about love, like my Anne. I sought out her brother at last, soon after his return to London . . .

"Edward! It is so good to see you again!" Thomas rose from his chair and embraced me with enthusiasm.

Laughing, I slapped him on the back. "You look just the same, my dear friend. Heavier, perhaps. But it suits you."

Thomas slapped his ample belly. With a wink, he indicated the gnawed bones on his plate. "I like to eat. I have done nothing else since my return from Jamaica."

"I see."

"Please, sit down, sit down." He waved the waiter over. "Whatever the gentleman wants—what do you want, Edward? A good English beefsteak? A rasher of bacon? A saddle of lamb?"

"I am not such a glutton as that. But I will have a small steak, grilled rare. And a mug of ale."

The waiter nodded, took up Thomas's plate of bones, and headed for the kitchen. My friend sat back inside the spindled arms of his sturdy chair, content to pick his teeth. My gaze wandered elsewhere. His sojourn in the West Indies had not improved his manners, but he looked robust and happy.

I had come looking for him at once, advised by my butler, the worthy Decimus, that my boyhood friend had called unexpectedly at the house and asked me to dine with him at the chophouse in Soho.

The place attracted a raffish lot, artists and the like. I had been here once before with Quinn, who enjoyed himself royally wherever he was, shouting insults across the table at his chief rival, the painter Will Fotheringay.

Fortunately neither was here today—I doubted they were even out of bed at two in the afternoon. Thomas and I could talk without raising our voices, the only men among the artists' models and prostitutes who had come in for a late breakfast. I spied Corinne in a corner, nibbling at a lambchop she held in her fingers, her feet crossed at the ankles. She was the very picture of ladylike decorum and did not even glance my way.

Thomas and I had much to catch up on—I had not seen him in ten years. An hour passed before he casually mentioned his sister, a topic I had hoped he would introduce. To seem overly interested might give me away, but I was perishing of curiosity. The London scandal sheets did not cover the humdrum news of the country as a rule. The Leonard family was very old and its most illustrious members had distinguished themselves in various ways, but they had lived quietly in Devonshire for centuries. At the time of Anne's marriage, she had left that life and that name behind, a further hindrance to my finding out what had happened to her.

Beset by my youthful jealousy of the unknown man she was to marry, I had asked no questions then as to his name or occupation. Showing up at the ceremony would have been unthinkable and I had received no invitation in any case. I was convinced my presence would have upset Anne. Her hasty explanation of her impending marriage on the night we became lovers told me little.

Looking back, I would interpret her words differently than I did at the time. Her guardian expected her to please him by marrying the man of his choice. Anne had accepted her fate, no doubt not wanting to be a burden to her family.

"Edward!" Thomas said loudly. He clapped his hands. "You are daydreaming! Is it the ale or—" —he cast a meaningful look in Corinne's direction as she patted her mouth with a napkin— "or has that little tart caught your eye?"

"Neither," I replied absently. I pushed my plate aside. "Shall we go?"

"Don't tell me you are not interested in so pretty a girl. I have heard that you are a great lover."

I rose, grinning. "I suppose I ought to blush."

"Only if it is true." Thomas scraped back his chair and used the table to push himself to his feet. "Ah, my knees are not what they used to be. You are hale and hearty, Edward. What is your secret?"

"I do not drink or eat to excess, and I take regular exercise."

He looked at me narrowly. "Spoken like a prig."

"I assure you that I am not."

Thomas slapped the table. "Glad of it! Let us repair to Hyde Park and look at the women. It is a pleasure to see so many English roses in bloom again."

A hired carriage brought us there in good time, and we alighted near Rotten Row. Our equipage and coachman might as well have been invisible. I smiled to myself, enjoying the edifying sight of the rich at play. Phaetons and curricles passed swiftly by, an inconvenience to those who merely promenaded and complained bitterly of the dust.

A lovely rider went by without a look to the right or the left, holding firmly to the reins of her gelding.

Thomas nodded approvingly. "Lord Gilberte's wife, Fiona. I have heard much about her, but I expect only half of it can be believed."

"And what might that be?" I looked at her back, admiring her fine seat upon her steed, and the glimpse of glossy brown hair under her hat. "You are more up on the latest tittle-tattle than I, my dear Thomas."

"He is old and very rich, and a dreadful lecher. She finds her pleasure elsewhere."

A familiar story. He went on, but I only half-listened. The subject of his gossip was far ahead of us by now.

By the time we parted, I had obtained the information I sought: Anne's address in London.

* * *

I found the house with some difficulty—the door was non-descript and the dark stone of the exterior was forbidding. The high, narrow windows were swathed in some dark stuff and not a flicker of light could be seen in them. I raised my hand to the doorknocker and hesitated. It was made of heavy brass, and depicted a nameless creature whose lips curled back over pointed teeth. From the nose hung a heavy ring. I imagined the ponderous sound it made when employed, producing an effect that was anything but welcoming. The creature's blank eyes seemed to offer a sullen warning: *go back*.

I felt my spine stiffen. I would not. My hand seized the ring and I knocked three times slowly as Thomas had specified. Someone on the other side slid the cover from a peephole in the door that I had not noticed. The faint sound drew my attention to the eye that looked at me for a long moment, greatly magnified by the bulbous glass. Cold and green, there was something reptilian about the eye and a blackness in its depths. With a tiny click, the peephole was closed again, and the eye's owner opened the door.

The man had but one. The other was covered by a patch of black silk that emphasized the aristocratic cut of his features. He bowed to me and gestured me inside. I entered with a feeling of trepidation, noting the luxury of my surroundings. The man led me to a parlor and said in a low voice that the mistress of the house would be down to see me.

I took the opportunity to study my surroundings. Red and black were the dominant colors, and the effect was oppressive. The windows were completely covered by several layers of drapery. The outermost ones were of the darkest shade, progressing in gradations of scarlet that were the color of flame at the center. Each window resembled a fireplace, to draw a polite comparison—or the mouth of hell, if one wished to be rude and honest.

So it was here that Anne lived. I scarcely believed it. Her sunny nature would be dimmed—she could never be happy in a house like this. Thomas had said that she had recently purchased it. He had done what a male relative was expected to do in the way of assisting her. Perhaps she had bought it with furnishings intact and was about to undertake its renovation. That explanation seemed satisfactory.

The man with the eyepatch reappeared with a glass of whiskey, offering it as if he knew that it was what I liked. No doubt Anne had told him of my preferences. I took a sip, cheered by its warmth going down. It put me in mind of summer days with her. However brief our affair had been, the memory of it would always be fresh.

I had been too young then, I mused, to truly appreciate her, or even to know her, for all my puppylike adoration. And as the years had gone by, I came to realize that she had held back much. The peculiar circumstances of her guardianship were still not clear to me. She had been married off in a hurry; I had always hoped that she had married well.

Thomas had informed me that she was a widow. I imagined her in the modest attire she had always favored, more expensive now perhaps. He'd said in an offhand way that her late husband's estate had been managed well enough and surely the income from her dower was substantial.

I sipped my whiskey, becoming aware of noises overhead. Footsteps moving across the floor, then coming down the stairs—I rose when Anne came into the room.

She was beautiful, more beautiful than I remembered. The years had been very kind. The roundness of her face had matured into an elegance that a young woman could never have. Her hair was still honey-blond but swept back from her face and pinned up, adorned with a diamond clip. She moved gracefully toward me, her dark-hued gown rustling over the floor, and I set down my glass with a bang that nearly broke it.

With joy, I rose from my chair and held out my arms to embrace my first love again.

No, her dress was not exactly modest. Her deep décolletage revealed her breasts as she never would have done in more innocent days. The wonderful sight stirred sensual memories. Without further thought, I kissed her—and she returned the kiss with passionate skill. With wonder in my heart, I thought to myself that she could still teach me a few things about love. Never, save with Xavi, had I been so intensely drawn to a woman, so eager to give pleasure as I had been on my one night with Anne Leonard.

Xavi's face faded from my mind as I pulled away from Anne to look at her face, touching a finger to the dear lips that had first kissed mine. Then I saw the spark that had enlivened her eyes fade away.

"What is it, dearest?" I asked. "Are you not happy to see me?"

"Of course I am," she said, patting my shoulder.

"Thomas told me that you were living in London now and that you had been widowed. I hope you do not mind that I sought you out."

"No, not at all. You have turned out very well, Edward. Are you happy?"

"Yes, I suppose so." Her question was simple but the answer was not. I could not tell her that I was madly in love with the wife of a married man, and that Xavi made me very happy indeed.

"Life in London must agree with you." She raised a hand to my chest, resting her fingertips there for a fraction of a second. "You must have an excellent tailor. He fits you to perfection." The light sensation of her touch went directly to my cock, as did her next words. "Yes, you are a handsome man and a masterful one."

"Anne—"

"Perhaps I should have married you."

Her tone was dry and she avoided my eyes. I thought to distract her by asking to see the rest of her new house. Then I hesitated. Perhaps she only wished to chat for a while and it was rather late at night. Still, her letter had specified the hour and here I was.

"I would like to talk to you, Anne. So much has happened since we parted—and you went away to be married."

She made no immediate reply but took my hand and brought me into a room filled with dark furniture and more scarlet draperies. There on a sideboard stood crystal decanters of whiskey and port on a silver tray, along with glasses to serve both. The glass of whiskey that the man with the eyepatch had brought to me had come from here.

The way the chairs were drawn up around the tables suggested a party about to take place, but we were quite alone. I pulled out a chair for her and she sat, gracefully tucking her dark gown under her bottom.

"That was a very different life. It is over," she said.

"Was he kind to you?"

She held her head high. "No. Please sit down."

I did, keeping a polite distance, even though I wanted to pull her into my lap and kiss her madly.

"What happened?" I regretted the question immediately. I should not have brought up the subject at all—former husbands make for dreary discussions.

"I would rather not say."

There, she had put paid to it. Good. I did not want her to think I was prying.

She ran a hand over the back of the empty chair nearest her and sighed. "Business is slow."

"What?"

She looked at me warily. "I suppose Thomas did not tell you everything."

I was baffled but unsure of how best to reply. "Perhaps not." That seemed safe enough.

Shaking her head, Anne rose to go to the sideboard and poured two glasses of whiskey, handing me one. "Then I will," she said, and drank hers down without a sound.

Back in Devonshire I had never seen her imbibe wine, let alone strong spirits. She licked her lips daintily. Most women would have coughed and spluttered. Very well. So she had acquired somewhat of a taste for drink. That was no reason to judge her. Perhaps her late husband had insisted that she share his midnight tipple.

The mysterious union between husbands and wives, especially the ones who hated each other, was ever a puzzle to me. Looking at Anne's composed but unhappy face, I thought of Xavi. Even she felt bound to her husband, under obligation to the lifelong sacrament of marriage, no matter how Don Diego neglected her or raged at her or how many others he coaxed into his bed. In the act of taking her virginity, she swore, his mind had been elsewhere.

Unlike me. Schooled by an older woman, my sexual nature unleashed in one deliciously wicked night, I had learned the secret of sexual bliss well before I lost my virginity to Anne: connection. I had listened to her, loved her well, took her seriously and teased her gently. And when she gave me her body, I gave her something like worship in return.

I hoped that was how she remembered it. Anne was lost in thought. I sipped my whiskey and studied her without speaking. Was I guilty of infidelity to my darling Xavi? Not yet.

The rush of feelings awakened at that moment eclipsed all others. (I will add at this point that I did not entirely believe Xavi's wide-eyed affirmations of her fidelity to *me*. Surely every wife must go now and again to her marriage bed, if only to forestall arguments about the subject. Men are simple enough to manage when their sexual needs are met.)

Cynical thoughts indeed, I told myself, for a man who has not married and does not wish to. It was possible that Anne had spoiled me for that. When we had parted ten years ago, I knew instinctively that I would never find another so passionate and so kind.

"Will you spend the night with me, Edward?"

Her soft-spoken question dumbfounded me. It had come out of nowhere but it could be said that she had only given voice to our mutual longing for each other, strong as ever. I could not say no. And so my sensual education began all over again . . .

5

When I left Anne's bed to go home the next morning, I slept for hours. Awakened by Decimus—the dear old fellow seemed to think that I had died, so deep was my slumber—I bathed and dressed, I went out again to the borrowed house in which Xavi and I met. No, not to see her, but to leave a letter in the locked cabinet. My reawakened passion for Anne, my night in her loving arms—ah, I had no idea what twists and turns lay in the road ahead where either woman was concerned. But in the matter-of-fact light of day, I felt compelled to forbid myself the pleasure of sexual intercourse with my naughty Xavi for the time being.

A tactful explanation was in order. I did not mention Anne and wrote only that I could not see her, Xavi, for the next several weeks. The borrowed house seemed to echo with emptiness—I stood for a while in the bedroom, all too aware of everything we had done there behind closed doors.

When I went to the library to leave my letter in the cabinet, I was surprised to see a missive from Xavi already waiting.

Here it is—I kept it.

To look at it again makes me wonder why I bothered. It is to the point, almost curt. In it she informed me that Don Diego seemed suspicious. She thought it best to "lie low." I wondered at the time where she had picked up the colorful language of thieves and beggars, chalking it up to the bad influence of vulgar plays and racy novels, which are every lady's vice.

(Another parenthetical note to myself: any novel, racy or not, in which the hero loves two heroines simultaneously will be thrown against the wall by female readers and never finished.)

So, I was off the hook. But that did not make me feel less guilty. In less than twenty-four hours, I had returned to my first love, a not very respectable but charming widow who was free to do as she pleased at last, and put aside my new one, the wife of another man.

Sin and guilt are relative under such circumstances, and I am no saint. Nor was Anne. Why do I say she was not very respectable?

Her house was a brothel. Nearly penniless after her husband's estate had been settled to the satisfaction of his greedy cousins, she had come to London and gone into business.

A very specialized sort of business. Anne catered to some of the richest men in London, charging thousands of pounds to satisfy unusual desires of all stripes. Her establishment was so exclusive and its clientele so afraid of blackmail that it was not even listed in Harris's Guide, a bible of the netherworld.

The hellish mood its décor evoked was perfectly suited to what went on there. I knew her as Anne; her clients called her La Belle Dame Sans Merci. The beautiful woman without mercy. Her late and unlamented husband had left her little choice. Anne had been forced to turn her own secret love of the birch into her specialty. It was a lucrative one.

She assured me that her brother was too complacent to be suspicious. He had never been above the first floor of her house, owing to his knees. I thought that Thomas simply did not want to know. He could figure out why his sister required so large a house near Grosvenor Square if he had to; he was a man of the world. But he asked no questions.

Anne was sure her brother did not frequent brothels, and as I said, hers was not listed. No, Thomas liked easy-going, cheerful affairs that lasted just long enough for both parties to feel comfortable and not so long that he grew bored. He preferred the company of females who loved to eat and drink as he did. As much as the complexity of women like Xavi and Anne intrigued me, I understood my old friend's delight in a sunny countenance.

Despite what she did for a living, Anne's sweet smile still appeared from time to time. I was glad indeed that it was not gone forever—she was not so hard as all that. But she swore up and down that she would never marry again. Her choice of profession would have made it difficult to do in any case.

So I felt no guilt on that score, and she would not have wanted me to. She made her own decisions and I could not dictate to her, nor did I want to. However, Anne did defer to my wishes in one way: I thought it best that our bedroom be furnished differently from the rest of the gloomy house.

It was a private retreat that we both loved, its windows flung wide open on fine days. The room needed no heavy curtains to mask what went on within, as it was on the top floor and no one could see in.

We often lay in bed after making love, watching the clouds go by during the day. The topmost branches of a tall old tree in front of the house seemed to try to catch them but they never succeeded. Thick with leaves in summer, the tree shattered the light into green-gold reflections that danced on our walls. The moon changed green-gold into silver when it rose, swelling into fullness as the days progressed.

In that room we were happy, unaware of time. It was bliss.

In my arms she became the dear Anne I remembered so well, and I loved her that way.

At other times, sitting in the parlor and taking tea, we were as proper as husband and wife. We discussed the change in her circumstances only once more—I knew that it was painful to her to have come down in the world in such a way. Yet she treasured her hard-won independence.

She scorned the least trace of pity, so I hid mine. Perhaps compassion is a better word for what I felt for her. Men control every aspect of female lives, and if women cannot or will not marry, there is no honest way for them to earn their bread. Yet I felt that the house might become a prison she could not escape.

Anne disagreed. I remember the fight. It was our first.

"It is outside this house that I feel oppressed, Edward. The city is so crowded—I am compelled to withdraw from its streets."

"Is that healthy?" I asked her.

"I am a country-bred widow and I was a poor one when I started out, with no social standing. The women of my own class wanted nothing to do with me, and the men followed their lead. Now they only stare. Too many know me by reputation."

"That is only to be expected," I said patiently. She would have bridled, and rightly so, at the least hint of judgment in my tone.

"How can I make you understand?" Her voice had a poignant catch. "The eyes of others—of people on the street—are my prison. Not this house."

I knew instantly what she meant. I could not argue.

"Within these walls, doing what I have chosen to do, I put on a mask and play my part. I am in charge—they may look at me only if I wish them to. It pays handsomely. And I have already set by a considerable sum for my old age, when I shall return to the country."

She sighed and turned her face away, and we discussed it no more.

With Xavi unavailable, I took more time to develop the business plans I mentioned, but the fortune I hoped to build seemed no more than an empty dream. I spent my free hours with Anne, who laughingly called me a libertine. She preferred an arrangement like that of my male secretary and his lifelong companion, whereby love was constant and lust might be occasionally indulged elsewhere.

She did not care if I followed my cock when it pointed to another female—in fact, she sometimes threw me at them so I would leave her alone. But she needed to know that my heart was reserved for her alone. Anne's own weakness was still for younger men, and to satisfy that, she had me. Like many a practitioner of the amorous arts, she was open-minded. As far as I knew, she was faithful to me. In her way.

Little trace of her country upbringing remained. Anne had become sophisticated to a fault. Her establishment had been designed to attract and keep clients who were used to the best of everything, and they paid handsomely to bring cherished fantasies to life. A man who had been overly stimulated in his boyhood by whipping from a governess not much older than himself could relive the experience in every detail.

I witnessed one such session from a comfortable hiding place behind the walls of the room set aside for discipline of this sort. Anne thought it wise to let me satisfy my sexual curiosity, preferring to keep me in her house to do it. She brought me into the hiding place, which had a separate door from the main room, installed for the discreet entrance and exit of clients who liked to watch.

In it sat an armchair and next to that was an assortment of good liquor, to prime the pump, so to speak. Before the armchair was a plump cushion, should a voyeur wish to pay extra for a woman to entertain him while he observed the man being whipped. Besides the transparent mirror directly in front of the armchair, the walls of the hideaway were lined with ordinary mirrors, to double and redouble the view inside, offering a dizzying profusion of whores for the price of only one.

Anne brought me in before the next session began, and made me comfortable herself. As she would be doing the honors and not one of her assistants, I was very eager to see it all.

The gown she wore was made to reveal as much of her splendid body as possible. It was black, of some lustrous stuff, and fit like a second skin. The neck was high to give her beautiful face an aspect of sternness but the front and back had been cut out to fully reveal her bare buttocks and lovely breasts. The dressmaker's art lifted her breasts up and out, and trimmed her waist into the bargain. Anne wore high-heeled boots underneath that the client had provided in advance.

Made of glove leather, they fit her shapely calves to perfection and were so soft that the shape of her toes could be seen. The high heels added several inches to her height, enabling her to command the ardent respect of the man she would punish.

Through the walls we heard the client enter, accompanied by the woman who would prepare him for the session. I looked at him through the transparent mirror on the wall. He gazed straight at me but of course saw only himself.

Good-looking and well-dressed, he seemed nervous. The woman with him took his clothes as he removed them, revealing a muscular body that made Anne's eyes sparkle. He was not unlike me, perhaps a year or two younger, but blond and blue-eyed. His attendant asked him to squat over a low bath, slapping his dangling cock in the water until it rose up, dripping. He seemed to enjoy it, but he had to struggle to keep his balance. Then she washed his cock and balls vigorously and rudely, using strong soap and a rough cloth.

He was already fully erect and his cock was enormous. The woman concentrated her attentions upon his buttocks next, scrubbing his pale skin until it glowed. Then she wrapped the washcloth around one finger and jammed it into his arsehole repeatedly.

The man flinched but sighed with pleasure.

"I assure you that he has asked for this," Anne whispered to me. "The rough scrubbing and strong soap make his buttocks more sensitive, and he will enjoy his whipping more."

I shrugged. I did not share his sexual tastes, but I suspected that what I was about to see would intrigue me.

Anne dropped a kiss upon my hair, and went out the door of the hideaway. I settled down to see what would happen next, and poured myself a glass of whiskey. She would make an entrance in good time—right now the woman with the blond man led him to the English horse, a padded contraption rather like a ladder whose use Anne had explained to me.

The client's wrists and hands could be strapped to it; his cock and balls toyed with or punished through an opening in the front. The client's face was also provided with an opening, perhaps to view the erotic play of women or men or both, and the chin rested on a padded rail. The horse could be adjusted to different heights, depending on the man, or even bent in half, for those with a very strong appetite for humiliation.

Our man had chosen to be bent over. The woman who had bathed him fastened the straps around his ankles first and then his wrists, leaving his hands relatively free. He was able to move but not much. He seemed restless, but then being forced to wait was part of his pleasure.

At that moment Anne entered. The man's eyes lit up at the sight of her, but she looked at him with scorn. She walked slowly around him, letting him look his fill at her bare behind and jutting breasts. He would not be permitted to touch either, but she might rub both in his face if she felt like it. Her voice low, she requested a set of hempen ropes that had been set to one side, which the other woman handed to her.

"You have asked to be tied. Understand that I am not gentle."

"I do not wish you to be gentle, mistress," he said. "I want to be made to obey. Command me as you will."

Anne went in back of him, spreading his legs by pressing her booted foot to his bare one and pushing it away from the other. The touch, the first she had granted him, made him grab the sides of the horse to steady himself. Knowing what he was about to get made him tremble.

She came around again and put her behind an inch away from his face.

"Please, mistress. Please push back," he whispered.

Luxuriously and slowly, Anne ground her naked buttocks against his face. He pressed kisses upon her silky skin, again and again. Then she straightened and went about the interesting business of humiliating him further.

My love made a loop in one of the ropes and placed it around his balls. Slowly, letting him enjoy the rasp of the hemp, she drew it into a tight circle. His balls looked even bigger. She tugged at the rope, securing the ends to a ring on the wall behind him.

Then she went to the side of the horse to reach through the opening and grabbed his huge cock, looking calmly at his face. He strained and bucked, held in place by the ball-encircling rope knotted through the wall ring, trying to control himself and not ejaculate too soon.

Anne made the horse rock. His balls bulged. She gave him another good face-grinding that left him breathless with lust, before she turned to pull down his foreskin. With delicate malice, she pressed the fine edges of her fingernails into the throbbing head. The sensation thrilled him—the blond man moaned with delight.

She made a loop in another piece of rope and placed this just under the head, tying the two ends to either side of the horse so that his cock was precisely in the middle and immobilized. Then she picked up a bundle of slender twigs.

"Are you ready?" she asked.

"Yes, mistress," he whispered.

She went in back of him once more, and gave him a whipping that could only be described as elegant. Many of her clients would return home to wives who knew nothing of the time they spent here, and the stripes they received could not be too harsh. The birching Anne administered was measured accordingly, and she reserved the most intense whipping for the part that showed the least: his balls.

His legs were spread to their utmost to show them properly. She had explained the importance of forcing a client like this to show his cock, balls, arse and arsehole to his mistress upon command and ask humbly for her mistreatment. The sensitive scrotum tightened and turned scarlet from her strokes.

He cried out with gratitude, begging for more, but Anne stopped. The woman who had prepared the man for his session left and came in with another prostitute, Perdita Wilkes, the house favorite because of her wonderfully round behind.

She stood in front of him in stockings and shoes, then bent forward until she could clasp her ankles. All I could see of her was legs and cunny. Perdita's hair tumbled over her shoes and her breasts were pressed against her thighs. Her best feature, her arse, was on full show. Anne came around to whip Perdita next, laying it on lightly but well.

The blond man watched intently, clutching the sides of the horse to steady himself again. He could not move forward or back between the cock ropes and the ball rope in the ring. The pleasure that his bondage gave him was obviously intense.

Anne's fine arse tensed and her jutting breasts bounced with each swish of the birch upon Perdita's quivering behind. I looked at the face of the man strapped to the horse, who was watching both of them with tears in his eyes. He was seconds away from climax. Anne signaled the first woman to birch his arse once more.

She picked up a second bundle and did so, with more vigor than Anne was using on Perdita, whipping fast and well. His muscles bulged as his arms and legs moved involuntarily in the restraints. Perdita straightened and came to kneel in front of him, wrapping her lips around the head of his bound cock and waiting only a moment more.

Screaming with pleasure, birched to orgasm, he came in great spurts that shook his body. Perdita sucked neatly, not missing a drop, aided by the tight bondage that prevented him from gagging her with wild thrusts.

Anne smiled and patted the blond man's face, wiping his tears of ecstasy away. Her voice was soothing, but I could not quite hear the words. Her manner toward him was entirely professional and I felt no jealousy...only arousal. To be bound and whipped was not my pleasure, yet I found that watching it was incredibly stimulating.

Her conduct toward her client was dominating, true, but not unkind. His submissiveness, his admiration of her, had echoes of my own feelings for her at a much younger age. His intense pleasure and explosive release was glorious to watch. Bound and thoroughly birched, he no doubt was thinking back to the woman, whoever she was, who had first excited him in this way.

Anne had given him precisely what he wanted.

But punishment of this sort was not all that my love provided in the way of entertainment. Nor did she care to work that hard. The more ingenious women devised scenarios of their own, and the loyal clientele kept coming back for more. Other women flocked in to get their share of the work: Belle Symonds, an experienced procuress, Emma Dighton, the former mistress of a great duke, and the female known only as

Mrs. Peek, whose ripped clothes earned her a small fortune. But they were outdone by a new girl who had lately joined the house. She charged the highest price of all.

I had no opportunity to see her in action—her chamber had no closet in which to hide or an adjacent room. Anne told me only that her name was Kitty, and would not otherwise satisfy my curiosity about the newcomer.

But one day, after we had withdrawn to our own chamber and I had satisfied her six ways from Sunday with my cock, my mouth, and my hands, she at last permitted me to visit Kitty, whose last client for today had left.

With some trepidation—was Anne testing my love for her?—I agreed to, if she would accompany me. I was curious as to what sort of reception I would get. Prior to Kitty's arrival, I had been readily accepted by the other women as Anne's fancy-man, to use their phrase. They knew almost nothing about me besides my first name and they asked no questions. Like Anne, they seldom left the house, and that was true of Kitty as well.

Relaxed from our lovemaking and perhaps a bit giddy, we abandoned our treetop chamber and went down the stairs. She made the introductions, not bothered by the girl's near nudity. Even in her house, the most expensive establishment of its kind in London, the women were not always dressed. It was not the sort of business that required it.

I nodded politely and entered the room, turning around when I heard Anne say good-bye. She went down the stairs with quick steps.

Her silent message was clear: *I trust you.*

Looking again at Kitty, I marveled at her beauty. Her hair was jet black, cut like a boy's but with a jagged edge. Her eyes were an odd shade of green and tilted at the corners, with a soft expression. It was no wonder that she had been nicknamed Kitty—she looked very much like a cat.

"Hello." The one word had as soft a quality as her unusual

eyes. I tried not to stare. Her bare breasts were high and her hips were narrow. Yet when she had moved to welcome us to her room I had noted an alluring and very feminine curve to her buttocks. She wore very little: black silk mitts that covered her hands but not her fingers and black half-boots, and a tiny triangle of strapped silk to cover her quim. It only made her look more naked.

There was a half-bath in the corner where she must have just bathed herself. I caught no musky whiff of sex about her person. Unconcernedly, she walked to her bed and sat down. I chose a chair near it. What was I to do? She smiled at me and I smiled back.

"I suppose Mistress Anne brought you to my room to tempt you," she said matter-of-factly.

My mouth opened and closed again. There was no safe response I could make to that remark. But what if Kitty were right? It was a test I would have to pass, for I loved Anne. I thought of the blond man struggling against the restraints he had requested and wished irrationally that I could be bound to the chair I sat in if I indeed was being tested.

Kitty opened her legs. The black silk triangle was tested too and it failed to cover her. One edge of it slipped inside her cunny. The wanton girl pulled on the thin straps until all of the black silk was folded within her folds.

She rose from the bed and used the little thing to masturbate. It must have been soaked with her sweet juice, but I dared not touch her and find out. The mitts on her hands drew my eyes to the slender fingers and what they were exploring. She held and stroked her clitoris, reaching an orgasm quite quickly that did not seem feigned.

Ignoring me for the moment, she sauntered over to her vanity table. There was a diamond clip upon it, small but pretty, a present from a wealthy client perhaps. She opened it and put it into her hair, as if she had forgotten all about the cunny she had just stimulated to climax and the man who had watched her do it.

I took the opportunity to look at her beautiful arse. Then I noticed she was watching me in the mirror and felt like a fool. I moved my gaze to her face, detecting for the first time a glittering instability in her eyes. Her youth and her air of innocence had deceived me at first.

But I would not give in. All the same, I could see why she charged the most. It was not so much what she could do, but rather who she was: an unknowable girl with a dangerous edge.

Kitty stopped what she was doing and flung herself back upon the bed. The sight of her in boots, and the white legs she kicked so freely was giving me a hellish erection.

"Would you like to see what I do for my clients?" she asked.

"Why not?" I hoped my voice was calm. Inwardly I was not. I would look a far bigger fool if I had to hang on to the chair to keep from touching her.

She walked away from me and brought over a tray that had been placed upon the table. I had noticed it as I came in, assuming she'd had tea brought up for her refreshment. But there was only cream in a small jug and a flowered saucer, rimmed with white.

This she set upon the floor a little distance away from me, pouring the cream into the saucer. She kneeled before it, then bent over to lap the cream with her tongue. The pose spread her buttocks open and I could see . . . well, what one sees there. Her flesh seemed very new indeed, tight and untried.

She took her time about drinking her cream, but she eventually sat up.

"Very pretty," I said. "Do your clients like to watch that?"

"Very much. I had a tail made, a long one, of fur. The short end of it is leather. That goes in my arsehole. Some men like to put it in for me as I lick up my cream." She rose from the floor, stroking her bare skin in a self-satisfied way. "And I will show you what else they like."

She went back to the vanity table and sat upon it, staring at herself in the mirror. She began to play with her high breasts, fondling herself gently. It was her look of absorption that was so erotic—it was very like happening upon a girl in the first throes of awakening sensuality, alone in bed perhaps. A girl who had no idea that anyone watched her.

My cock ached painfully. She rose and put one knee upon the vanity stool, then picked up a slender glass bottle. It held perfume but she did not spray herself with the fringed bulb attached for this purpose. No, she merely flicked the fringe at her cunny, smiling down at the hidden flesh she stimulated in such a feminine way.

Then she squeezed the bulb. A puff of sweet-smelling mist wetted the inside of her thigh and the perfume trickled down her skin. "Some men like me to hold their head between my thighs," she whispered. "Very tightly. So they can hardly breathe. Then Mistress Anne tickles their arses for them. She is very good at it."

Was she expecting me to agree? It was not known that Anne had permitted me to watch the blond man be tickled, as Kitty put it. And I had not known that Anne and Kitty worked together. But perhaps the girl was lying. Her artless demeanor made it more likely than not.

I thought of Lord Caringdel, whose degenerate tastes were notorious, and his procurer, the infamous Bowles. His lordship would love a girl as strange as Kitty. No doubt she would love him back, for the right amount of money. And then there was Lord Aspinall, who was worse than Caringdel and Bowles put together . . . He had probably tried to suffocate himself between her thighs already.

She walked idly back toward the bed, untying the straps that held the black silk triangle in place. Then she sat down and spread her legs again. She put her finger against her cunny and tried to put it in.

"I am a virgin," she said. "If I pressed very hard, my finger would go in, but that bit of skin commands the highest price of all."

How she had retained it this long was a mystery. Her manner was hard, for all the youthful freshness of her face and body. I heard Anne come in behind me and was grateful that my erection had waned. A shift in my seated position and there would be no evidence that my time with Kitty had aroused me at all.

Kitty sprang up and ran to Anne, kissing her full on the lips. "He does love you. He would not touch me."

Anne only nodded at the girl, evading her embrace. She looked at me, a wry smile teasing the corners of her mouth. "Edward, come away. I want to talk to you."

I rose and made a half-bow to Kitty, vowing to myself to avoid her in the future. She stared at me and again I saw her eyes glitter. She was a very strange girl indeed.

When we were alone, I told Anne that she would do well to be rid of Kitty and why. My dear love cast a level look at me. "I agree that she is half-crazy but she is safe enough with me. But she will not last long, I suspect. She takes opium. In fact, she cannot go without it for more than a few hours."

"Fie, Anne. You must make her stop—she will teach the other girls to use it."

"She already has. Some of them need it. I will not deny them the dreams it induces, or the sleep."

I could not hide my concern, but I said no more.

"She has already been turned out of another house for it, but I will not, Edward. A far worse fate would befall her."

"You are not her mother."

Anne stared at me unflinchingly. "Her mother sold her to me."

"In Christ's name, how could you enter into such a transaction?"

"As I said, there are worse fates." Her voice had an icy edge. "I have not told you everything about my life after we parted, or you would know what they were."

"Anne . . ."

"Unmarried women must take care of themselves as best they can." Her tone was unemotional but her words held a bitter truth. "I must look after her and the others as long as I am able."

I gentled my voice. "You should not, Anne. Close your doors and come away with me."

She shook her head. "No. Never. I would ruin you if I did such a thing."

That night we slept back to back, not in each other's arms. And the next day she told me to leave.

6

I did not think my peremptory dismissal was permanent. Perhaps it was best that I was forced to return to my routine. My frequent absences had concerned my housekeeper and Mrs. Mayhew's maternal fretting was something I wished to avoid.

I had been gone too often and too long, it seemed. Xavi had been so bold as to send letters to our house. For a courier, she had apparently used the ladies' maid, the English girl. Decimus's description sufficed for me to remember her.

He bowed and retreated. I looked through the sealed letters on the silver tray, recognizing Xavi's by the handwriting. These I tucked into my waistcoat to read at my desk. At least she'd had the common sense to leave her name off them.

There was one from Sir William Thurlow, a barrister and friend of mine who was advising me on matters pertaining to my business plans. That was far more important at the moment. He wished to see me at my earliest convenience, et cetera.

I went into my study and dashed off a reply, asking to see him this afternoon. I then opened my strongbox and removed a sum of money for Thurlow's fee, which I hid inside a pocket that could not be picked. The note I sent off to Thurlow at Lincoln's Inn with the boy who helped in the kitchen. The lad was barely presentable, but as far as I knew he was trustworthy. I lacked Xavi's advantage in that respect. There were no footmen in livery at my beck and call.

Whatever was she upset about? I took out the envelopes from Xavi and looked at the hurried handwriting. My name was barely legible. Bah. I felt deeply annoyed and tossed them down upon the desk. At the moment, I was sick of women.

For daring to suggest that Anne rid herself of Kitty, I had been banished. It was presumptuous of me to offer advice she had not asked for, but it was not enough of a reason to turn me out on the street. My odd encounter with the strange girl still haunted me, if truth be known.

Damn it all. Sex could be all-consuming. When I had bragged to Thomas that I did nothing to excess, I had not been entirely honest about that aspect of my life, despite his jab about my prowess as a lover. In sensual pleasure and no other, I was likely overindulge. And I had.

Decimus knocked and brought in the newspapers. He had ironed these, setting the ink with dry heat so I would not dirty my fingers. He was followed by a housemaid carrying a tea tray laden with food and, of course, tea. Such homey comforts were a welcome change from the louche atmosphere of Anne's house. The usual polite obsequies followed, curtseys and so forth. I nodded as patiently as I could, and leaned back in my chair, opening the first paper and quickly scanning the columns of print.

The gossip took pride of place over the news, as usual. I glanced at the recordings of social events and realized that I was mentioned, in cryptic fashion, to be sure, but mentioned.

An invitation from Lord D—means only one thing to the ladies of London. They must surrender! By all reports, he is a masterful lover and we have heard they find plea-

*sure beyond their wildest dreams. He has spent much time
of late in the company of a certain scandalous widow, a
Mrs. A—*

Infuriated, I gritted my teeth and threw the newspaper on the floor. Whoever had provided that information? Of course, there was more than one Lord D— in the peerage but the veiled mention of Anne narrowed the field of possibilities.

We had parted courteously not three hours ago, but she seemed distant and said she felt unwell. I took her word for it—it is never a good idea to call out a woman on a white lie—although I assumed the circles under her eyes were the result of lack of sleep.

If she saw this scurrilous report, she would be upset, despite her remarkable sang-froid. Such coolness was necessary in the business she was in, but Anne was more vulnerable than she liked to admit. I wondered again about her refusal to end her involvement in her lucrative but unsavory profession. She was driven by great fear of poverty, that much was clear.

I was awash in guilt. To play the hero and rescue her was not something she wanted. It began to dawn on me how deep her distrust of men was, although she had never turned her affections toward her own sex. Her marked avoidance of Kitty's embrace was something I had noted.

Anne's behavior was a puzzle that I could not solve at this moment. I sighed and looked again at the unopened letters from Xavi. I opened them all, not knowing which had arrived first, and flattened the folded paper inside. The scent of her perfume reached me before I read the words, evoking sensual memories of her that distracted me from the business at hand.

I ought to join a monastery, I told myself. I needed the rest.

Quickly I read the letters, noting again the hurried appearance of the penmanship. The lines were closely spaced and difficult to read. To make matters worse, she had written up and around the margins, adding endearments, second thoughts, and pleas for urgent assistance. Making sense of it all was impossible in my distracted mood. I began by arranging the letters in ascending order of the emotions they conveyed, from mild agitation to frantic haste to utter hysteria.

Then I read them.

At last the reason for her risky attempts to contact me directly became clear. Just last week, engravings of a nude woman that looked very much like her—but who was not her—had appeared in a different printseller's window. Not the one that had sold the reproductions of her demure portrait. Like those prints, these were unsigned, but the style was Quinn's. Her maid had told her of them, surprised at the likeness to her mistress. Xavi beseeched me to help her.

Diego, she wrote, had not seen them, but she was terrified of his wrath. He would assault her, break her nose, make her so ugly that no one would ever want to look at her again. And he would do the same to the maid, assuming the girl had lied about where her mistress was and what she was doing—

Damnation!

Quinn was a loose cannon on his best days. And he was a great one for getting drunk and doing outrageous things on a dare. In my exhausted and irritable state, I was willing to believe that he might have done it. Or had he merely been careless, imagining a naked Xavi—there was not a pretty woman he didn't imagine without her clothes on—and drawing away? Quinn's risqué prints were enormously popular and an original drawing on which an engraving could be based was well worth stealing. He threw most of his drawings on the floor of his studio, anyway, and left them there for Miss Reynaud to pick up.

Either way, he deserved to be thrashed. But the first thing to do was go and see the prints for myself.

The reproductions of her original portrait were no longer for sale at the other shop, of course. Not caring that Quinn declared them forgeries of his style, Don Diego had discreetly bought as many as he could through intermediaries, had the plates destroyed the same way, and threatened Quinn with castration if it happened again. Xavi had said at the time that Diego had not blamed her—but—I could fill in what would happen in this case.

I feared for Xavi. Diego might go instantly on the attack if he thought she had posed nude—wanton as she was when we made love, I knew she would never, ever do such a thing. As it was, the idea that her beautiful body could be the object of leers and sniggers made me wild with jealousy.

And frustration. As she pointed out in a postscript that I had not noticed right away, she would not be able to see me until the matter was resolved. She longed with all her heart to see me again . . . but it was not safe . . . I could almost hear her sobs and my heart ached for her.

I folded the letters and hid them with the rest of our papers in the secure place appointed to them. The tea in the pot had steeped too long, but I poured a cup and drank it cold, grimacing at its bitter strength. My mouth was dry but I needed it. I was about to do battle.

Quinn's voice floated down the stairs, giving Rob instructions for the errand he was about to run. I shoved past the apprentice and burst through the half-open door, ready to break every bone in Quinn's body.

"Edward! How nice to see you—but you look angry, my dear fellow—whatever is the matter—argghh!"

His face turned a shade of red-purple that would not have been out of place in one of his lurid sunsets. That was because I was holding him by the throat. By the merest fraction I relaxed my hold and let him breathe, but I kept him against the wall.

"Damn you, Quinn," I snarled. "I demand to know why you did it!"

"Agh—what—are—you—" He grabbed my wrist and pulled my hand away from his throat, regaining some of his strength with what little air I had allowed him. "What the devil are you talking about?" He could not roar the words, but he tried.

I stepped back. Quinn was a burly man and I knew he could take me on, although he was older. Still, I had the advantage of surprise.

"The engravings at the printseller's—Mr. Martin's—I saw them on my way! In the window! With her face!"

He shook his head. "Have you gone mad? Whose face?"

I grabbed his ear. "Must I drag you there like a schoolboy? You know what I am talking about!"

Quinn bellowed, confused and furious with pain, and knocked my hand away with his upraised arm. Out of the corner of my eye I saw Rob edge back into the studio, looking warily at both of us.

The artist lowered his head and charged me like the bull he was. I dodged him swiftly and he landed a-sprawl on the floor, but scrambled up and seized a chisel from among his tools. Holding it over his head—the sharp edge glinted in the light—he charged me again and I ran for the door.

I had no wish to have my features sculpted anew by a renowned artist. My boots made a tremendous noise as I galloped down the stairs, and a woman on the ground floor peeped out of her door to see what the commotion was.

Bellowing louder but still one flight of stairs behind me, Quinn threw the chisel. It stuck in the doorframe near the woman's head and she slammed the door shut with a terrific bang. I heard the intended instrument of my destruction fall, but I was already at the street door and did not wait to see if Quinn had picked it up again.

I dashed into the street, heading more or less in the direction of Mr. Martin's shop before I thought better of it and pressed myself into a deep niche in a brick wall. The rough bricks grated against my back, but I kept still, hoping that Quinn, if he had followed, would run past without seeing me.

Sure enough, he did, the chisel clutched in his fist. A minute later, I heard people curse and his loud voice cursing back, and looked out. He had scattered the crowd gathered under the green-and-white striped awning that shaded Martin's bow window and was peering inside. He shook his head and frowned.

I had not lingered there after my first glimpse of the nudes. The style seemed identical and my eye was not untrained. The likeness of Xavi was very good—oh, God. That above all had triggered my rage. But Quinn's bafflement, which I could see clearly, was not feigned. He had no idea I was observing him.

Perhaps the sensual nudes were not his after all. My heart sank. The man was my good friend and I had not given him the chance to defend himself or explain. Did I dare venture out and confront him again? Quinn's temper came and went as quickly as a thunderstorm, and I had certainly provoked him. But if he was not responsible, who was? I had to find out for Xavi's sake, get my hands on the damned things, see to it that the engraving plates were destroyed. I had gone off half-cocked myself.

Keeping that in mind, I left my hiding place and surveyed the scene. Perhaps the people in the street would keep Quinn from fighting openly with me—no. They did not have the genteel appearance of art-lovers, but were a rough lot who would undoubtedly egg him on.

I decided upon another plan and edged into an alley that I hoped led to the back of Mr. Martin's shop. Several steps later, I found that I was right—but I narrowly missed being drenched by the filthy water the shop assistant pitched out the door. The dissolved acid in it would have made holes in my clothes if not my skin.

I stepped carefully around the puddle and went into the rear area of the shop, looking for the proprietor. Mr. Martin, who obviously manufactured the prints he sold, was wiping his inky hands on a long, green-and-white striped apron.

I took a deep breath and began. "May I ask the name of the artist who did those prints in your window?"

He smirked at me. "Do you want the naughty ones of the whore, then? That is the last set."

His insolence enraged me but I kept my voice calm. "There are others?"

"I have already sold six sets. There are no more."

I only nodded.

At that moment, Quinn walked in through the front door, still holding the chisel. I supposed he had heard my voice inside. His expression was chastened and his anger had vanished. "Not my style, although the girl might be—"

I coughed to interrupt him before he could say Xavi's name or mine and took him outside through the open door, out of earshot. I was unsure whether he was telling the truth about the prints, but I would have to apologize and make him believe I was sincere.

Xavi had not been identified on the mezzotint replicas of his now-famous portrait of her. And the same was true of the much more cheaply done erotica in this fellow's window. I wanted to keep it that way.

My impulsive confrontation with Quinn might get us all in trouble if the printseller remembered such details. What if Diego heard of this latest outrage from someone who knew his wife and had seen the pictures by chance? Questions would be asked.

"You must not reveal Xavi's name or mine," I hissed at him. "She is frantic about the unexpected appearance of these pictures and afraid of her husband, who knows nothing as yet. The news of it sent me into a jealous rage and I assumed the worst. I am sorry for what I did to you, more sorry than I can say."

"Good. Let's go."

"We can't. We have to get those prints. So play along. For her sake."

"Yes, yes—of course. I understand."

"Does this man know you?"

"Martin knows my work. And he probably knows me by sight. This neighborhood is crawling with artists."

An apt phrase. "Good enough."

We went back into the shop.

"My dear Quinn!" I said loudly. "They are very good! I recognized your style—"

He waved the chisel grandly. "Fred, you are mistaken. My style can be copied and someone obviously did. I suspect Fotheringay—the bastard hopes to discredit me before the academy show."

I scowled at him. "You and Will have always quarreled about who is the better artist."

"I am," Quinn said, as if all the world knew that to be true.

He set the chisel upon a worktable and sat down on a chair piled with fresh-from-the-press etchings of rustic subjects. Entirely innocent and quite uninteresting, I thought. The shop's proprietor squawked with dismay.

"Oh, dear." Quinn rose and looked down where his buttocks had left double dents in the damp paper. "However, my imprint will only improve them. I did look before I sat down and I know they are Fotheringay's." He picked one up and squinted at it. "I recognize his work. Weak line, poor composition—the man has no talent whatsoever."

Quinn tossed the etching back upon the chair with disgust.

"His art sells well enough," Mr. Martin said. "But the rustic pictures are not so popular."

"I should think not. Cottages and chickens. Bah." He waved dismissively. "I would rather look at a woman's—"

I gave him a steely look and he shut up.

"The ladies like cottages," the other man said. "But men are different. Fotheringay can do both, you know. He's a dab hand at a naked female. Good for business."

"Are you saying that he did the etchings in the window?" I asked.

The printseller gave me an alarmed look. "N-no, sir. Those are not by him."

I stared at him for a long moment, as if the sheer force of my gaze might induce him to tell the truth. The man said no more, but turned away and made himself busy, ignoring the two lunatics who had blundered into his shop.

"Well, I will take the last set," I said. "How much?"

Martin turned around and named an extravagant sum, on the general principle that a fool and his money are soon parted. I dug into my hidden pocket and tossed down a handful of guineas.

"We want the engraving plates also," Quinn said.

"Certainly not. They are far too valuable. I can make thousands of prints from them."

"Exactly my point. We will pay you double what you think they are worth. Name your price."

The ink-stained wretch thought it over. I blanched when he came up with a figure he thought reasonable. But the plates had to be destroyed and there was no other way to get him to part with them.

"We wish the set we just bought to increase in value, you see," Quinn said blandly. "If the plates are destroyed, then no more can be made."

The proprietor hesitated and I wanted to kick Quinn. Did he not know that there was such a thing as too much explaining?

I put all the money I had brought with me on the counter and added my gold watch. Mr. Martin seemed quite pleased with it.

"Done," he said at last. "The plates are yours." He took up a pad of lined paper and a pencil to jot down the details of the transaction: a description of the set, its price, a note to the effect that the engraved plates had been sold with it, and the day's date. He paused and looked at me. "Name and address?"

"Ah—" That was not information I wanted to give out and my mind had gone blank.

"In case you wish to resell them through the shop, sir. So I can contact you."

Quinn stepped up. "Give me that pencil, Mr. Martin. You can have my address. Fred here must be discreet about this purchase." He elbowed me in the ribs and laughed.

"Quite right," I said, relieved. I watched him put down his name and address. Mr. Martin took the receipt from him and filed it in a metal box with an ingenious slotted drawer. Even if he was covered with ink and kept a sloppy shop, he was meticulous in matters that had to do with money.

Quinn snapped his fingers at the assistant. "Quickly now. Bring the plates here. I believe there must be ten. I can count, even if I am an artist. There were that many pictures in the window."

It seemed to take forever and we continued to josh each other. Affable to a fault, Quinn promised the proprietor a first look at other, better, far filthier engravings than these in future. Finally the assistant returned, lugging the plates in a wooden box. Quinn looked them over, then watched him wrap them in canvas and tie it up with heavy string.

Mr. Martin brought out a green-and-white striped portfolio and handed it over. "Would you like to look at them before I wrap this up?"

"No. We have no time for that—"

"Oh, but we do," Quinn said. He took the portfolio and opened it, leafing through the images with the air of a connoisseur. I realized that he was counting them to make sure there were ten, as promised, and came to look at them again. They were risqué but not obscene, and rather well done.

The model was shown in different alluring poses, utterly wanton and beautiful, as if she were about to jump from the page into her lover's arms. I had seen Xavi in quite a few of those poses, wearing little or nothing.

I reminded myself that the woman I was looking at was not her, but some unknown girl who resembled her or who'd been got up to look like her, and shook my head to clear it. Viewing all ten prints was having a curious effect upon my mind.

I closed the portfolio, asked Mr. Martin to wrap it up too, and we left. Quinn carried the heavy plates and I carried the portfolio.

We were at the end of the street before Quinn spoke. "Not the end of the matter, Edward, but it is a good beginning. If we had been too serious he would have suspected something. I thought I did well by playing the buffoon."

"It comes naturally to you."

He slapped me on the back. "You can say thank you at any time. If Martin had not wanted to buy from me in future, he might have had second thoughts about selling you the engraving plates."

"Thank you. And yes, I know that."

Quinn adjusted his grip on his parcel as I hurried him along, eager to get away from the neighborhood.

"Now all we have to do is find the other sets."

I multiplied six by ten. "There are sixty etchings unaccounted for. Let us hope the sets have not been broken up."

"They have only just been sold. And there is a receipt for every one in Mr. Martin's ingenious box. With the name and address of each owner. We shall have to get our hands on that box, find the receipts, copy the information we need, and return it with no one the wiser. I volunteer for that." Quinn threw me an odd look. "Buying back all six sets will be interesting."

"What if the owners don't want to part with them?"

"Then we shall have to steal them."

Was I willing to risk gaol or the gallows to protect Xavi's reputation? I might well be protecting her very life and that of the English girl. I would have to. "I will."

Quinn laughed. "By yourself? I don't think so. I say we get drunk first."

I rolled my eyes. "It is not yet noon."

"But it will be when we are finished drinking."

"We might as well," I said. "Lead the way."

We stopped in a public house and quaffed far too much ale while we attempted to figure out exactly how to do the dirty deed. The ale did not aid our powers of reasoning and as a few hours went by the whole business began to seem like a play with some very odd characters. Thundering husbands, naughty wives, and hopeless romantics—in my beery haze I felt that my life had turned upside down and inside out, and I was beginning not to care. Drink made us low fellows for a little while, thoroughly coarse and maudlin by turns.

I set down my mug, feeling ashamed. At least I had a true friend in Quinn. He'd had to assure me repeatedly that he had nothing at all to do with the prints, knew nothing about their provenance, and at last I believed him. He had known from the beginning of my affair with Xavi, and I had trusted him implicitly to keep things quiet. That he had not betrayed that trust, as I had been too quick to believe he had, was a great relief to me.

He finished the ale in his mug. "We must get the receipts tonight and begin at once. Gossip travels quickly in London. We made ourselves conspicuous."

"A fight in the street is not news."

"But this one was more amusing than most, at least to the onlookers. One man tells another of it, and so it goes."

"What of it?"

"If Don Diego should somehow find out about those etchings—if we fail to find them all—and if he figures out who did them before we do, he will skin the man alive," Quinn said, chewing thoughtfully on the bread the barmaid brought for us to share, along with some cheese. He used the chisel to break off a chunk, looked at it closely and frowned. He threw it to the dog curled up in one corner. The animal lifted his head to snap the treat out of the air.

"To say nothing of his wife."

"It could happen. And do not forget Diego is very likely to suspect me again. If he thought I would sell cheap copies of her portrait, it is not so big a jump to think I would do worse."

"True."

"I can't offend a man who knows so many people at court, Edward. Dukes and whatnot are my best customers."

I nodded. "Then I will handle the matter myself. Perhaps it would be best if you went up to the country for a while."

Quinn tipped up his mug and swallowed the last of his ale. "Not a bad idea. But we shall get the receipts first and you can begin."

"Leaving me to my fate?"

"Yes. For now." He laughed at my somber expression. "Edward, you know I will help you. Come back to the studio with me. I can pack a bag and take the coach to Surrey. Rob and Miss Reynaud can manage without me for a while."

We settled the bill and departed.

Relaxed by the ale, I stretched out on the long divan in his study, my arms folded under my head, contemplating the ceiling. Quinn's studio was light and airy, a pleasant place to take a nap. Despite my worries about Anne and deep concern for Xavi, I succumbed to sleep. Some hours later, my eyes flew open when Quinn set a wooden case by my head with a thump.

"Wake up, my beauty. There is a midnight coach leaving from the courtyard of the Hare and Bells. You and I can get riproaringly drunk before I leave."

I yawned. The Hare and Bells was around the corner. Good. I had managed to sleep the afternoon away. But ... I had missed my appointment with the barrister. And there was something else. "What about the receipts?"

"Mr. Martin closes early on Saturdays. But I paid the shop a visit anyway. Through the window."

He grinned and handed me six folded receipts, stained with ink. I looked at him with surprise and tucked them into my shirt. "And the portfolio of prints and the plates?"

"Safely hidden. Not here, though."

I could not ask him more because I heard Rob's voice in the next room, talking to Miss Reynaud. So the assistant had returned, unafraid of his master when it came right down to it. Miss Reynaud shuffled in wearing carpet slippers and set up to resume her copying.

She cast a mild look in my direction and a tiny smile appeared on her face. I smiled back politely, wondering what it was Miss Reynaud did for fun. If Quinn was away, she was likely to take as many naps as she wanted upon this very divan. He buried her in work more often than not, and she deserved a rest.

In another hour, Quinn and I departed for the Hare and Bells, where we ordered stronger stuff than ale while we discussed what we knew of Diego. He was an undeniably powerful man and well-connected in high circles, certainly able to make trouble for both me and Quinn ... but it was his notoriously foul temper that cast the longest shadow. To chase it away, we became more determined than ever to have a very good time.

By the third round, Quinn began to feel it. He said, just in case suspicions had crept into my mind as I'd slept, that he'd had nothing to do with the damned engravings, he would never dream of doing such a thing to Xavi although he was certain her naked body was far more beautiful than the new etchings for which Fotheringay, the idiot, was undoubtedly responsible and deserved to be thrashed. He added that I must be head over heels in love, which made me a bloody damned fool, because only a bloody damned fool would lay the wife of a jealous Spaniard.

After a while I told him to shut up. I assured him that he was no longer a suspect. We had known each other too long for him to lie to me and get away with it, especially when we were drunk.

He belched and wiped away a tear.

By the time we were well in our cups, he had somehow acquired a barmaid upon each knee after a while, plying him with drink. I pitied his fellow passengers that night—he was sure to vomit out the window when the coach hit a rough patch of road.

With his teeth, he bit down upon the scarf that concealed one barmaid's bosom and pulled it out. Her shabby gown was very low-cut and her breasts almost popped out. She only laughed.

"Now, Ellen," he said coaxingly. "Show us the scenery. I am a great lover of scenery like yours, my girl." He held his glass of whiskey to her pretty lips and tipped it up.

Ellen swallowed the rest in one gulp and looked over her shoulder for the innkeeper. Mr. Cobbett was nowhere in sight. Harriet, the girl on Quinn's other knee, helped out by reaching into her friend's bodice and pulling out her big breasts. One nipple brushed his mouth and he wasted no time in sucking upon it.

"Mmm." His cheeks hollowed with the force of his sucking, which the girl seemed to enjoy. Her friend tugged upon the other nipple, giving me a flirtatious look. It was clear that we could have them both for a few shillings and the price of a none-too-clean room upstairs. But I demurred. Let Quinn

romp with barmaids. My taste in women was rather more ele-
vated than that.

I finished my own whiskey and ordered more, which came
quickly. I drank that too. And another. The girls were looking
better and better. Harriet jumped up from Quinn's knee and
came to sit upon mine. Well, I thought. Don Diego and his evil
minions might be lying in wait in the alley. Life was short. I
might as well enjoy myself.

It was late in the evening and my whiskers had grown out to
stubble that rasped her ear when I whispered in it.

"Shall we fuck you and your friend together, then? Is that
what you two want?"

She nodded eagerly and wriggled in my lap. Harriet's arse
was soft as a sofa cushion and the thought of slamming into it
was exciting me.

Ellen had guided her other nipple into Quinn's mouth to be
sucked next, and the sight of the first one, shining and pink and
stiff, made me reach into Harriet's bodice and see what she had
to offer.

Her breasts were not so large as Ellen's, but the one I cupped
filled my hand with pleasurable warmth. She sighed softly, and
I caressed the other in due time, enjoying the way she was now
bouncing upon my lap.

Quinn had his hand up Ellen's dress, I noticed. In another
minute, he would slide beneath the table and have his head between her legs, eating her cunny. He often talked of his craving
for this part of a woman, bragging that, blindfolded, he could
distinguish between females by their flavor alone.

I knew that he had even gone so far as to advertise for partners in this practice in the magazines that women read, in careful words. And he'd had no end of replies. If he'd had his way,
he would have posted signs on Covent Garden walls, of course.
*Ladies in Need of a Good Licking, See Quinn the Cunny Man!
Satisfaction Guaranteed.*

I stopped fondling Harriet and reached across the table to tap Quinn on the arm. He gave me a groggy grin.

"What?"

Harriet and Ellen got up at the same time and grabbed our hands.

"Upstairs, Quinn. We can share a room. Four of us won't be too much of a squeeze."

His eyes widened. "No—I mean yes. Not too much of a squeeze at all."

The raucous customers paid no attention to us as we threaded our way through the benches and deal tables of the bar room. Ellen and Harriet went up first, followed by Quinn, who managed to fondle both their arses. I admired his dexterity and concentrated on making it up the rickety stairs.

The room they led us into was not as grimy as I had feared, and someone had brought in a candle and provided fresh sheets. There was straw upon the floor that gave off a sweet, summery smell and even a nosegay of flowers in a small vase by the bed.

Ellen and Harriet wasted no time in stripping down to their stays, and Quinn was nearly as fast. Naked, he looked like a satyr. A set of horns would not have seemed out of place upon his forehead.

"Lie down," he told them, indicating the bed behind them.

The girls giggled and did as he asked, lying side by side and opening their legs so that their knees touched. Their juicy quims gleamed in the candlelight.

"Is that not a fine sight?" he asked me.

"Indeed it is."

He kneeled in front of them, fondling and playing with both cunnies at once. I decided to keep my cock out of it and have the pleasure of watching for now.

"Which one of you would like to be licked first?"

"Me!" Ellen cried.

"Very well." Quinn patted Harriet's thigh. "You may watch if you like."

Harriet seemed quite content to do that, rolling onto her side to watch Ellen be done first. Quinn gently spread her friend's labia, and found the clitoris, applying the tip of his tongue exclusively to that sensitive bit.

She wriggled her arse upon the sheets, pushing up into his face, and Quinn thrust his tongue deeply into her cunny. He did it strongly, forcing in with every thrust, and the girl responded. "Oh! Harriet does not do it so well as you!"

Quinn sat back and wiped his mouth. "Really? Shall we have a contest, then?"

"You're on," Harriet said. She got on all fours and put her head where Quinn's had just been but kept her cunny over Ellen's face. The girl on the bed stared dreamily up, trapped between her friend's knees and unable to look at anything else.

I took my cock from my breeches and stroked it as I stared too.

Harriet began to lick and suck her friend with intimate skill. I could see that the twosome quite enjoyed such affectionate play, and who could blame them?

For my part, I loved the show. I was rather drunk and the whiskey quite dissolved my inhibition. Harriet raised her head and caught a glimpse of what I was doing to myself, and winked at me, then returned to pussy-sucking her dear friend.

Quinn, feeling rampageous, got on the bed and got behind Harriet. He licked her cunny from behind, treating her to the same deep thrusts of his tongue he had given to Ellen.

Harriet was not distracted for a moment. She continued her attentions to Ellen's cunt, but I could see that she was thrusting back slightly to take advantage of Quinn's stimulation.

The lascivious sounds of two tongues hard at work filled the room, punctuated by Ellen's soft moans. She was in an excellent position: able to watch her friend being tongue-fucked while she got the same. The difference was that Quinn went at it hard and fast, and Harriet was more gentle, but both methods were equally stimulating.

Quinn rose halfway and stayed on his knees, unable to wait for his own satisfaction. He positioned himself behind Harriet, who understood that she was about to get a cock shoved into her as far as it would go. She brought her face up from Ellen's dripping pussy and looked over her shoulder at Quinn.

"Have at," she said cheerfully.

He spread her arse with large, strong hands and fucked her hard, making her rock on the bed. Ellen, neglected for the moment, whimpered underneath them, and then reached to amuse herself with Quinn's big balls. The man was very well endowed, and his heavy sac soon tightened from her feminine teasing.

Ellen raised up a bit and extended her tongue to lick his balls. Quinn gasped and fucked Harriet vigorously indeed, banging against her bum, until his groin tensed. His climax shook his body, both girls, and the bed, and I sprayed into the air at the same moment, shouting as the hot jets of cum fell onto the straw below.

We men collapsed, he on the bed, I onto a chair, and the girls finished each other. In another hour, when we had recovered sufficiently to make our way downstairs again, I put Quinn on the coach to Surrey, and headed home singing.

7

My head was rather the worse after such a convivial evening, to say nothing of my conscience. But I could not undo what I had done. Besides, an intoxicated dalliance with willing barmaids simply did not count as true debauchery by the standards of London, at least not for a man. I justified my lapse as a reward of sorts for undertaking the difficult task of preserving Xavi's reputation, to say nothing of her life. My conscience would have to be satisfied with that.

I thought no more about last night. The matter of the engravings was far more pressing. I took Xavi's letters from their hiding place and read them again, paying more attention than I had the first time.

I had missed something important: she planned to attend a masquerade ball and hoped to see me there, although it would be dangerous. Still, if I were masked and she could slip away— she did not think Don Diego would be there— I understood what she was getting at. The ball would take place tomorrow night. The name of its giver, Lord Colefax, was familiar to me. However, it was not likely that I would receive a belated invitation, for many reasons. But I could contrive a way to meet her there.

The problem of the erotic engravings I intended to address at once, on my own. Since Quinn had not done them, that left Fotheringay to be investigated . . . and beaten to a pulp if he was the culprit. Mr. Martin's denial had not been convincing. But I would still have to track down all the existing sets. There were six and I had the seventh, or Quinn did, in some safe place. I might as well begin.

The folded receipts were hidden in a cubbyhole of the desk, put there upon my return from the inn. I took them out and studied the names and addresses. To my surprise, I knew two of the names, and one of those was a woman. But I decided to begin at the two bookshops that had each bought a set—at a slight discount, I noticed. Mr. Martin was enterprising and no doubt wished to expand his business.

I went into the showroom of Woolf's, looking about at the shelves holding thousands and thousands of books. The glass dome overhead, a wonderful novelty, brought a great deal of light into the room that made reading easy and attracted many customers. Comfortable armchairs had been placed in here and there, paired with sofas. Young ladies had commanded these to read together.

The few men in the place looked down on them kindly, no doubt imagining such pretty creatures in their own libraries, sighing over the handsome volumes they planned to have bound in matching leather for their own shelves. Volumes which were unlikely to be read, of course, even by bookish young ladies. Such sets were produced to convey the impression of intellectual brilliance. Thick with the weight of accumulated knowledge in them, they made excellent doorstops.

With so many sweet-faced females about, I was reluctant to go to the desk and enquire in a low voice as to whether, ahem, *etchings of a certain kind* were available. I saw no clue as to where a portfolio like the one I sought might be found. So I wandered about, pretending to browse the shelves.

I came upon a room with curtains drawn back over the arched entrance. It seemed to be for private use, but it was empty. I glanced around to see if anyone was looking at me— no one was—and I slipped inside.

Perhaps parties were given here to celebrate the publication of one book or another. I had been to a few of such gatherings, at other booksellers. They were dismal affairs. The guests tended to be few in number, clutching the books pressed on them by the newly minted author, who signed the title page with a flourish and high hopes of immortality. Most would sink into oblivion.

Which was what I wanted to happen to those damned engravings of the woman who looked like Xavi.

I walked out again and turned to the left, to a section marked Art & Antiquities, where perhaps the hunting would be better. Here a clerk was shelving new stock, and not only books. And then I caught a glimpse of distinctive green-and-white stripes.

He was intent upon his work. I hoped it was the one I sought, but that foolish thought was dashed when I saw not one but twenty portfolios in the rack he was filling.

I would have to wait for him to go away to examine them all. Fellows who haunted the aisles of bookstores looking at such things without buying had a way of being discouraged. Or guided swiftly out to the street and treated to a hard kick in the arse.

Still, I was well-dressed and looked every inch the gentleman. I pulled out a book at random and flipped through it, gradually feeling the uncomfortable sensation of someone's eyes on me. I looked up—it was not the clerk, who had finished his work and gone away.

A woman smiled at me pertly. A delicate pair of spectacles was perched on her nose, but they only added to her attractiveness. "That is a very good book," she said, indicating the volume in my hand.

"Is it?" I turned to the title page to see what it was she thought I was reading. *Fanny Hill. The Memoirs of a Woman of Pleasure.* I closed the book with a snap and she went off into peals of laughter.

Several curls escaped her charming coiffure as she did. Was there no end to the temptations to be found in London?

"I assume you have read it," I said boldly.

"Yes. I have."

I had no idea what to say next. My virtue, such as it was, was not safe even in a bookstore. She brushed past me, running a fingertip over the shelved green-and-white portfolios.

"And have you looked at those as well?"

"No." She looked at me over her shoulder, a pose I have always found fetching in the female of the species. "Should I?"

"My dear young lady," I began, realizing that I sounded exactly like the sort of pompous jackass who went to bookstores to meet dear young ladies and try to impress them. "It is not for me to say, but—"

At that moment a man came around and took her by the arm to lead her away. He gave me a suspicious look that I ignored with all the hauteur I could summon up. I could have taken him in a fair fight, but these hushed aisles were hardly the place for a manly battle.

I was grateful to have the aisle to myself again and went through the rack of green-and-white portfolios as fast as I could. When I found the images of Xavi—no, the woman who looked like Xavi but was not her—I took the portfolio up to the counter and bought it straightaway.

* * *

One down, five to go. When I had got the thing home, I hid it under an armoire in my bedroom. I went to my study and looked through the receipts again, drawing a line through the one Mr. Martin had written out for Woolf's bookshop and moving it to the back.

The next name was Fotheringay's and the address was in Soho. Mr. Martin had hesitated when he said Quinn's rival was not the artist who had created these sets, but it didn't mean he was lying. The printseller could have been telling the truth. Why would Fotheringay buy his own work?

He might have done it to cover his tracks, I supposed, but that seemed like a bit of a stretch.

I was reluctant to go after his set alone, for doing so would undoubtedly mean tangling with the man, who had a disagreeable temper. No, I needed Quinn's help and I would have to wait for him to return from the country.

Recovering another set from the second bookseller would be easy enough, if it had not been sold. I tucked the receipts in my pocket, permitted myself a sigh, and went out again.

I arrived a little too late. A customer had one of Martin's distinctive portfolios under his arm and was paying for it. This shop was nowhere near as spacious or well-stocked as Woolf's and I spotted the other green-and-whites at once, in a rack on the floor. It was the work of an instant to go through them. My heart sank when I realized that the one I wanted had undoubtedly been bought by the man now walking out the door.

I would have to follow him.

Only a moment after his exit, I went out too, walking in a nonchalant way. He moved with long strides, whistling as if on his way to some pleasant assignation. Good. His mind was elsewhere.

He strode on for nearly half a mile. I found that following someone was a very odd business. I had to stop when he stopped, go when he was going, but not be obvious about it. Even the best neighborhoods of London had their footpads and thieves, plying their trade in broad daylight, and I did not want to be taken for one.

The man came to a town house, waving as he looked up at the second-floor window. It was framed with roses growing on a trellis and a woman leaned out to cut one and throw it down to him with a smile. A romantic gesture, but I was sure she was his wife. He blew her a kiss and entered when a maid, who cast a curious look at me, opened the door for him. He disappeared inside.

There I stood, a little unsteady on the cobblestones, my feet aching after my long walk. The man I had followed knew that he was going home to loving arms and his steps had been accordingly light, as if he was walking on the air of this balmy day. I could not very well knock on the door and ask if he wanted to sell his portfolio to me. I was not particularly surprised that he had brought it home as a gift to his little wife, for I supposed that to be the case. A happy couple might share such pictures to excite each other.

There could not be a safer place for the portfolio to be hidden. I walked the way I had come, more slowly now, my hands clasped behind my back. The familiar look of London, the humble chimneypots of its houses and the graceful spires of its many churches, both reaching toward the same sky, put me in an odd sort of mood. I turned my thoughts to the missing portfolios once more, glad to have the time to consider the problem at my leisure. Our plan to find them all had been hatched in haste, and Quinn and I had not even discussed the possibility that one or more of the sets might not be recovered.

Once back at my own house, I sat in silence. I felt lonely after following the stranger and somewhat disgusted with myself for doing so.

My gallant attempts to recover the portfolios were sure to be rewarded with ardent kisses and caresses from Xavi, but I could not help wondering if the effort was worth it. Once everything was destroyed and her husband's suspicions calmed, we could resume our affair . . . but what was the point? It would end badly, the usual result of affairs in which one or both sinners are married to other people.

Anne had dismissed me, Xavi was likely to do the same. I loved both; I had neither. Was there a woman in London who would someday be mine—all mine? A sadder question came to my mind. Was I worthy?

Probably not.

I enjoyed carousing with Quinn, I had a taste for sexual adventuring, and I came and went as I pleased at all hours. Our amorous encounter with the barmaids had provided welcome relief from thoughts of Diego and—I had to admit it, if only to myself—the mixed emotions that had bedeviled me in the last weeks. I liked my freedom.

Bah. At the moment I didn't want it. The glimpse of domestic bliss I'd been granted between the unknown husband and his rosy wife had put me in a cynical mood.

I put the receipts with the ever-growing pile of paper I hid, and some note-sheets of Xavi's fell out. I smiled inwardly as I read them again.

She had rewritten the tale of the Frenchwoman, her brother's mistress, on these, not finishing it. It was hard for her to imagine her younger brother as a lover, and she left off abruptly after a description of Veronique Joubert.

Veronique's eyelashes fluttered and her bosom heaved with every breath she took of the warm air of Jamaica. Before her darling Thomas had come from England to succor her, a lonely young widow, Veronique had been forced to call upon her manservant, Tremont, known as Tree for his height and the length of his . . .

I read no more. Still, the wildly romantic tone was amusing and perhaps she meant it to be a parody. I smiled to myself. We were two of a kind: fools for love. Lightheartedness was a necessary counterpoint to the strong passions that drove us to risk so much. What I needed now was to see her, reassure her, hold her close, and that I would do at the ball.

My bad mood dissolved.

The musicians hired for the occasion were playing merry airs and the dancing had begun when I entered. There were no other guests upon the stairs or in the hall when I bowed to the brass-buttoned personage at the door and made a leg in the old-fashioned way. I knew that Henry, Lord Colefax's butler, would recognize me. I lifted my mask for a fraction of a second.

He did and kept his voice low. "Lord Delamar?"

Henry had never thought ill of me for dallying with Lord Colefax's wife. It had happened a long time ago and Henry had dallied with her too—at a different time and place, of course. Lord Colefax, who was universally disliked, had seemed to be none the wiser, and the young lady in question went on to take many other lovers, highborn and low.

"Hush," I whispered. "Yes, it is I."

Henry collected himself and pretended to take the invisible card I extended to him. Lord Colefax was not a complete fool, and he had never invited me to his house again. The protocols of entrance observed, I grinned at Henry and joined the throng in the ballroom.

The dancers had joined hands for a quadrille and went through the measured steps in time to the music. There were no bumblers among them and the sight was pleasing. I had been too long away from polite company. Its manners and mores encouraged self-restraint.

My heart got me in far greater trouble than my cock, I

thought. It beat wildly at the sight of Xavi; it throbbed with fondness when Anne came back into my life. Worst of all, my wayward nature was not interested in choosing one or the other, but insisted on loving both.

If only I were like most men and let my cock direct me. That organ gave a twitch as a lovely woman danced by. Her hand clasped in her partner's and held high, her pretty chin tilted up and her eyes sparkling behind her domino mask, the dancer was the picture of grace. I wondered who she was . . . and then reminded myself of the reason I had come.

Where was Xaviera Innocencia? Taller than most of the guests, I scanned the crowd. She had not mentioned what she would wear, and it was possible she had on a powdered wig like many of the women as well as a mask.

I thought that I spied her, but I wanted to be sure. Edging through the guests and murmuring my apologies, I made my way to the side of a lady with a figure very like Xavi's, whom I could see only from the back. She wore a fitted gown in a garnet color, a shade that my darling particularly liked, and her dazzling white hair was adorned with tiny diamonds.

When the woman turned around, I realized my mistake. The lady wore no mask and her white hair was not a wig. It was gloriously thick, though, arranged in an elegant coiffure. Her beauty was of the mature sort but no less compelling than many of the younger women present. I made her a slight bow and moved on.

Ah—there was Xavi, in sapphire silk. Her mask was in the Venetian style, with upswept wings at the corner that wrapped around her dark hair. Her eyes flashed when she saw me, but she said nothing to me until she murmured some excuse in her charming accent to the handsome young man she had been talking to.

He could not be Don Diego, I thought, remembering Quinn's phrase for the Spanish ambassador: old goat. I glanced discreetly about for someone who might fit that description, but the company in general was quite attractive.

"He is not here," she said softly, taking my arm when the young man moved away.

"Do you mean your husband?"

"I do. He is in bed with the ague. I sent my own maid to comfort him."

"Was that wise? A very young woman might be the death of him."

Xavi snorted. "I don't think so."

So there was life in the old goat yet. How unfortunate. "I went to look in the printseller's window," I whispered.

She stiffened and would not look at me.

"I think I will be able to help you, Xavi. Only seven sets were printed and two are in my keeping." That was not quite true. Quinn had one and I had the other, but I thought his involvement might make her uneasy. "A third . . ." I hesitated, not wanting to describe the rose-covered house and the damnably happy turtledoves living there. "A third set is safely hidden elsewhere."

"What about the engraving plates? Thousands more could be printed from them." There was a desperate tone in her voice.

"I bought those and they too are hidden."

She smiled slightly. "Thank you."

"Rest assured," I went on, "that Mr. Martin's window now has a new display. People will forget what they saw very quickly."

"Oh." There was the faintest trace of pique in her reply. "Well, what did you think of the etchings?"

I looked at her with some surprise. "Have you seen them, Xavi? I understood from your letters that you had not, only that you had been advised of their sudden appearance."

"Oh—no, I have not." Her reply was breathless. "I am not allowed to go about as Englishwomen do, in a free and easy way."

I felt a pang. It seemed unfair for her to be confined so much at home and to have to employ such complicated strategies to make an occasional escape, as she had tonight.

She was talking very softly now and I bent my head down to hear better.

"My maid described them to me in detail. She cannot read but she remembers everything and I trust her completely."

"Do you mean the English girl who was with you at Quinn's?"

"Yes. After the portrait he did of me was copied, it is not so surprising to find my face on another woman's naked body, eh?" She tapped my chest with her folded fan, playing the coquette for the benefit of those around us. They were not listening, preoccupied with their own conversations. "Do you have any idea who the artist is?"

"Not yet."

She pursed her lips. "I would guess that it is not Quinn."

"You are correct, but why do you say so?"

"I think you would have killed him for it."

"Xavi, I almost did."

She murmured her dismay and looked around to see if anyone had overheard.

"But I came away satisfied that he did not do it. And a good brawl with a good friend can clear the air."

"How very English of you," she said dryly.

I laughed a little, and pressed a kiss against her dark hair. It was no use explaining the joys of a masculine fight to a well-bred woman like Xavi.

She was lost in thought. "I thank God that my husband has not been informed."

"I was wondering about that and I have been worrying about you. Do you feel quite safe?"

"Until he finds out, yes."

I wanted to caress her shoulders, rub away her obvious unease, but I could not do it in public. "He will never find out,

Xavi. And even if he does, he will have to agree that it is not you in the pictures, but only the copied features of an unknown beauty."

"Hmph. I am glad to be wearing a mask tonight."

She looked even more stunning in it. "This will all blow over soon enough." I hoped that was true. I wanted it to be true.

"If it does not, Diego will . . . ah, there is no telling what he will do."

I led her away to a quieter part of the ballroom when the musicians struck up a lively schottische. "You must not worry. Still, I am surprised that he let you come out unchaperoned."

"I am not alone," she said lightly. "Another maid came with me. She is over there—" Xavi nodded at a mousy girl flirting with a lieutenant in scarlet regimentals. "We are safe enough."

"I see. Then let us do as they are doing and enjoy a glass of punch."

A liveried servant was passing by with the bowl upon his shoulder and his companion served from it, filling the glasses on the small tables around the perimeter of the ballroom. We refreshed ourselves and exchanged small talk with another couple at a nearby table for a while. When the exuberant music ended they turned to talk to their arriving friends and I lifted Xavi's hand to bring her to the dance floor.

"Shall we dance?"

She nodded and we joined the next group, going through the steps as if we had been dancing together many times. It was an odd feeling to be out in public with her—every one of our meetings had been in some secret place.

She had never seemed to mind. Perhaps growing up in a convent had prepared her for it—the thought was ironic indeed, considering the mischief we got up to.

We led the dance hand in hand, and broke apart to step to the side of the dancers in rows behind us, and went back to the beginning again.

When the music ended again, we bowed to each other and mingled for a while among the glittering throng. It would not do to be seen exclusively in each other's company. Lord Colefax hankered after celebrity and sent over a list of his illustrious guests to the *Tatler* after every party he gave. Although I had not been invited and my name did not appear, it was possible that some busybody might recognize me and add my name after all.

Don Diego might have sent a busybody of his own to keep an eye on his wife. And there was no telling who that someone might be. The popular image of a spy as tall, dark, and dashing was simply absurd. The least visible of men were the most ordinary in appearance. I caught myself—her watcher, if there was one, might be a woman, perhaps one that Diego was sleeping with himself. The white-haired beauty in the garnet dress was a likely candidate but she did not look in Xavi's direction, preferring to flirt with a circle of officers.

I observed my love as she drifted from one acquaintance to the next. It seemed that she had made many during her months in London. But no one seemed to be close to her—she had no bosom friends. No wonder she was so passionate with me. Our affair meant much to her, perhaps everything. It was good that she knew nothing whatsoever of Anne, and vice versa. My first love was in no way a rival to my second, but women are women, and cats will scratch.

"Meet me in the garden," I whispered. "But leave after I do and make sure no one sees you."

She looked at her mousy maid, who was now being bounced on the lieutenant's knee, sipping a glass of wine and giggling at whatever he was whispering in her ear. Giddy with delight, the girl spilled a drop on his white breeches and brushed at the spot, moving her hand up his manly thigh.

"She is bold," Xavi said softly.

"And growing bolder by the minute. Get her more wine and I will see you in the garden."

I left the ballroom unnoticed when the music began again. Even if Xavi could not manage to find her way to me, the night was beautiful and I was content to be alone. The moon floated in the sky, full but half-shrouded by wisps of moving clouds. The garden was framed by tall cypress trees and against these were marble statues, gleaming whitely in the dark.

I wandered down the close-clipped lawn, my footfalls making no sound, and stopped at a nude Diana, depicted as the huntress of myth. The figure held a marble bow, drawn back to its utmost point, and looked high overhead with unseeing eyes. Had the arrow in it been released, it would have hit the moon above. The marble doe at her side was so lifelike that it seemed to tremble for a moment . . . but the illusion was caused by the passing clouds.

I sighed. I heard the rustle of silk and Xavi appeared. Her steps had been as noiseless as mine. She did not speak, but pressed her lips to mine for an ardent kiss that went on and on. Her dark sensuality fired my blood. My hands roamed over her, forgetting everything that had happened since our last meeting.

"It has been too long," she whispered. Not for me. Remembering the encounter at the inn, I was assailed by guilt and rightly so. My cock, however, rose to the occasion. The seductive intimacy of her voice, the pressure of her supple body, were too much for me. But I would do penance by giving her pleasure, I decided, and denying myself.

I dropped to my knees and looked up at her. "Xavi . . . will you allow me to satisfy you intimately?"

She stroked my hair as I pressed my face against the folds of her gown. "Yes. Of course." Her hands clutched her skirt and she lifted them to show me her cunny. I nuzzled her there, giving her loving little licks. Xavi sighed.

Although the dark concealed us, someone else or perhaps another pair of lovers might come out to enjoy the beautiful night. I had to be quick about what I was doing. I had her set her feet far apart to make room for me as I kneeled before her. My tongue went far up into her cunny and I savored the womanly taste of her, selfishly happy that only I had this privilege. I thrust it slowly in and out, remembering Quinn's lascivious skill and how readily he had brought the buxom barmaids close to climax.

Xavi was near her own. She ran her fingers into my hair and clutched it, pulling my face against her mound and grinding wantonly away. Her little moans came faster and faster, and I kissed her cunny as wantonly as I liked to kiss her mouth. When a shadow passed over the moon and the darkness grew more intense, I heard her scream. The sound died away but I quickly raised my head and wiped my mouth.

Had something frightened her? Had we been seen? We were still masked, it was hard upon midnight, but even so . . . I could not quite shake the feeling of being watched. But there was no one.

She dropped her skirts with a rustle, smoothing them down, as I rose. "And what about you, my love?"

I shook my head. "Not now. Not here. But soon. Very soon."

8

A month later, a letter came for me. The faithful Decimus held it out upon his silver tray without comment. My surprise must have showed on my face.

"Oh! One from Anne, is it? And not—?" I caught myself. I had almost said Xavi's name out loud.

He merely smiled. I turned Anne's letter this way and that in my hand, thinking it would be interesting to hear his opinion of the pros and cons of loving two women. Old Decimus had long cherished a tenderness for the cook, who kept him supplied with the sweet rolls he adored, but he also admired the house-keeper's comfortable bum. Both women seemed happy in his presence. No doubt I, at thirty, seemed like a young fool to him. But he was too respectful to say so.

I set the letter aside to read in private. The younger maids were cleaning the windows and I enjoyed looking at them upon the ladders, scrubbing away and joking with each other. Living amidst women had always come naturally to me.

But I could have used manly advice now and again. For that, I could ask my secretary, Richard Whiston, who was back in

London. He thought nothing of having more than one lover, and might well be able to tell me exactly how to maintain the delicate balance and keep my own sanity.

Quinn was happy to offer his counsel whenever he thought I needed it, but the artist lived so far outside the bounds of polite society that most of his advice would have landed me in the dock, with him right beside me. He was apt to encourage the wildest schemes, fuck any woman who wanted him, and was generous with all that he owned.

Especially to poor, shabby Miss Reynaud. Why she kept herself on such a tight string, I didn't know, but I had slipped her a few guineas myself. Noblesse oblige. I had taken her into my confidence and showed her what was in the green-and-white portfolio I had, supposing that she had seen the engravings in Mr. Martin's window anyway. I hoped she might shed some light on the artist who had done them, but she pronounced herself quite unfamiliar with the man's style.

I came back a week or so later with a further question, for which I had procured one of the engraved plates from Quinn's hiding place after an exchange of letters asking and answering the question of where it was. She had examined the plate with a strong magnifying glass and come to the conclusion that the plates had been engraved some years ago, even if the prints made from them were recent. The lines etched into the metal showed traces of older ink, dried out, and there were also signs of wear. Far more than a mere seven sets of ten each had been pulled from them.

The evidence of the old ink was proof that the model could not possibly be Xavi, who had not been in London anywhere near that long. But it was very curious. The likeness was remarkable, especially when viewed through a magnifying glass. Miss Reynaud ventured the opinion that the resemblance was coincidental. I agreed but the prints were still guaranteed to infuriate the volatile Diego.

I wished that Quinn had taken the whole file-box from the shop, instead of only the six receipts. There had to be some record of payment to the artist, even if he—or she—had engraved the plates years ago. The meticulous Mr. Martin would have written down his name.

I could go back and steal the box myself, I supposed, but I was not as reckless as Quinn. If more stealing needed to be done, I volunteered him in absentia.

The matter did seem to have blown over quite quickly, as I had hoped it would. Xavi and I were not able to see each other as frequently as we had during the first months of our affair, but we found enough time to discuss it, when we were not making love.

I still wanted to retrieve the remaining four portfolios. Fotheringay's . . . well, I would wait for Quinn to storm the barricades with me. The one that had been sold to the address with a woman's name—the answer to that might be found in the letter from Anne that had arrived today in reply to my own. The remaining two were in parts of London that I did not want to enter alone: one in St. Giles's and the other, the last, in the far more refined vicinity of Regent Street, not far from St. James's Palace.

I might be robbed in the teeming slums of the first, and as far as the second . . . I imagined myself knocking upon the door of some august personage attached to the court or encountering a royal mistress who was expected to live close to the royal cock.

I would not risk either.

Xavi was no longer pressuring me in any case, and I was willing to wait. It was high time I outgrew my natural impulsiveness in any case.

First things first. I picked up Anne's letter and broke the seal, quickly reading the few words on the folded paper inside.

I saw you at the ball and ever since . . . I miss you, Edward. Come as soon as you can.

Astonishing. Had I walked right by her without knowing it? How her heart must have ached to have been cut by me in that way—Anne would not have known that the slight was inadvertent. I would go to her at once and explain. I dipped my quill in the crystal bottle of ink, dashed off a note and folded it without benefit of blotting sand. The wet ink bled through. I sealed my hasty missive and rang for a servant. The lad would bring it to her house within minutes. I knew it would do—she loved me as I was, impulsive as I was. And I still loved her.

I bounded up the stairs of the stone house, grabbing the heavy ring of the doorknocker and pounding away. The brass monster that bit the ring had been polished recently . . . I could swear the damn thing winked at me. Someone new let me in, a big fellow I did not know—the reptilian doorman had slithered away in my absence. The new man waved me upstairs. I took the stairs two at a time, not looking upon the landings to see if the whores I had met during my time with Anne were anywhere about.

Even in a house as well-run as hers, the women in residence changed quickly. It was a hard life. No amount of finery could conceal the viciousness at its core.

I came at last to the top floor and entered without knocking. There was Anne, sitting in the sun in a billowing robe of Chinese silk that caught the light. The window was open and I could hear the leaves of the tree rustling outside. She smiled when she saw me come in and stood, reaching out to let me take her in my arms.

"Anne . . . oh, Anne. Why did you send me away?"

"I had to." She kissed me with passion. "I was growing too fond of you."

I held her close and rocked her a little against my body, kissing her honey-colored hair. "I thought as much," I said smugly, wanting to provoke her.

She laughed at my rude reply and gave me a slap, precisely placed, that stung my cheek. But it felt good.

"Skillfully done, Anne. Would you like to birch my arse next?"

"Not you. Never you."

"Ah, why will you not let me experience that strange pleasure?"

"Because you are not suited for it. You are not in the least humble and you hate to hold still."

She was right on both counts. But I had never forgotten her in that unusual dress, her breasts and buttocks bared, whipping the balls of the man she'd tied so expertly. His erotic agony had been hotly anticipated and completely fulfilling.

"So," she said hesitantly, "when I saw you at the ball, I thought you no longer wished to speak to me."

I led her to the bed and we sat on it together. "No, Anne. I am so sorry that happened, but it was entirely unintentional. If I walked by you, it was because I did not see you. Were you masked?"

"Yes. And my hair was powdered. Even so . . ."

"I swear that I meant no insult. But were you invited? I was not. Do you know Lord Colefax?"

She smiled slightly. "There is a man who needs very firm discipline. He likes to be over a woman's knee to get it."

"Really?" Sharing salacious gossip again was great fun. And I hoped to distract her from unpleasant memories. "Tell me exactly how. I dislike the man."

"That is because you slept with his wife several years ago."

I tipped up her chin and made her look into my eyes. "And how did you know that?"

"Colefax mentioned it during one particularly vigorous session with our new spanking girl, and got three extra blows of the paddle for whining. Sally doesn't allow it."

"Good for her."

"He expected Lady Colefax to be perfectly faithful when he never was and he was proud of his cruelty toward her."

"Precisely what she said."

She patted my thigh. "He is not ill-favored. Some of my women think he is handsome. Of course, he always brings little gifts."

"Colefax was never generous with his wife, the blackguard."

"He mentioned that as well. Sally gave him two extra for that offense and made him tie his cock in a knot."

"I see," I said, laughing at his fate and Anne's joke. "I will have you know I provided his forlorn lady with pretty things and all the lovingkindness she desired."

She pressed an approving kiss upon my cheek. "Then she was lucky for a little while. Like me."

"A good-hearted rake bestows diamonds in equal measure on wife, mistress, and whore alike. But you would never let me give you any."

"No. You were sweet to try. You are still sweet."

"Thank you very much. I intend to try again."

She shook her head. "No. You are in love with someone else. I saw her at the ball. Why did you not tell me?"

"Ah—"

She put a finger to my lips. "Do not apologize. I won't listen."

"Very well. But we were trying not to look like we were together."

"I know you too well, Edward. Who is she?"

I explained as best I could without giving too much away and I left out Diego, who had not been there. Anne prided herself on keeping up with the *ton*, but Diego was not really a part of it, despite his influence at court. She certainly was not. Anne knew the men who came to her house and not that many others.

She nodded when I got to the part about the portfolio with the nude engravings that looked so much like Xavi.

"Which is why you wrote to me," she sighed. "And why you went to the trouble of getting the receipts for them from Mr. Martin, by hook or by crook. You must have been surprised to see my name."

"I was."

"And here you are. She wants them all in her possession, I suppose. Does she . . . have a husband? She is very beautiful."

Female intuition was a remarkable thing. "Yes. She does. And she is no more beautiful than you, Anne." I meant it sincerely but she waved away the compliment.

"I find mirrors much less fascinating than I used to. And that is all I have to say on the subject."

"Would you tell me, though . . . why you bought one of the portfolios?"

Anne shrugged. The billowing robe slipped off one of her shoulders and I saw the thin gown beneath. Her magnificent breasts were revealed under the silk and I longed to bury my face in them. I suspected that she knew what I wanted and understood my unspoken desire, but she kept it to herself.

"I happened to walk by the shop and saw them in the window. I liked them and went in. I have bought sets from Mr. Martin before. But I haven't looked at that one since."

I wondered if her girls had posed for others, but it was not a question I was going to ask. And trying to buy it back from her would serve no purpose.

"We sometimes give a portfolio like that to clients in advance," she said thoughtfully. "Anything to get them excited quickly."

That was the last thing I wanted to hear. The more men who

saw the pictures, the more likely that word would get back to Don Diego.

"But I won't use those now that I know. I had no idea that your Xaviera was the model," Anne said. "Of course, she was wearing a mask at the ball and—"

"She was not the model, as I said."

Anne raised an eyebrow and gave me a quizzical look.

"The resemblance is striking, however. If her husband found out, she would be treated very severely indeed."

My love favored me with an ironic smile. "More severely than if she was caught with you?"

I rose from the bed and paced the floor. "She is not going to be caught. But it is best if there is not the slightest breath of scandal where she is concerned."

"Well, then she must be careful. Indulging in private infidelity while maintaining the appearance of public virtue is difficult." She coughed. "Your Xavi and I are in the same business."

"Anne! What are you saying?" My temper flared but she continued to look at me steadily.

"Oh, nothing. The truth is never welcome."

"Enough." My anger swiftly ebbed away and suddenly all I wanted from her was a kiss, a real one. I sat on the bed again and took her hands in mine, bending down to press my cheek to hers and nip at her earlobe. I could feel the blush rising in her cheeks under my gentle treatment. La Belle Dame Sans Merci, my beautiful lady without mercy, needed mercy desperately.

I caressed her as lovingly as I could but sensed a steely resistance. All the same, I put my lips over hers and teased her mouth open with my tongue. Anne yielded at last, able to surrender only to something as simple as a kiss.

But she pushed me away when it was over. I felt put in my place. Very well. If I was not to have her this time, it was not the end of the world. We might as well talk.

"So." She wrapped the robe tightly around herself, like

armor. Beautiful, soft armor. "Tell me more about your Xavi. Something that I don't know."

I nodded. "Did you see the first portrait of her that appeared in the shops? The reproduction, I mean. Everyone was talking about it. But she was not named."

"Clever of her."

"She is, but that was not her doing. In fact, she had nothing to do with it at all. Nor did Quinn, even though he painted the original."

"Oh, that man. One of his girls came here, looking for work."

Nonplussed, I simply stared at her. "Which one? There are so many."

"I expect you have slept with several." Her tone was acerbic.

"I haven't. Not recently."

"Hmph."

I nodded, thinking I would have to be careful not to trigger Anne's obvious jealousy again. "You did not tell me the name of the girl who was looking for work."

"Corinne. She was with me when I bought my portfolio and she bought one as well."

Quinn's model—so the St. Giles's address was hers. The link had escaped me. Mr. Martin had scribbled her name, no doubt distracted by Corinne's snow-white prettiness. "Why?"

Anne shot me an impatient look. "A girl may go where she pleases in London."

"I mean, why did she buy the portfolio?"

"Not for the sake of art," was Anne's crisp reply. "She wanted to try out the poses and see if she could make more money at a different sort of modeling."

"I am not sure what you mean."

"Emma Hamilton posed naked upon tables for dukes and earls and managed to marry one, to say nothing of bedding Lord Nelson. I suppose Corinne thinks she can do the same thing. If she becomes famous she can even look abroad for a peer. It seems to be quite the thing to do."

"I see." But I didn't, not quite.

Anne sighed. "It doesn't matter. I am so tired of the silliness of young women. They seem to have no idea how soon their looks will go, yet that is all they think of."

I was not sure whether I could find out anything useful from her. It was madness to expect her to want to help Xavi. I should not have even mentioned the matter of the portfolio.

It was impossible to blame her for being upset, even if she had been the one to tell me to go before she ever knew about Xavi.

Anne sat for some minutes in silence, I having decided to let her direct the conversation.

"I did see the reproduction of the portrait," she said at last. "In this business we sometimes have to make conversation while clients are waiting—dear God, how I detest it!—and someone mentioned what a stir it was causing. I suppose the original was even more lovely?"

"It was. It may even be Quinn's masterpiece."

"And where is it now?"

The question was reasonable but for some reason it startled me. "Why—her husband has it, I suppose."

"I have always found it disconcerting," she said dryly, "to look at a portrait and the person who sat for it at the same time."

"Why is that?"

"Because they are so different. The artist paints away all ugliness and presents the person as an ideal."

"Xavi's portrait looks exactly like her."

"Then she can consider herself lucky. Obviously she is perfect to begin with."

"Not at all."

"Is she smiling in it?"

"Not exactly."

"Those vague half-smiles." She shuddered. "I think that artists get them all out of the same book."

"An odd observation but quite possibly true."

Anne relaxed a little. "In any case, Quinn is the best portrait painter in London. Far better than that filthy Fotheringay."

The back of my neck tingled. Something about the disdain in her voice when she mentioned Quinn's rival told me she knew him very well indeed. "So you have met him too?"

"Of course. He comes here often. He does have money and there is not a vice the man does not have. He drinks, he whores, he gambles—"

I had to laugh. "Anything else?"

"He will tell you as much himself." She seemed exasperated. "Can I not speak freely to you, Edward? You and I have known each other for so long—well, the less said about that, the better."

I was silent for a little while. The delicate balance of our relationship was swinging wildly. But if I could get her to tell me something about Fotheringay, it might prove very useful.

"Tell me, Anne—do you think he could have done the etchings of Xavi?"

"Do you mean the naughty ones?"

"Yes."

She made a wry face. "Well, he does hold orgies in his studio. But rolling around with lots of bodies doesn't mean you can draw one."

I laughed. "I think it would make it very difficult to do."

"Edward, why are you asking me about all this? What does it matter who did the drawings? She is not named—who will care?"

I reached out and stroked her tumbling hair. Pleading Xavi's case at this point seemed like a tactless thing to do. "I just think

Fotheringay might have done them, if only to make Quinn look bad."

"Hm. An interesting point."

I agreed with a nod. "And if another set of engravings like that appears, and Fotheringay is responsible—"

"He could probably get her husband to kill Quinn and have him sent to the gallows."

"Xavi would not cry."

"Oho." She patted my cheek. "Is she that heartless?"

"Anne, you know what I mean."

She stood and stretched. "I think I do. Well, I will give you my set back and I can give you his address. He is not that easy to find sometimes."

"I have it. But I do appreciate your thoughtfulness, Anne."

"How nice of you to say so. And now, my dear friend—"

That was the first time she had referred to me that way. It stung far more than her playful slap.

"So is it friendship now?"

"You will find that it lasts longer."

"Oh, Anne . . ."

"Do not sigh." She flung off her robe and pulled the gown underneath over her head. Anne stood before proudly naked. "We can be lovers for another hour."

"Thank you," I whispered.

We hurried through Soho, ducking through narrow alleyways that I never would have let her walk down alone, our way lit by a link-boy with a torch. It sputtered but we went on. A steady drizzle turned the stones of the houses slick and unpleasantly cold to the touch.

It was a dreary change from the cozy bed we had abandoned to come here. I had not wanted her to go out and was struggling to hold an umbrella over us both, but Anne was eager to walk, hoping to get to the streets with brightly lit shop windows in time to look her fill. Many stayed open well after dark to attract the custom of theatergoers digesting their cheap supper after the play.

Walking after dark was a new habit of hers. Evidently she had heeded my advice about her house becoming a prison. She dragged me from one window to another, shopping without spending money. The hubbub on the streets was comforting. It was a sound into which one could disappear if one wanted, enveloped by it and the darkness. Even during the day Soho was shadowy and people here knew better than to look at each other for too long.

We passed by the chophouse where I had met Thomas but we did not go in. When the rain came down, the artists left their chilly studios and headed for the gregarious warmth of the taverns. Fotheringay was bound to be in one or another of them.

I had no plans to confront him, thinking only that an introduction might make him less guarded. He had undoubtedly seen me with Quinn, his archrival in his trade, more than once. Finally Anne stopped on Romilly Street, at a sign proclaiming the public house below it, built below ground level. The entryway held a puddle of dirty water and a wobbly stone to step upon, which she did, hoisting her skirts nearly to her knees. She entered in this way, to loud huzzas from the men gathered inside.

"Annie!"

"Come, please sit with us! Here is a chair!"

This polite fellow had his nose mashed in by the hand of a more enthusiastic admirer, who braced himself on the other man's face and waved to Anne.

"No! Sit on me lap!" he yelled.

"I will sit on the table," she said diplomatically.

"Move down! Make room for Anne's arse!"

I took the men at the table for artists, recognizing the paint under their fingernails and generally wild-eyed demeanor as the hallmarks of the breed. She perched upon the cleared space and leaned back on her hands.

"Anne, I have given up painting to become a writer and, ah, I wrote a story," said a shabby fellow. "Shall I read it? It is dedicated to you."

She wrinkled her nose. "What kind of story?"

"A filthy, dirty, funny story."

The men roared with laughter.

"Huzza!"

"Read away, Diggory!"

Diggory pulled out several sheets of paper from his patched overcoat and cleared his throat. "Sweets For The Sweets, or, The Cook's Story."

The waiter approaching the table put his tray under his arm and stopped to listen. The shabby man nodded to him and began to read again.

"My conscience is always clear but then I am a pastry cook. Temptation is my stock in trade. Gwen was a tempting morsel, as fluffy as whipped cream. If I chose to dally with her, it would not involve penetration of her cunny or her mouth, a necessary precaution against the great pox."

One of the men interrupted him. "Is this a filthy story or a physician's tract?"

Diggory replied with severity, "A filthy story." He cleared his throat and resumed reading.

"No, we would but fondle one another to climax and be done with it in a few minutes, no more grave a sin than I had committed many times. The thought of Gwen lying back upon the bed, bared to my view, her dress pulled up and her legs spread wide was tempting. I could simply ask her to play with herself while I watched closely, or have her put some big thing into her cunny and give herself a very good fucking with it.

"Once out of the kitchen, Gwen requested that I put her down so she could lead the way. Feeling oddly merry (I had stolen a bottle of wine from the butler) and having—most unwisely—set aside all thought of the wedding cake I was supposed to be icing, I followed her up the stairs.

"I wondered if there were other women upstairs, and whether they might be persuaded to join us, then chided myself for being greedy.

"Gwen would do very nicely. She had her dress in hand and was lifting it a fraction of an inch with each step up. By the second floor, I was running my hands over her smooth thighs, by the third, her naked arse—but only for a moment.

"Nimble and light on feet shod in heeled slippers of silk, she stayed just ahead of me, not permitting me full liberties with her flesh. She was an expert tease, bringing the folds of her dress down a little and snugly wrapping the material around the fine buttocks I had just glimpsed. Round and firm, they were working as hard as her pumping legs to get her up the steep stairs ahead of me.

"She stopped suddenly, pulled her dress to her waist again, and I stumbled, unable to keep from pushing my face against her naked bottom. Such soft skin and so yielding! Gwen laughed and looked over her shoulder as I regained my balance. 'You are impudent, sir!'

" '*I* am impudent? Why, you—'

"She scampered up and away, keeping her dress at her waist. Ah, if there is anything more delicious than a pretty woman half-dressed, slowly revealing her bare behind, I do not know what it is. My cock was ready to poke through my apron. I would have taken her upon the stairs, so great was my lust.

"Gwen reached the door of a chamber and went in. I followed eagerly, wanting only to throw her down and have my fun. Without my noticing, she had undone her bodice too on the way upstairs, and her breasts were as bare as her arse. They were a magnificent sight, large and full, heavier than I had expected.

"Wicked thoughts assailed my intoxicated mind—thoughts of tying her arms over her head so that the twin globes would look larger still, their long pink nipples jutting out. I might suck upon them to my heart's content and she could not stop me.

"Squeezing my cock through my apron, I waited breathlessly for her to undress all the way. Ripping it off would have been faster, but girls like Gwen seldom had more than one dress. Even a whore deserved gentlemanly consideration. And waiting only made desire stronger.

"She made quick work of shedding her clothes, pirouetting before me wearing only the heeled silk slippers and a black ribbon around her neck. 'What is your pleasure, sir?'

"'To tie you up,' I growled, and mentioned a few other amusements I had in mind that would not involve my cock in her. She seemed clean and sweet, to be sure, but I wished to leave without a case of clap to remember her by.

"Gwen mentally added up the cost of my requests and directed me to place the sum within the drawer of a small table by the bed. I withdrew the pouch in which I kept my money, and did as she asked . . . delighted to see just the sort of big rod I had imagined her sticking into herself inside the drawer.

"The object lay in a satin-lined box. Made of ivory, it had a leather surround at its base attached to a leather pouch that was not unlike the one in which I kept my money.

"I winked at her and picked it up. Instead of golden guineas, the pouch held heavy balls that moved within it, larger than any man's. I noticed that the leather cuff had been pierced in four places, no doubt for the thin leather straps that were still in the box.

"'The women in the house like to use it upon each other,' she explained. 'It ties on, you see.'

"Stepping her legs apart, she traced her fingers over her hips and down between her thighs.

" 'I should like to see it on you,' I said. The intoxication caused by the two glasses of wine had not worn off, and Gwen's open-legged stance was only intensifying it. Not quite dizzy, I was nonetheless not myself. 'Very well,' I heard her reply.

"Gwen took the dildo from me and picked up the straps from the box, unrolling them with a flick of her wrist. The tip of her tongue licked her lips, which I captured for a moment in a kiss, clasping her to me and roughly fondling her arse. Pressed to my chest, she nearly dropped the thing in her hands, but surrendered to my embrace after a moment.

"I let her go and removed my own clothes. My usual method for a fast fuck—lowering my breeches and lifting my apron, without bothering to remove my clogs, would make too brisk a business of this interlude. No, I wished to stay a while, and be a naked Adam to her Eve in this garret Paradise. The little room was papered with a flower-strewn pattern that suggested as much.

"I watched while she set the dildo on the bed, neatly attaching the first three straps and working on the fourth.

" 'Do you need my assistance?' I asked, amused by her thoughtful concentration upon the task.

" 'No, sir—there. It is ready.'

"Gwen kneeled upon the bed and picked up the ivory cock, letting it dangle in front of her while she tied the top two straps around her waist. I could hear the balls clicking faintly inside the pouch. It was clear that the thick leather was meant to soften their swing against intimate flesh.

"She drew the other two straps between her legs, nonchalantly setting the rod in place, and pulled them over her buttocks, fastening them to the waist strap from behind.

" 'I see you have done this before,' I said.

" 'Yes. Few men are so large and we do enjoy it.' For the

first time, she looked downward at my member and smiled. 'But you measure up, sir.'

"I shrugged. My cock was long and thick, true, but the one she was sporting was an inch longer. Still, the sight of her wearing it was exciting. All I could think of was how it would look to see her thrusting into another woman in every possible position.

" 'Shall I get one of my friends—'

"It was as if she had read my mind, but then the thoughts and emotions of a man about to have sex are as naked as he is.

" 'No,' I said. My imagination would have to do for this brief romp, I told myself. 'But get on all fours. I want to see how it hangs.'

" 'Certainly.'

"She obliged me and put her head down upon her folded arms. I looked my fill at her womanly arse, excited by the thin straps that cut into her skin a little, and intrigued by the sight of balls dangling between female thighs. I reached down and made the leather pouch swing until it touched the ivory cock.

"Gwen murmured her encouragement. I played with the cock part too, judging its heft. It was cool to the touch but the ivory would quickly take on the heat of the cunny it penetrated as it was slid in and out.

"I let go of it and fondled her breasts, hot and full, swaying beneath her. Her nipples were extraordinarily long, as if an infant had been suckling them. Did she have a child? I stroked her belly, which was soft and giving. Perhaps she had. Women in her profession did not tend to mention their offspring to clients.

" 'Do you not want another girl with me, sir? Are you quite sure?'

"I could not contain my curiosity. My reputation as a cook was well-deserved and the mere promise of being stuffed with sweets had tempted many into my bed. I had enjoyed two women at once many times, but as it happened, I had never seen one woman fuck another with anything but fingers and tongue. 'No—I mean yes.' Desire had taken over.

"Gwen got up, her strap-on bouncing, and went to the door. She used it to shield her nakedness as she called softly. Someone female answered at once and in short order, another woman came into the room, letting a robe of fine silk slip from her shoulders.

"Her hair was dark red, impossibly long, and it flowed over her white skin like a waterfall of fire. The curls upon her cunny matched it. She was a beauty indeed. She only nodded to me in greeting, led quickly to the bed by Gwen.

" 'Lie down, Jane.'

The redhead did.

" 'And lift your legs high and spread them, so the cook may see.'

"This she also did, using slender white fingers to open her red-fringed cunny.

" 'I want your big rod, Gwennie,' she said softly. 'All the way inside me.'

" 'And you shall have it.' Gwen turned to look at me and smiled. 'Shall I tie her ankles and give her a good banging, sir?'

" 'By all means.'

" 'She does like it deep.'

"The woman on the bed looked from my cock to Gwen's. 'I would like to be fucked by both of you in turn.'

"Gwen clasped her friend's ankles with swift strength and lifted her slightly off the bed. The other woman stayed that way, her ankles crossed and her cunny squeezed between her thighs as Gwen bent down to spank the redhead's bottom very hard and repeatedly.

" 'You are not giving the orders here, Jane.'

" 'No, Gwennie,' she whispered. 'I must not—oh!'

"Gwen redoubled the pleasurable punishment. The other

woman's legs tensed but she kept them up and kept her bare bottom where Gwen could get at it, clearly enjoying the stinging slaps. 'More!' she cried. 'Ah, give me more!'

"As suddenly as she had begun the spanking, Gwen stopped. 'No. Move back. Put your arse in the middle of the bed. You will get more later.'

"Thus persuaded, the redhead moved to the middle, watching as Gwen took scarves from a basket near the table. She wrapped each of the other woman's ankles with one, leaving long ends. Then she tied Jane's legs far apart, using the rails at either end of the bed so the taut scarves would not interfere, I surmised, with the fucking she was about to do.

"She thrust several firm pillows under the redhead's arse, lifting it up. I would have an excellent view of what was to come. My erect cock throbbed in time to the pulse that rushed through my body. I heard its steady beat and little else. Gwen nodded to me and clambered over her friend.

"Again I saw the dangling balls between her thighs swing as she grasped her strap-on and gave the redhead the tip. Gwen kept it there, bending down to stroke Jane's heated face and kissing her ardently. 'Do you want my big cock, love?' she murmured into the other woman's mouth. 'Do you need a good fucking?'

" 'Yes . . . yes,' the redhead whispered. 'Give me all of it.'

"Gwen thrust her tongue deeply into the other woman's mouth and rammed the dildo in all the way in one swift thrust. The leather pouch smacked against Jane's uplifted bottom, the heavy balls within moving in a way that excited both women.

"I came closer and spread Gwen's arse cheeks apart, liking the feel of the hard-working muscle in her otherwise very feminine bottom. She screwed as hard as any man, pounding vigorously and giving her friend a great deal of pleasure.

"The redhead writhed under her as much as her ties allowed, and moaned when Gwen cupped her breasts. With a woman's skill, she pinched Jane's soft nipples—the redhead's nipples were not long, with the well-sucked look of Gwen's, but rather like the flat pink petals of some sensuous blossom. Her areolas showed the half-moon marks of Gwen's fingernails with every pinch, and each made her whimper with pleasure. The redhead in her turn clutched and scratched Gwen's big fine arse, driving her to stronger efforts and harder strokes.

"Their roughness with each other was unbelievably exciting to me. The submissiveness of women could change quickly in each other's presence, something I had not known.

" 'Look—look in the bottom of the basket,' Gwen panted, stopping her movement for several seconds to speak to me.

"I did and saw a very small dildo, shaped like a tulip bulb, also of ivory, with a string through a hole in the slender top.

" 'Yes, I have it.'

" 'Put it in my arsehole.'

"Her enthusiastic swiving had made all her flesh so moist that I saw no need for oil.

" 'Hold still.' I parted her buttocks with one hand and gently pushed the wide part of the little bulb against the tightly puckered hole that Gwen wished stimulated. She relaxed atop Jane, and whispered something in the other woman's ear.

"Reaching around, the redhead assisted me in spreading Gwen's bum wide open and the bulb slipped in as if her hungry little arsehole had wanted it very much.

" 'Ahh,' Gwen groaned. 'That is very good.'

"She began to fuck her friend again, but not so wildly, tightening her buttocks with each downward thrust to keep the bulb inside the snug hole between them. Only the slender end of the thing stuck out, the end through which passed the string that I had wrapped lightly around a finger. I splayed my hand across her arse, feeling the slight tugs upon the string as she continued to fuck her friend.

"Her motions were more side-to-side now, rubbing and

rocking, bouncing her false balls in this way and that. Their cunnies were swollen and so juicy that they were wetting the sheets. But the redhead could not move away with her legs tied—still, I guessed that the wetted linen under her arse was flattering evidence of Gwen's desire for her.

"I took the liberty of pressing my hand into Gwen's behind, adding my strength to hers to stimulate the woman beneath her. The redhead began to lift her hips to meet Gwen's, straining upward again and again as much her bonds permitted.

"I pushed down, Jane pushed up, and Gwen lost control. Her arse was shaking now under my hand; her cunny pressed so tightly to her friend's that their orgasm was simultaneous and explosive. They cried out at once, and I gave Gwen a frisson of extra pleasure when I made sure that the little dildo stayed where she had wanted it: up her arse.

"Gasping, they held each other tenderly, letting their desire ebb away, exchanging mutual endearments as they kissed away the feminine tears that streaked their flushed faces. I let go of the dildo and gave Gwen's arse a final pat.

"Gwen gave a sigh and heaved herself off Jane's body, blowing her breath over the redhead's breasts to cool her. She reached around to pull out the little bulb with the string and put it aside. Then, her dauntless cock bobbing in her friend's face, she untied Jane's legs one by one, and rubbed them affectionately.

"The redhead rolled over and got up, looking dreamily about on the floor for her robe. She slipped it on and exited without a backward look. Gwen was untying the straps of the dildo and soon set that aside as well.

" 'And now for you, sir . . .' She yawned. 'Forgive me. I gave the girl my all.'

" 'Indeed you did. Well worth the money.' I began to stroke my cock, shivering with the intense pleasure of touching my own neglected flesh. The sexual explorations of two women are always stimulating to the male of the species, and the variation upon that theme I had witnessed was especially so.

" 'What would you like?' She patted my cheek absentmindedly as she spoke, her desires so satisfied as to be nil.

"I brought her close to me and let my engorged member press against her soft belly. She answered my movement against her with slight undulations of her body, kissing and nipping at my chest and my shoulders, a series of sensations that went right to my cock. I fought, not very hard, against my mental languor, reminding myself silently of my vow to come away with no ailment to remember her by. How to have a woman with no penetration? There were many ways.

"It was entirely possible that I could ejaculate simply from what she was doing now. Or I could command her to stroke my cock in her tight-clasped fingers, sliding over the skin with sweet oil until I shot in high arcs. Or—I looked down and saw her dreamy eyes narrow as she looked over my shoulders. Some instinct made me turn around.

"It was the bride. I had forgotten all about icing the cake. But she saw what I was doing and lifted her dress ..."

The table erupted in loud cheers and cries for more. Diggory had read it well, with dramatic rolling of his eyes to emphasize every thrust and wiggle.

"To Gwen and Jane!" said a booming voice.

Anne raised her glass with the others, laughing. The constant company of women was not good for her, I thought. She seemed to brighten up considerably in this group, who obviously adored her. And they had something in common: artists and madams alike made the most money from the careful presentation of female flesh. Their models became her girls and vice versa—and an occasional lucky one did very well for herself indeed.

The artists and writers looked down on the artisans and the shopkeepers, who toiled hard for every penny. But Anne was drawn to this world too. She looked through the glass of the windows as if the vulgar bric-a-brac and trumpery things were fine indeed. It was clear to me that she could never go back to her old life in the country, no matter how much money she saved. Anne was a woman of London, for better or worse. And more and more, she was not the Anne I had once loved.

9

We did not find Fotheringay that night or the next. Anne was willing to go out with me but she kept me at a distance, and her determination to do so was not something I wished to trifle with. It had been selfish of me to want both her and Xavi.

I was not like Quinn, who grabbed at life with both hands. He cared nothing for the opinions of others so long as he had his pleasures. I missed him greatly and wondered how he fared in the country. The drizzle that had dampened my night out with Anne had turned into a rain so steady that it must be drenching the whole of England.

We were walking under an umbrella and it felt good to have her under my arm again, when she stayed there.

Anne had not exhausted the possibilities of the Soho shops. As we turned a corner, I spied a printseller's up ahead but thought nothing of it. Surely she would stop at the jeweler's next to it first.

I felt her head turn against the sleeve of my coat as she looked out from under the umbrella. And I saw what she saw in the same instant: More erotic pictures of the woman who looked so much like Xavi. But they were different.

I looked more closely. Quinn and I had bought the plates for the ones that were sold in the green-and-white portfolios—I thought wildly that we would have to try to buy these. But where had they come from? I wanted to put my fist through the window and take them away. Anne must have felt the muscles of my arm tighten because she patted me quickly.

"I am sorry. You must not be angry," she said softly. Despite her natural jealousy, her sympathy was real, although I daresay she felt more sorry for me than Xavi.

"But I am."

"Shall we go in and ask about them?"

"No." At that moment I began to have the curious impression that someone, somewhere was out to get Xavi. Her name had yet to be connected with these erotic engravings—this lot was titled only *A Beauty Bare*. Yet whoever was printing them was making sure that they would be seen.

It was futile to track down the remaining portfolios or try to establish their connection to the addresses on Mr. Martin's receipts. More would only pop up. I could not shake the feeling that I was also a target in some way. Certainly our secret love affair made her position doubly precarious. As Anne had pointed out, private infidelity and public virtue made strange bedfellows. Xavi was guilty only of having a face so lovely that her image became valuable.

Who was behind this?

I doubted I could stop it simply by buying up each new set that appeared. My intuition told me that whoever it was would only do it again. The new etchings were more roughly done than the others in the seven sets, as if to satisfy a demand that had grown without my knowing it.

When Xavi learned of this—she would learn, someone wanted her to learn. She had no one to turn to but me for help. Of course I would do my utmost, I thought, moving with Anne a little distance away from the printshop window. Nonetheless, for Xavi's safety and my own, I would have to end our affair.

We came to Anne's neighborhood after a silent walk. There was no one on the streets. The curtains were drawn in all the houses and the doors shut tight and bolted. Her man would let her in and then I would be on my own. I was glad of it, my mind still troubled by what we had seen.

We found a shadowed place to kiss good-bye and took our time about it. Then, hearing a noise, Anne peered into the darkness and we both saw a dark figure some distance away move slightly out of shadows of his own. The man wore a wide-brimmed hat tipped down over his eyes, but he raised his head just long enough for her to get a glimpse of his face.

"It is Fotheringay," she breathed.

"The very man I want to talk to."

She pointed at his back. He was walking away quickly. "Not unless you run after him."

"I cannot leave you here, Anne."

"He is going to the gaming hell. I have seen him here before." She told me how to find it and I walked her to her door, waiting to see that she was safely inside. She blew me another extravagant kiss. So much for friendship.

"Be careful, Edward," I heard her call.

I turned the corner as she directed and found the place. A small brass plaque was the only marker. I tried the knob. The door was not locked and I entered, then made my uncertain way down a flight of narrow stairs, keeping a hand on a banister of well-smoothed wood until I stepped onto the landing at the bottom. A balding fellow in a shabby tailcoat showed me into the room beyond.

Though it was not yet midnight, the table was surrounded by exhausted men, whose undone shirts and wrinkled jackets attested to the length of time they had been there. Playing cards had been tossed down upon the cloth, abandoned along with the gamblers' hopes of making back what they had lost.

Anyone could see that a few had risked all for kings, queens, and jacks, the stone-faced swallowers of great fortunes and estates—and lost. These unfortunates sat slumped in their chairs, the fever that attended their play broken at last. Others, with more sense or less to risk, perhaps, seemed calm enough, smoothing their disheveled hair and finishing up the dregs of drink in their glasses. No one talked. A sense of despair pervaded the atmosphere, already thick with stale smoke and the sweat-smell of nervous men.

Only one seemed at ease amidst the scene. A tall man with black, piercing eyes was standing near a wall observing the men at the table—whether he had just entered, like I, or had been there for a while, I did not know. He moved away, avoiding the light of the sinumbra, the shadowless lamp at the center of the table—a lamp that brightened many a slide into hell.

A dark fire flashed within his eyes when he suddenly looked my way, and I recoiled, as if from the sound of a gun. But no shot had been fired. I dismissed the odd illusion. In a moment, I became aware of ordinary noises: the sighs and the dull scrape of chairs as the gamblers rose, ready to stumble home.

More would soon come down the narrow stairs to replace them and the play would continue until dawn. I glanced around, avoiding the gaze of the dark man, whom I took for the proprietor, his suspicions awakened by my entrance. A pretty wench entered and pressed herself against him, kissing him to distraction. Well and good. I examined him from across the room. His clothes were impeccably cut and elegant, although he did not look English. Why, I could not say.

He seemed too aristocratic in manner to be the proprietor, James Townly, whose name I had noted on the small brass plaque by the street door. Who else could he be? The dark man had not been among the players at the table, but only watching as I came in.

Will Fotheringay was nowhere to be seen. I supposed he might be in one of the curtained alcoves to the side, where other wenches relieved the occasional winners of some of their wealth—I was familiar with the operation of such establishments.

A young man entered, setting the dirty glasses upon a large tray and sprucing up the uneaten food with a little fresh parsley for the next customers. He nodded at me and asked what I wanted to drink. I asked for wine—it did not go to my head as a rule. The young man took the full tray into an antechamber and I made myself comfortable enough in one of the chairs as a few men, casual acquaintances, came in, talking loudly of the operetta they had just seen.

I recognized Sir Peter Moncrieff, a dissolute friend of my cousin, and young Lord Sperry, whose first name escaped me, although he would not have bothered to remember mine. Being ignored did not trouble me. I thought to stay a while so long as I could remain in the shadows, but if Fotheringay did not appear I would leave.

The young man reappeared with a glass of dark red wine. I thanked him and once more noticed that the dark man was looking at me on the sly. He gave the wench he had been kissing a resounding slap on her arse and told her to try her luck elsewhere. At the moment she was trying her coquettish wiles on the opera-lovers. None seemed interested in her charms.

"Who is that fellow? Does he own this establishment?" I asked in a low voice. The young man kept his head down and did not look in that direction.

"No. Far from it. He is Don Diego Mendez y Something," he said. "A great man in his own country or so I was told. He came here with a friend, but the poor sod lost a thousand pounds in five minutes and stormed out."

So this was the husband that Xavi so loathed. What in God's name was he doing here? My curiosity about the man made me study him anew, but more discreetly than before.

Our paths had never crossed until now—I had taken great pains to make sure of that and so had Xavi. It was pure coincidence that we should meet in such a place, but then, I reminded myself, anyone with money was welcome here.

He was younger than I had thought he would be, yet his true age was difficult to determine. He exuded an air of self-possession, clearly accustomed to command others and to have his commands instantly obeyed. And I had mistaken him for the owner of a gambling hell . . . but then he did look like a Lucifer. Whether his manner was a consequence of his noble birth or his important position at court, or simply the natural result of his height and powerful build, I could not decide.

The wench crossed the room to me and smiled prettily. I motioned her to sit in my lap. What else could I do? If I were not occupied, Don Diego might attempt to strike up a conversation. I could not very well slip away until he left the room.

My new friend needed no further invitation. She dropped onto my thighs, wriggling with evident pleasure and scarcely permitting me to finish my wine. It had little effect—the pressure of her squirming arse made my cock stiffen, which she felt. The young man saw that my glass was empty and brought another without my asking. I drank that down and dug in my pocket for a coin, giving it to him along with the second, now empty glass.

"What is your name?" I murmured into her soft neck, pressing a kiss to the black velvet ribbon around it.

"Bess," she said simply, as if she had no last name worth mentioning. "Shall we go upstairs?"

Here was my reason to leave the room and not be followed. All thoughts of the previous events of the evening vanished, along with the memory of Anne's face. I rose with her in my arms, looking straight ahead and heading back toward the stairs. No one remarked upon my departure—I guessed that my pretty friend serviced several men a night, and most of them were regulars.

But when I heard a deep voice call my name, I turned around. Diego was asking to talk to me.

I put Bess on her feet and told her to run along. The play at the table had resumed and the gathered men concentrated their attention on their cards.

He was taller by an inch or two. I refused to be intimidated. "Yes?"

"Come with me. We can talk over here where it is quieter. I know who you are, Lord Delamar."

What could I do? No gentleman would cut and run. I had no idea what he would say.

I took the chair he indicated and sat, looking him squarely in the eye.

"So. Mr. Quinn is your friend, I believe."

I inclined my head. "He is."

Diego gestured to the waiter. "More wine." He did not order any for me, not even pretending to be civil.

He waited in silence before it arrived, every inch the Spanish grandee. "He is no friend of mine. I believe my wife is having an affair with him."

That caught me off-guard. "I—I could not say."

"You hesitate."

I shook my head. "Don Diego, you are a gentleman and so am I. You cannot trap me, or ask me to incriminate Mr. Quinn."

His eyes blazed. No matter what I said, he would think the worst. Quinn might get his throat cut for my sake.

"My apologies," he said evenly. "There is the matter of the engravings. Have you seen them?"

"I don't know what you're talking about."

"Yes. You do."

He did not seem like the sort of man who would bluff but I could not answer him. If someone who knew him had seen me in front of Mr. Martin's printshop, I was doomed. And I doubted that whoever had spotted me had done so accidentally. He must have had someone watching Quinn, and they had seen it all.

The men at the table grew loud and boisterous as the play progressed and bets were placed. Turning an apoplectic red with anger, one man rose to argue with another who sat across the table, grabbing his lapels and dragging him out of his chair.

The lamp in the middle of the table fell over and cracked and the tablecloth caught fire from the spilled oil. An outward-spreading ring of tiny flames reached the edge of the table and leapt up as the folds caught. The room filled with smoke as the waiters tried to put out the flames, throwing pitchers of water at the fire. Pushing, screaming, trampling upon each other's feet, the gamblers tried to get out, clogging the door to the stairway.

I rose, coughing, and shoved my way out. Diego was right behind me. I dodged a fat fellow who tripped over someone else, and he took the Spaniard down with him.

Pushing past the others on the stairs, I came out onto the street, taking great lungfuls of air, grateful to have escaped.

Then I heard Don Diego's voice coming from inside. So he had escaped as well. Given his sheer strength, it did not surprise me. He bellowed my name before I saw him and I deliberated for only an instant. I took to my heels and ran.

Later in the week . . .

Richard Whiston settled himself in the chair by my desk and looked about, not idly. "I see you have some new pictures. The one of Mount Etna is very nice."

"Thank you."

"No one else would put an erupting volcano on the wall. Does it . . . signify anything?"

I snorted. "Only you would ask a question like that."

"And what is the answer?" His pleasant voice was dryly humorous.

"It is only a volcano."

Richard nodded and smoothed his hair. "Very well. If you say so. Now tell me why you had to see me in such a hurry."

"I need to pick your brain."

"Then begin."

"You are quite the social butterfly, Richard."

He nodded thoughtfully. "I suppose I am. If it is gossip you want, I'm your man. I even know a few facts about some rich and important people. Who sleeps with whom, that sort of thing." His irreverent smile broadened into an out-and-out grin. "And who are you sleeping with these days?"

Since he had been my secretary for the last seven years, and had started with keeping my social calendar, the question was a reasonable one. But he had taken on greater responsibility when I inherited this house and began to invest the money my father left me. Richard had a good head for business and gave me very shrewd advice on it.

"Let us concern ourselves with rich and important."

"As you wish." He looked at me expectantly.

"I want to know more about a man at the Court of St. James's."

"Ah. He travels in exalted circles."

"He is the Spanish ambassador."

"Yes," Richard said thoughtfully. "Don Diego. Someone pointed him out to me. Striking man. Tall, dark, menacing."

"That is him. And where have you seen him?"

Richard shrugged. "He goes to the boxing matches."

"Oh."

I must have looked dubious because Richard smiled. "Everyone does, from dukes to dockworkers. But they go for different reasons. I just want to look at the men, of course. I leave at the first bloody nose." He held up a hand. "In answer to your next question, I doubt that is why he attends."

"Would you care to speculate?"

"I think Don Diego likes bloody noses. And broken ribs. And pain. The wilder the fight, the more intent upon it he is." Richard looked at me levelly. "I do hope you are not planning to import olive oil or some such thing from Spain."

"No. Unless you think it would be a good investment."

"I couldn't say." He paused, drumming his fingers upon one knee for a few seconds, then picked up the newspaper folded upon my desk, peering at the front page and reading one headline aloud. "Fire Breaks Out In Gaming Hell. All Saved. How inspiring."

I could not speak to that.

He put the paper down. "Is there something else you want to ask me?"

I sighed. I could not put off confessing to at least some of what I'd done. "Yes. I have a question on an entirely different matter. Is it possible to love more than one person at the same time?"

"I take it this is not a rhetorical question."

"No, it isn't."

He pondered the matter while pressing the tips of his fingers together and humming under his breath. I was half-expecting a skeptical answer but his was thoughtful. "If everyone is agreeable to the arrangement, it can be done."

Should I take him into my confidence about Xavi? I decided not to. He hadn't mentioned the Spanish ambassador's wife. I would have to talk around the matter.

"What if one of them is married?"

Richard shook his head. "Well, that is different. In my world, some men are and their wives know nothing at all of their affairs with other men."

The parallel world of men who loved men was his milieu, of course, and I knew that the situation he described was common enough. Of course, affairs were equally common among men who loved women.

"I think," he said slowly, "that the sacrament of marriage is meant more for the procreation of children than the preservation of love. Many go looking outside their homes for that."

I nodded.

"And many go looking for sex as well," he added in somewhat of an afterthought.

I had found both without ever having gone looking, really, not expecting it to happen, and certainly not with two very different women at the same time, if not in the same place. They shared the same experience of having known great unhappiness in marriage. Anne would not even tell me what had happened between her and her late husband, but it was clear that she loathed him. And Xavi lived under the thumb of a violent and unpredictable man.

"I think that is especially true in a miserable marriage."

"Yes." Richard said the one word quite carefully. "But the partners in it will still remain married. Divorce is next to impossible. The remaining solutions are melodramatic: running away to sea, committing murder, that sort of thing. Or mundane. One packs one's bag and moves into a house five streets away."

"Well, I have no desire to commit murder, I assure you."

"I am glad to hear that. But since you are not married, perhaps what you are getting at is that someone may wish to murder you."

His tone was light and I knew he was joking. However, he was close to right. And I was not the only person in jeopardy, far from it. That Diego would suspect Quinn had not occurred to me, although the conclusion was understandable.

My decision to end my affair with Xavi had been made in haste, but I could not simply cut all ties to her. She was still at risk of a beating or worse, for something she had not done. On principle, that bound me to her more tightly than our illicit lovemaking. She had no one, I mused, who would come to her aid now but me.

"And what do these elliptical questions have to do with the Spanish ambassador?" he asked. "You have gone from the specific to the vague. Never a good sign."

"Ah . . ."

"I see. You are involved with his wife."

His guess was a shrewd one, and I would not deny it.

"Edward, may I say that the probable complications are probably not worth the pleasure?"

"There is rather more to it than that."

He frowned. "One of which is her husband's taste for violence."

"Yes."

He surveyed me with a worried look. "Would it not be better to leave well enough alone?"

"Not at this point."

"So the hole you have dug for yourself is too deep to climb out of."

"Something like that. Richard, we fell in love."

He nodded sagely. "A grand and glorious emotion. It seldom lasts."

"Are you saying I should give her up?"

"You know as well as I do that the lady in question is all the more desirable because she is unattainable," he said crisply. "And there is the matter of her husband's honor. Some men are tolerant of their wives' affairs, some are not."

"He is not."

"That is to be expected," Richard said. "A pity, though."

"Don Diego is not faithful to her."

Richard made a wry face. "You have her word for it, I suppose."

I was silent.

"Edward, he is still her husband and he has the right to do as he pleases, unfortunately. And you are the odd man out."

"But—"

Richard rose and began to pace about. "Do you like boxing, Edward?"

"Yes. So long as no one is too badly hurt."

He stopped in front of the calendar on the wall. "There is a match this Friday. The East End Terror versus Billingsgate Bob. It starts at nine o'clock, and if the Terror is lucky, it will be over at five minutes past nine. Do come."

"Perhaps I will. Thank you for the invitation."

He took a pencil from my desk and jotted down the other details.

"Most likely Don Diego will be there," he said casually. "He often is on Friday nights."

"I do not want him to see me, Richard!" I blurted out.

"Oho. So he knows who you are."

"But not what I have done." I was thinking of Quinn, of course. I had not explained Diego's suspicions concerning my friend to Richard.

"You did not tell me that."

"I—I did not know how to."

Richard clasped his hands behind his back and rocked a little on his feet. "He is not a man you want to provoke, Edward."

"I know that," I said almost savagely. "So why are you trying to throw us together?"

"I am not. He will sit in front, where the lights are brightest and he can see everything. He gets there early and leaves late.

You and I shall do the opposite by arriving late and leaving early, and we can sit far in the back, in the dark."

"I have not said yes. And I still do not understand why you want me to go."

"Know thine enemy, Edward. That is all."

The place where the matches were held was nothing much to look at: it was a low building of brick with no windows, on the south side of the river Thames and not far from it. A loose crowd of men—as Richard had said, they were a mixed lot, with top hats among the greasy caps—and even a few women milled about outside. Richard and I sat in the hired carriage waiting to see if Don Diego would appear. He was nowhere to be seen. When the hour drew close to nine, Richard opened the door of the carriage and jumped out.

"Wait here. He may already be inside, but it is best to check."

He made his way to the entrance, ignoring the rude comments from the people around him and spoke to the man at the door, then went in.

I saw him come out a minute later. He walked quickly to the carriage and gestured to me. "Come. He is here. Down in front, where I thought. There is a woman with him."

I made no comment to that but got out, and followed him. A slouched hat provided some concealment for my face, and the high collar on my coat would do the rest. Richard had assured me once more of Don Diego's intense concentration upon the fight and the contestants. The others who had waited were now mostly inside.

Agreeing to go with him had been an impulsive decision and a last-minute one. Perhaps it was male instinct that did make me want to know my enemy, as Richard put it. And observing a good fight ought to keep me on my mettle.

We squeezed past several pairs of knees belonging to the on-lookers in the back row of benches, muttering our apologies.

"He is there," Richard murmured, pointing to the back of Don Diego's head. As he had said, there was a woman with him, small in stature, sitting pressed against his side. The crush in the front was considerable and perhaps she had no choice.

I could not see his face or hers. She wore a neat bonnet that covered her hair and a dress and jacket of some dark material. A latecomer attempted to find room next to her, but Don Diego reached out swiftly to push him away with one long arm. He wrapped it around her almost protectively.

The two combatants entered the roped-off square, illumi-nated by a battered lamp high above, hanging from the ceiling. They waved to the audience, who cheered and yelled, rooting for their favorite champion well in advance.

The East End Terror sported bizarre tattoos that covered most of his chest, shoulders, and arms, and much of his face. The odd design looked pagan—there were no hearts, flowers, or sweetheart's names, just thick blue lines that swirled over his skin. I supposed him to be a sailor lately come back from the South Seas. He looked quite capable of consuming human flesh.

His opponent was no less ferocious. Billingsgate Bob had only one tattoo, and it was of a fish. His heavy muscles slid and moved under his skin as he clasped his hands and flexed his arms. The crowd roared their approval.

The air was soon thick with a fug that made me cough. I was still feeling the aftereffects of having been caught in the fire, and the oppressive atmosphere made me feel weak. But I could not take off my hat or coat, even though we sat in the dark, and so I suffered in my own silence.

The shouts were nearly deafening as the boxers circled each other, crack-knuckled fists up at the ready, sweating hard. Their bodies gleamed under the light from the lamp, which cast strong shadows on their features, making them look even more fearsome. They were bare-chested, wearing only thin breeches tied just above the groin, and their calves were bare as well. The soft shoes that enabled them to move quickly were not unlike a dancer's, an incongruous note.

Punches whistled through the air and were dodged with lightning speed. Bob landed the first one, a heavy blow to the ribs that made his opponent grunt. But the Terror was game and fought on, keeping his fists near his face as if he expected Bob to hit him there next, protecting his chest with his forearms.

He got in the next one—Bob did not even see it coming. The Terror stepped nimbly back, and his arm shot out again, hitting the other man just above the eye.

"First blood," Richard said, wincing. "No—he is not cut. It is only swelling."

But I saw Don Diego lean forward. He was so close to the combatants that a stray punch might have hit him. I had the impression of a wolf sniffing the air, as if eager for blood that would soon flow. A lump rose above Bob's eye, beginning to close it.

The boxers circled each other again, throwing jabs and lighter punches. Their savagery was contained to some degree by their desire to put on a good show before half-killing each other. The onlookers cried out for more, determined to get their shilling's worth of mayhem.

The woman at Don Diego's side nestled against him. She was not much bigger than a child. I felt a wave of disgust.

And then the battle began in earnest. Circling once more, than grappling in a clinch, they pounded each other's bodies. The thud of fists on flesh sent a visible thrill through the onlookers, as toffs and workingmen howled for blood. They got it.

The Terror had Bob bent over, the other man's head under his tattooed arm. He punched him relentlessly, opening deep cuts where skin stretched over bone. His mighty fist came down on his opponent's swollen cheek and I heard the teeth inside Bob's mouth crack.

Head hanging, eyes swollen nearly shut, he spat them out and reared up like an enraged bull. He charged the Terror, slamming his battered face into the other man's belly. The pride of the East End went down on his arse, his legs in the air.

Everyone in the place rose to their feet, shouting hoarsely. Almost everyone. Don Diego and his companion did not. And I did not. Richard was standing but his gaze was averted from the carnage in the square.

Billingsgate Bob had his man where he wanted him, and gave no quarter, kicking his ribs and his ears. The Terror clutched his head, keening in agony. He struggled to get up but could not. Gasping, standing his ground in the blood-soaked sawdust, Bob raised a triumphant fist. He had won.

A collective groan of satisfaction came from the audience. An older man came out, a bucket of wet towels in one hand, and kneeled by the Terror. He wrung out a rag and stroked away the blood on his face, not listening to the ebbing force of the combatant's ragged, noisy breaths. I saw the Terror's tattooed chest heave upward once, twice . . . and then it moved no more.

The older man continued to wipe the boxer's face before he realized what had happened. He put his head down over the fallen man's heart and listened, then pressed his fingers against the side of his neck.

"He is dead," was all that he said.

No one present seemed to care in the slightest. Many were already on their way out, jostling each other. I tipped the brim of my head down when I saw Don Diego rise, and extend a hand to assist the woman with him. He spoke to her as they made their way out also—I could hear him but not see him. His voice was invigorated, deep and loud, and he moved more swiftly than his companion.

Standing by me where I sat, Richard understood that I wished not to be seen and moved slightly so that his body blocked mine.

"Coast clear," he said softly.

I looked up from under the brim of my hat. Don Diego had gone on and the woman who had accompanied him had fallen behind. She was trying to get past a knot of louts who were chaffing her and gave as good as she got, kicking one viciously with her small half-boot. I noticed the spikes of black hair escaping from her neat bonnet next and then I saw the gloves she wore when she reached up to tuck the hair back in: fingerless black mitts. Her slender figure edged by the men in her way and as she did so, she looked straight at me. I remembered those strange, glittering eyes at once. Kitty smiled at me.

10

Mrs. Mayhew wrinkled her nose and looked at our disreputable clothes when we entered my house, but made no comment. I asked her to send up a cold supper for us, as was my routine after an evening out, but I knew I would be unable to eat it. I wanted to vomit; I could not. She nodded and withdrew with a perfunctory curtsey.

"I expect she knows where we have been," I said. "The air was bad and we smell of the place. Her late husband was devoted to the sport. I have never seen a match like that, though."

"Nor have I. And I am sorry, Edward," Richard said. "It was butchery, nothing more."

"They were evenly matched," I answered wearily. "Either might have killed the other."

"Yes, that is true."

"Was that the lesson? Have I learned whatever it was you wanted me to know?"

"Perhaps," he answered. "Come, let us go into your study and have a whiskey. You need it."

"I do. I don't know if I can keep it down."

"Try."

He poured himself a double shot and handed me just one. I sipped at it, feeling its reliable warmth erase the chill in my bones.

"Who was that girl who looked at you, by the way?" Richard asked. "You seemed suddenly afraid."

The sight of Kitty had been a shock to my system that I wanted to forget. Why she was with Diego was a mystery, perhaps one that Anne could answer for me. My last visit to the house had been only to see my former love. Kitty had been nowhere about.

"She is a strange one." That was true enough. "You might have guessed that by the look in her eyes."

"You were the one who was looking into her eyes."

"For a second. She was right in front of me."

"Why didn't you acknowledge her? She smiled at you."

I gritted my teeth.

"She is only a whore."

"Oh? And does she ply her trade upon the street?" There was a thin edge to Richard's question.

"No. She is in a house."

"And do you and Diego share her as well as his wife?" The edge grew sharper.

I shook my head.

"Really, Edward. You cannot expect me to believe that. I thought that—oh, never mind."

"Go ahead. You never did tell me if I had learned my lesson tonight. Or what it was."

Edward went to the door to open it when he heard Mrs. Mayhew's knock. He took the supper tray from her capable hands. "Thank you, Mrs. M. We shall make short work of this."

"Good-night, sir. And sir."

I nodded in her direction. Edward set the tray on a side table and ignored it.

"I hoped that seeing Diego's bloodthirstiness might knock some common sense into you. But I see that is impossible. We will have to get Billingsgate Bob to do that, perhaps."

"Thank you. I look forward to it. Oblivion sounds good."

Richard looked down at the tray and picked a crust off a sandwich, chewing it thoughtfully.

The next day . . .

I was consumed with the need to see Anne. The afternoon was drawing on. She would be up and about in her house, preparing for the clients who would stroll down the quiet side street in Mayfair in another hour or two. I dashed off a note and enfolded it within two envelopes, each one with its own dot of red wax. In case the outer one was accidentally opened, the one inside was also addressed to Mistress Anne, in strictest confidence. If Kitty were there I would have to meet Anne outside and our discussion would be less private.

I sent it off with the boy and had a reply in less than an hour.

"She is not here any more, Edward," Anne said. "The girl left of her own accord."

I felt relieved. At least Kitty would not know of my presence here today. I wondered if seeing me at the boxing match had startled her, and then I thought of her opium habit. Her unnatural tranquility was in part owing to it.

"Was there a quarrel?"

"No. I don't argue with the women as a rule. They know what is expected of them."

"Then why did she go?"

Anne gave me a quizzical look. "Kitty never said. I expect she found a protector. Sometimes they do."

"And you will not run to her rescue."

"I don't even know where she is."

She composed her features, looking into the mirror on the wall as she brushed her hair into a thick strand, wrapped it around her hand and pinned it up. The temptation to kiss the silky nape of her neck was something I would have to fight.

I had not seen Xavi in far too long, and I yearned to bury myself in Anne's sweet flesh and forget everything for an hour.

But she had given me the information I had come for, and she would soon be attending to her clients.

"I thank you, Anne. I will be on my way then—"

"You have not told me why you want to know," she said calmly. She looked at herself in the mirror again, turning her head this way and that.

"I saw her by chance in public. I was curious. That is all."

"A very thin reason."

She had given me an opportunity that I was not going to resist. I came to stand behind her and cupped her warm breasts. She took out the pins that held her hair and turned around in my arms.

An hour later, I left.

I had other appointments and the day was drawing to a close. A changeable sky hung over London and the vast bulk of St. Paul's showed white and then gray as I hurried past to the Inns of Court some distance away. Sir William Thurlow had granted me a rare hour of his time to discuss the business matters on which I still hoped to build my own fortune.

Magnaminous of him, considering how much he charged.

That done, I treated myself to a chop and potatoes and an excellent bottle of wine. I was hungry to the point of starvation after my romp with Anne, but otherwise physically satisfied. When Decimus let me in, I gave him a manly wink and handed him my hat.

He merely nodded and took it away to be brushed.

I went up the stairs two at a time, very much in need of a

bath, for which I called down to the maid in the hall. She did not hear me.

Oh well. I would do without. My good dinner had cheered me up and I was feeling rather reckless. It would not do to be eaten alive by worry and fear. The complicated nature of my life seemed somewhat less daunting at the moment. Xavi, the prints, even her sinister husband, receded to the back of my mind.

The door to my bedroom was ajar but I thought nothing of that. I went in and stopped where I stood.

Xavi had come to me.

"Dear God! How did you get in? Did anyone see you? You cannot stay here—"

She rushed into my arms. "I have not seen you for so long! I had to!"

"But—but—" She pressed kisses to my mouth and kept me from talking. The danger we were in mingled with a sense of arousal. Damnation. I had just come from Anne's bed—I could not be feeling desire for Xavi. But I was. I pushed her away gently.

"The servants must have seen you."

She shook her head. "I sent my maid to the door first and waited where I could see her but I could not be seen. She asked Decimus about Mrs. Mayhew—you mentioned their names— and whether there was work for a new girl. He is kind, Edward."

"Too kind, perhaps."

"He abandoned the door to show her the way to the kitchen and I seized my chance and ran in."

"Where is the maid?" I asked, looking around. "Is she here as well?"

"No. If work was offered, she had been instructed to say she would ask her mother for permission. I expect Mrs. Mayhew thought well of that. She left after I was upstairs."

"Xavi..."

She stretched up to cover my mouth with an even more wanton kiss. I gave in, thanks to the bottle of wine. If she too required a good fucking like Anne, I might very well oblige her. The problem of getting her out remained.

"You will be missed at your own house."

"Diego is not there," she said contemptuously. "He seldom comes home. I think he has someone else."

A fact I could confirm. But I said nothing of seeing him with Kitty.

"But what about your servants?"

She only shrugged. Xavi went to the mirror to take her hair down, just as Anne had done for me.

"Come, Edward. Run your hands through it."

I did. She arched like a cat.

She was in a mood of feverish excitement, and her own recklessness was exciting to me. Xavi gave me a heated look in the mirror and picked up a brush, which she handed to me.

I used it upon her hair with assiduous care, then gave it back to her.

"May I specify where you will apply it next?"

"Xavi, we must get you home."

"I will not go."

"Then I will make you."

Apparently that was not what she wanted to hear. She hurled the brush at me with all her strength, hitting me squarely in the middle of the chest.

"I hate you! You have not written—there were no letters for me in the library cabinet—you were far too calm at the ball—and you were—oh!—polite!" She almost spat the word. "You have someone else, I know it! You are worse than Diego!"

The blow itself did not hurt, but her final words unlocked a great deal of emotion on both sides—and a surge of hot desire was the greater part of it. My gentle Anne had satisfied me fully but Xavi needed to be put in her place. I would not tolerate the insult of being compared to that filthy bastard.

"Am I?" I said softly. "We shall see. Take off your clothes!"

With frantic haste she undressed, not arguing. I locked the door and did the same. She might as well learn now that she was not always in charge—she was making my life ever more complicated and I could not have her bollocks-up my desperate attempt to help her. Coming here as she had was the height of foolishness.

If the nuns in the convent had not disciplined her, then I would. It was high time . . . and there were many intriguing ways in which to do so. I was in no mood to discuss anything with her. She was soon to find out that obedience can be a very pleasurable virtue.

Naked, she kneeled upright upon the bed for the punishment she wanted.

"Give it to me, Edward."

She took the brush which I held out to her. The bristles were short and flat and the other side was smooth wood, a fact she appreciated.

"I want both. The smooth and the prickly."

I took it back, caressing the smooth side. It would make an excellent paddle.

"How many strokes do you want, Xavi?"

"Ten."

"Then you must count them."

My hand came down for the first, my fingers curled tightly around the handle of the brush.

"One," she said.

I clasped her left buttock in my other hand, holding it apart from the other. That received a smack of its own.

"One-half," she said pertly.

I let go and clasped her right buttock.

"One-half again. That makes two in all."

I grinned. She wanted to make it last.

"Clench your arse for me."

She did.

I angled the brush and gave her another on both buttocks.

"Three."

"Does it feel good?" I inquired.

"Yes—oh yes."

"Then here is another."

"Four!"

Her cunny was wet—I could smell its succulence. Down came the brush again.

"Five."

Her bottom was a healthy pink. She grabbed her breasts and rubbed them together.

"Should I paddle those next?"

Xavi gasped. "Not yet. My arse! Back to work!"

"You are a demanding creature."

"And proud of it."

I set the brush on the bed.

"Why are you stopping?" she asked indignantly.

"Because I think you need something in your arsehole. If you are so interested in discipline, you may try to hold a dildo in it and not let it fall out."

Her eyes glowed. "Put one in then."

I had one in my bedroom that a lady love had left some time ago. Sentimental as I was, I had kept it. But the question was where had I put it. I ransacked through several drawers and finally found the thing under my old shirts. It was smooth and thickly rounded, but no more than five inches long.

Perfect for what I had in mind.

I returned to the bed and swiftly gave her another one stroke, just to keep her in line.

"Six. Why such a small dildo?" She was pouting.

"You shall see."

"Why does it have the bulb on the end? And why is the bulb flat on one side?"

"It is an ingenious design, is it not?" I said blandly.

"Why will you not tell me what it is for?"

I made no answer.

"I suppose it is a handle. The other end looks like a cock and head."

"It is not a handle, but the cock and head does go first."

"Well, then. Begin."

I spread her cheeks apart. "Hold yourself that way."

Her tiny hole needed cream and I had that too, in a jar. I found that next and swiped my fingertip through, dabbing it upon her arsehole puckers without actually touching them. I imagined that the coolness of the cream would be pleasurable on its own.

I was right. She cooed at me. "That feels lovely. What now?"

"Watch."

I applied the thick cream liberally to the small dildo, especially the head.

Xavi's eyes widened. "The bulb must be a handle. You are not creaming it."

"Bend over and shut your pretty mouth for five seconds," I said, exasperated. "Please, Xavi."

"I can't bend over if I must hold open my arse. I will fall."

"You are impossible. Here it comes."

I pressed the tip against her tight puckers without being able to see them through the dab of cream. Still, her arsehole opened—it was more obedient than she was—and the dildo went in a little ways.

"Mmm. But that's not far enough, Edward my love. I won't be able to hold it."

I paused. "Is this not about your discipline? You need it and you asked for it."

"Yes." She sighed. "Yes, sir. I must be made to mind. Give me more."

Such impudence excited me. I did give her more, perhaps another inch and a half.

"And now we resume," I said.

Assuring myself that the dildo was properly positioned, I took up the brush again. The smooth side of it tapped only once, lightly, against the flat side of the dildo's bulb. It went in another inch.

"Oh!" Her cry of pleasure was very satisfying to me.

"You can hold it easily now, my darling."

Her eyelids lowered over her dreamy gaze. The inside of her thighs was wet and slick, her cunny dripping with the stimulation that the part next door to it was receiving.

"Do you want more?" I asked her.

"Yes. Oh God yes. Should I be counting? I think that was seven."

I shook my head, although she could not see it when I was standing behind her. "No. When this rod is snugged all the way in—the bulb on the outside—then your buttocks shall be paddled with the brush again."

"Very well. How many inches are left of the dildo?"

"Perhaps three."

She murmured her desire to feel the bulb at its ultimate resting place outside her arsehole when all three remaining inches had gone in.

"Another tap?"

"Yes, Edward. It feels so good."

I grasped the brush and gave the flat side of the bulb another gentle tap, and she took another inch in the arse, groaning with wanton delight.

"You are beautiful, Xavi. And I alone of all men in London am privileged to see you this way."

"Tell me what I look like," she whispered.

Demanding. And vain. That was my Xaviera Anything-But-Innocencia.

"A lovely woman kneels upon the bed. She demands that her bottom be paddled. Her lover thinks of a new way to amuse her, and she is intrigued."

"Yes."

"She spreads her behind and receives a dab of soft cream. But she is puzzled by the object in his hand and wants an explanation. He is not quite forthcoming but she is ready. The head of the object goes into her arsehole."

"Yes. And she—I mean, I—holds it like a good girl."

"Indeed you are."

Tap.

She was not expecting that one but receiving another good inch delighted her. The dildo was slightly thicker in the middle and her arsehole accommodated it nicely, prepared as it had been.

"There is one more inch left. Keep your cheeks spread."

"Yes, my love." Her reply was so low it was almost inaudible.

I put the brush down and caressed her breasts, loving the way they jutted out when she held her arse open for me. I sucked and nipped at each nipple.

"You must not move," I said when I brought my head up. "And you shall obey."

"Oh, Edward . . ." She moaned and I captured it with a rough kiss.

"The last tap is going to feel very, very good. You have been waiting for it."

I squeezed her breasts firmly and repeatedly. She did an excellent job of holding herself completely still. The dildo in her arse did not bob or wiggle.

Her nipples were erect but bent in my tight grasp. These would be next.

"Keep your arse open," I instructed her. I took her nipples between my forefingers and thumbs, rolling them. Had I tugged, it would have unbalanced her. I wanted her to feel the sensation completely. I pressed each nipple between finger and thumb, an action that was just short of a pinch. Then I pressed harder, again and again.

"Would you like another woman to do this to you?" I murmured.

"No," she moaned. "Only you."

"But women understand each other's bodies so well. Imagine that a big, strong young woman has been called into the room. She especially loves nipples."

I was thinking of Sally, the goddess who paddled men over her lap at Anne's house. She would do very well, although I could not make her image jump from my mind to Xavi's.

"Go on," Xavi whispered.

"Your nipples can take more." I pressed without pinching, harder and harder. "She is going to tie your nipples to her own. Close your eyes."

Alas, the flat small ones on my own chest could not stand up and make the fantasy real. But my voice and the repeated pressure from my fingers holding her nipples seemed quite effective.

I let go and caressed her breasts, moving my hands in light circles over the nipples I had made so sensitive.

"Those are her breasts brushing against yours." I took hold of her nipples again, pressing precisely upon each. "Hers are as erect as yours."

"Mmmm . . . oh. Oh oh oh."

To my delight, Xavi was very close to climax.

I rolled her nipples vigorously, then pressed very hard for the last time. "Your nipples are tied to hers . . . it feels so good . . ."

Then I let go, grabbed the brush and gave the dildo in her

behind a firm, final tap. The bulb snugged up against her arsehole and she swayed, ready to faint with pleasure, all filled up
by the thick rod. I reached down and spanked her pussy gently—one, two, three!—rotating the dildo as I did.

Xavi cried out and came in my hand, rubbing frantically and
squirting her juices into my palm with every contraction of her
cunny.

"Screwed and spanked and tied," I breathed into her ear.
"How good it feels." A second climax, stronger than the first,
began. She went wild and it took all my concentration to do her
cunny and arsehole for this one, lightly spanking the first and
turning the creamed rod around in the second.

"Oh! Oh! Oh!" she screamed. I held her at last, absorbing
some of the intense sensations she was experiencing with my
own body. I felt a sudden wetness between us and I shook all
over. She grabbed my arse and held on.

I had come without knowing it, so aroused had I been by
our rough play.

And we had never even finished counting.

I awoke some hours later to see moonlight streaming across
the bed. Christ. Xavi was still with me and there would be hell
to pay when Diego discovered she was gone. But it was too late
now. She smiled in her sleep, and threw her arm across my
chest. What had I done?

I had lost my temper at her, and the result had brought us
both intense pleasure. It was as if her reckless mood had merged
with my own upon her arrival, redoubling our willingness to
risk a night together.

Her full lips parted as she breathed in and out, as peacefully
as a child. I put a finger to them and she woke.

"Where am I?"

Her lifted head turned from side to side, trying to make
sense of her surroundings.

"In my room. In my house."

"Oh, no," she breathed.

I pulled her back. "We will figure something out."

She nestled against my chest, playing a little with the fine hair upon it. "Are you drunk?"

"No."

"Then you must be insane."

"Possibly."

"How am I going to get home? In a balloon?"

"Explain where your bedroom is, and give me an idea of the outside of your house."

"It is in the back. Diego never comes to me."

I blew out a breath. "Well, that is in our favor."

"My maid will help. She hates him. He has tried to molest her."

"Good. But right now we must act alone."

Xavi patted me and struggled to sit up, bunching the tangled sheets around her middle. "Not quite. I told her to sleep in my bed just in case."

"Would he not punish her for her deception? What if he happened to come in?"

"I told her to flash her cunny. That is all he cares about. She will have to endure his grunting and humping but it is better than being beaten."

"She is remarkably loyal to you."

Xavi's shoulders moved in a shrug. "I pay her well."

I sat up too. "Even so."

"You are right—forgive me for falling asleep—and forgive what I said to you."

I kissed her in the middle of her forehead. "I have already forgotten it. There, you have a kiss to take home."

"Is it magic?" she said wryly. "I need protection."

"I am doing what I can, Xavi. There is no time to explain it all now."

I hopped out of bed and jammed one leg and then the other in my breeches. Boots next, shirt, jacket. The strings of the shirt were untied and my chest hair showed.

"You look like a highwayman," she said admiringly.

"More like a madman, I should think."

By providential luck, I got her inside before anyone saw us. The house was immense, with a stable in the back. She had me check there first.

Don Diego's carriage was gone. Two lighter equipages were inside, but the space where the carriage had been was quite empty. The lantern that had been carelessly left lit showed wheel tracks in the scattering of straw—what one would expect to see, of course, but I wondered how recent they were. I took the lantern from its nail and bent down. It was impossible to determine but the stub of a cigarillo glowed amidst the particles of straw.

"That is the carriage which brought us here from the docks," she said. "With all our worldly goods, it seemed."

"Why would he use it to go out at night?"

"I think that he is gone for longer than one night."

"Then that is our great, good fortune. I will not have to hoist you up the trellis upon my shoulder."

She smiled fondly. "My hero."

"Your fool."

We tiptoed up to her bedroom, finding the little maid where Xavi had said she would be. The girl rubbed her eyes and woke.

"Where is he, Maggie?" Xavi asked.

There seemed to be no question of who he was. Dominated as the household was by him, the women in it preserved a shred of dignity by not even honoring him with the title of master when he was not around.

"He left for a week and took several of the servants with him. And a small woman with black hair and strange eyes."

Kitty. So he was so bold as to bring a whore into his own house.

All Xavi knew was that he had brought a woman she did not know here and away with him. It did not seem to surprise her. I assumed it had happened many times before.

Xavi's infidelity seemed of no consequence whatever compared to his. However wild our sexual games became, they were a mutual exploration of pleasure for us both. She loved me and only me; her husband loved no one but himself. His overweening pride and violent nature compelled him to act purely on instinct and never reason.

Such were my thoughts as the maid said good-night and quietly padded away to her own attic chamber but not before I gave her a guinea for her trouble.

"Very odd," I murmured.

"No, it isn't. He has gone away before, but not like this, quietly in the night."

"Why?"

"There are several great ladies who find him thrilling. He is invited to country house parties and I am not."

"You and I might have met more often, had I known."

Xavi shook her head. "The time of his return could not be predicted. He hates to tell me where he is going or who he is seeing."

She sat down upon her bed, smoothing the satin of its cover where the maid had wrinkled it. The ornate furnishings were of Spanish manufacture, richly carved and gilded, with an abundance of red everywhere.

Even the wallpaper twisted and writhed, its florid velvet exhausting to the eye.

I looked around and noticed no mementoes of the sort that

women cherish, no little paintings of sisters and brothers or a mother and father.

"Did you grow up in a house like this, Xavi?" She had never mentioned her family, only the convent.

"No. My house was plain and small. And the convent where I was raised after the deaths of my mother and father was an austere place."

"Tell me about it."

"In a moment." She flung herself back into the pillows. "How strange it is to have you here, Edward. In one night we have seen where the other lives."

"After months of meeting on the sly, it is odd," I said. "At least this room is yours." The thought of Don Diego pressing her unwilling body down into this gorgeous bed was revolting.

A dutiful wife would spread her legs and pray for a hasty ejaculation.

In one corner stood a *prie-dieu*, the low stool upon which good Catholics petition God in velvet comfort, although there was no crucifix near it or anywhere else on the walls. The rosary with which she had been portrayed in Quinn's painting was nowhere in sight. I supposed she was not genuinely devout. No doubt Diego had requested that it appear.

He was a blackguard, through and through, but mindful enough of the opinion of others to insist upon the appearance of piety.

"Do you pray upon that little stool?" I asked her.

"Yes. For his death."

"Oh, Xavi . . ."

"He used to make me kneel upon it for hours. I was supposed to look at him naked in front of me. If he wanted to fuck another woman in front of me, he did. If he wanted to jam his cock into my mouth and have me clean off her juices, he did that too."

So much for kneeling before God. In this house Don Diego was the only god and a law unto himself.

She hummed as if she didn't have a care in the world, had never cared, would never care. Her tone had been unemotional, so much so that I found it chilling. She was a very different person under her husband's roof, in some indefinable way his creature. The man cast a long shadow.

"And—and what did you do?"

"I steeled myself to endure. Eventually he became bored and looked elsewhere."

"Let us talk of happier things, Xavi. You said you would tell me of the convent."

"Yes. We—we were strictly schooled." I took her slight hesitation for a painful memory. "But I found some things beautiful. The chapel, for one—and the way the light came down from above. The garden that the nuns kept."

The serenity of the picture painted by her words were so at odds with her glorious wantonness . . . I could not comprehend how her nature had been formed in such a place.

"And were you married there to Don Diego?"

"Ah—yes." That memory must have been painful indeed. "A virgin bride of sixteen . . . it seems like a very long time ago."

I was taken aback. I had no idea of how old she was. "But you are now just . . ."

"Twenty-three."

"And Diego?"

"Forty-six."

"He seems younger. Quinn described him to me as an old goat, so I thought of him that way."

She snorted. "He seems younger because he is pickled in spite. There is no blood in his veins. But he likes to see it flow from others."

I was silent, remembering the fight. More and more, I felt it was my duty to rescue her from the brute. But how to do it and not be killed was a puzzle I was not yet ready to solve.

"Are you safe in this house?" I said suddenly. "Is that bad?"

I thought of how I had seen her at first, sitting for her portrait, calm and utterly beautiful. Without the opportunity to meet in society, our passion had been intense, explosively so. The undercurrents I felt more and more now had not pulled so strongly at me then. And I had Anne, who simply loved me. And was honest when it was over. "Xavi—answer me."

She seemed far away.

"England is . . . better. I am not locked in my room here or followed by a duenna. Time moves much more slowly in a country like Spain. You live more slowly . . . and if I were there, I would die slowly too."

I heard a noise—a rattling of wheels—and Xavi sprang from the bed. "He has returned!"

I went to the window and opened it, seeing a hack go by over the cobblestones.

"No. It is only a hired coach. But I cannot stay."

"Then go."

She stayed where she was upon the pillows, her hastily donned clothes in a tangle about her.

She was sulking again. Xavi could be highly sensual, sophisticated, provoking and childish by turns. The more I learned about her, the less I seemed to know. It had been a very odd night.

"Good-night, my love." I leaned over her to kiss her cheek.

"The trellis should hold you."

Her matter-of-fact tone made it clear that she wanted to be left alone. I went to the window and opened it, then climbed down and got away.

11

Quinn's return was a rowdy one. Rob had come round to tell me that his master was arriving at noon at the Hare and Bells and I made sure to be there. He clambered down from the coach with a pair of chickens under his arm in an openweave basket, clucking madly.

"Chickens? Quinn, whatever were you thinking?" I asked.

He winked. "I need them for a painting. I shall give Fotheringay a run for his money in the cottages-and-chickens line."

"I am surprised you are not leading a cow on a tether." Miss Reynaud's timid voice made itself heard.

"Thought of that. Couldn't get one in the coach."

He handed me the basket of chickens and gave the copyist a mighty hug. Then he presented the birds to her. "For you, Miss Reynaud."

"But I don't want them."

He didn't seem to be listening. His ruddy face beamed with pleasure at seeing us all again.

"And how are you, Edward? Still killing the ladies?"

His choice of words was unfortunate but I managed to smile. We made an odd procession on the way back to his studio, Rob laden down with bags and boxes, Miss Reynaud exchanging beady-eyed stares with the chickens, and I carrying his rolled canvases.

"You are a good sport, Eddie," he said. "For a nobleman, that is."

I frowned at him but he only grinned back.

"So how goes the great cunny hunt?" he whispered conspiratorially.

"What?"

"The etchings. Have you retrieved them all?"

"No. More have appeared."

His expression grew sober.

"Really? Where? At Martin's again?"

"No, in Soho, at another shop entirely."

He kicked open the street door to his studio. "Hmm."

We got through the business of dragging all his things upstairs and Quinn sent Rob out for something to eat. He gave Miss Reynaud the rest of the day off, but she didn't leave.

"What shall I do with the chickens?" she asked fretfully. "I am not going to take them home."

"Very well. Put them on the balcony for now. I will build them a box to live in. Perhaps they will lay eggs, eh, Miss Reynaud? Lovely fresh eggs."

"You have gone mad," she said. "The country did you no good at all."

"Well, I was not there for my health, strictly speaking," he told her.

I shot him a warning look.

"I was there to paint pictures! Lovely, lovely pictures! Of chickens!" He gave me a maniacal smile.

"Completely mad," Miss Reynaud said.

She did eventually leave and Rob did too, once Quinn's belongings and supplies were stowed away.

"Now then. What the devil is going on?"

"I found two—no, four of the portfolios." I had forgotten Anne and Corinne for a moment. " I think Fotheringay has one and you kept one. The last belongs to an address I have yet to visit."

Quinn thought that over. "I thought Foth might have done them, though. Why would he buy his own?"

"I don't know. I haven't asked the man."

"But you must, Edward."

"I followed him into a gambling den and was nearly burned alive."

"Dear me. I had no idea that playing cards were so flammable."

"There was a fight. Someone knocked over a lamp."

He raised his eyebrows. "How exciting. I am sorry I missed it. But there I was, buried in the country."

"I should think you would have buried your cock between a milkmaid's thighs."

"I did. Several times." He guffawed and slapped his leg. "And you?"

"Is this a fucking contest?"

The idea intrigued him. "An excellent suggestion."

I laughed—I had to. Quinn's good nature and common sense dispelled the turbulent emotions, good and bad, that I had been weathering. It was refreshing to see him. "Then we shall have one."

"You won't," he scoffed. "You are far too much of a romantic."

"You may be right."

"Of course I am. Come, let me show you my paintings. I went around and persuaded the gentry that they needed paintings of the houses they lived in."

"Anything else?" I knew him too well.

"Oh, I painted their dogs. Good sitters, dogs. Cats are not."

I admired his work, which was well-done as always. But I could not put off telling him of Don Diego's suspicions for long.

It was no longer a question of losing patrons at court or scoffing at the empty threats of an enraged husband.

"Quinn, Xavi's husband was in the gaming den."

"What, with Fothy?"

I nodded. "Fotheringay may have led me inside. Diego insisted on talking to me. But he wanted to know if I was your friend."

"You are. That is no secret."

"You don't understand. He thinks you are Xavi's lover."

"But I'm not."

I put a hand on his shoulder and shook him a little.

"He tried to get me to incriminate you, but I would not."

"Good. Very wise. I still think you are overreacting."

The painter was far too blithe for his own good. "He is dangerous, Quinn. And he lives according to his own law."

"Explain."

What I knew was in part supposition and not fact. But the sinister demeanor of the man—and Xavi's toneless recitation of his cruelty toward her—and most of all, his conduct at the boxing match, made me afraid. He had watched a man die an utterly miserable death and it had seemed to invigorate him.

"He is cruel, deeply cruel. Take my word for it. Is that enough?"

Quinn studied my face. "I do believe you are serious."

"Then what are you going to do?"

"Go back into hiding. But not in the country."

"Then where?"

"Corinne's. She wants me to paint her picture again. I look forward to sucking her delicious toes."

He picked up one of the bags he had emptied and started

throwing things into it: a clean shirt, a parcel of paints, and so on, until it was full.

"I have a very grand painting planned, in the style of the old Italian masters. I shall be God, riding a cloud, and Corinne and that lot can be the angels. What do you think?"

He was very good at making me laugh. "I think I would like to see it."

"I am going to call it *The Apotheosis of Everett Quinn.*"

"That is a very grand title."

"It is time I did something different. I am tired of painting the portraits of rich men's wives, especially when they come after you bent on mayhem. Tell Miss Reynaud to take care of the chickens. Off I go."

I saw him out and headed home. There was one way to keep Quinn in place: have a buxom woman literally sit on him.

My friend would be safe enough, perhaps, but then he was a man and well able to defend himself. The thought of Xavi, incommunicado and alone in her splendid gaol with only a maid to talk to, was deeply troubling. Still, emboldened by my absence or her own frustration, she had come out on her own. She might go to the house where we made love and attempt to meet me again. I would leave her a letter there.

My darling—

Our last meeting was not enough—there is never enough time to love you as you deserve to be loved.

When can I see you again? I long to kiss you and . . . no more need be said until we meet again.

> All my love,
> Edward

I went again and again, but there was never a reply.

Once, just once, I saw Xavi, in Diego's coach. My heart

leaped and I ran after it, fool that I was. She shook her head and frowned in a haughty way when I came close enough for her to see me. Her eyes were cold when she opened the window, her words soft with malice. "Get away from me."

I was too startled to reply and had I not stepped back, would have been dragged under the wheels of the coach. It rumbled away. So she was alive. But something had happened. Her mind had been poisoned against me.

A week passed and then another. The last time I found the cabinet empty, I vowed to stop. That very night Richard came by and found me brooding. Our conversation was not a cheerful one and he soon left me to my own devices. I got up. My ill humor might be dispelled by a walk. The lonely streets were no comfort.

I made my way to the banks of the river Thames and sat upon the stones of an old wall. The swiftly flowing water reflected the moonlight but the sight was unromantic.

A soft cry came from an alley and I turned my head. There was nothing. I supposed it was a cat, fucking or giving birth or dying. Then I heard footsteps, precisely placed, and not very loud. I turned around.

Kitty had come out of the shadows and stood so close I could touch her. I got up.

"No need to be a gentleman. It is only me."

"What do you want?"

"I saw you sitting alone. I thought I would keep you company."

Her voice had the curiously unemotional tone of Xavi's, I realized. What was she doing here? Diego must have tired of her.

She sat when I did, primly adjusting her skirt beneath her narrow buttocks. There were faint circles under her eyes, but they only heightened the strange beauty of her face.

"Do you want to know why I left Anne's house?"

Her confiding tone surprised me. "All right."

The moonlight was bright enough for me to see her face. I might learn something about Diego—and hence, Xaviera. Or I might not.

"It was because of Don Diego. He asked me to go away with him and I said yes."

I had thought as much. The heaviness in my heart seemed to swell. Why I felt sorry for her I could not say.

"I was surprised to see you at the fight, sir. It was a good one."

Her conversational tone, considering the ugly fate of the boxer, struck me as odd.

"A man died."

Kitty only shrugged. "Men die all the time. What of it?"

"You are young to be so hardened."

She turned her head to stare at me. "I am not so young as that and I have done all right."

"I suppose in your terms you have."

Kitty kicked her boots against the rocks of the wall. "I made a lot of money at Anne's house."

"Really."

What else could I say? *How perfectly splendid! Huzzah!* It would be utterly wrong for me, a rake, to pass judgment upon whores, high and low. I had spent far too much time trying to persuade women to give away what she charged for. I was feeling very low and her company was not helping.

But my mind took up the puzzle of why she had wanted to be with Diego in the first place. It was possible that he had simply needed someone to keep him company when he went slumming, as he seemed to like to do. I had no idea of how long he had been with her, and Anne had said only that Kitty had left her house, not when. He must have dallied with her for several weeks, perhaps longer. It was no use asking her. Everything was all the same to Kitty.

And now she had returned to the streets. I imagined her in his big black coach, driven out to the country-house parties to be viciously used by scoundrels who called themselves gentlemen. He had brought her back out of boredom, or because some other broken girl had caught his attention.

Unless he was somewhere about. He was the kind of man who fucked one woman in front of another just to see her cry. The devil only knew what games he got up to with Kitty.

I had the feeling that she had edged imperceptibly closer. My irritable solitude had been pierced and I wanted her to go away.

"What are you doing here, if I may ask?" Perhaps if I asked her enough bothersome questions, she would leave.

"Oh, I came to meet a friend."

"Is it someone I would know?" My polite tone would not have been out of place in a drawing room. Ours was made of rocks and strewn with rubbish. My nostrils filled with the stink of the river. It didn't seem to bother her. Nothing seemed to bother her.

A man approached, stumbling a little.

"There he is."

He was roughly dressed and reeking of drink. I could smell it when he came closer. He looked me over and then looked at Kitty. "Is 'e your pimp?"

She giggled. "No. He is a friend of mine from—from before."

"I am yer friend," the man said. "Not 'im." He reached down and grabbed her by the arm, hauling her to her feet. She made no protest at his rough handling, but I picked up a rock and got ready to use it.

"Naow, naow," he said, backing off. "You put that down."

I did but I kept a wary eye on him. He approached again, circling like a stray dog. This time he was quicker. With one arm around her waist, he threw her over his shoulders and disappeared into a low tunnel.

I ran after him. It was too dark to see and I felt my way along the curved walls. After several minutes, despairing of finding my way, I came out on the other side in a neighborhood I did not know—and then I saw Kitty, brushing her dress and looking not too much the worse for wear.

"Thank you," she said. "But we have finished. He only wanted what he came for."

Being taken for a pimp and failing at an attempt to be a hero—well, at least my response had got me off my arse.

I nodded and walked with her a little ways. No one paid attention to us. She stopped by a brightly lit window and looked at the paste jewels winking on their velvet trays.

"How pretty. I had a diamond clip once."

"I seem to remember it."

We went on our meandering way and soon she stopped in front of another shop that sold cakes and sweet things. She hummed.

"Would you like one?" I asked. She had just earned a shilling or two, but I thought I would treat her.

"No, sir."

I told myself again, now that my spirits had lifted, that she might prove to be a source of useful information about Diego. All it would take was money. There was no telling what he would do next.

What with one thing and another, I followed her for another hour. She brought me to a slum, a three-story edifice on the verge of toppling over, and stood in front of its ramshackle door. "This is where I live."

For a fraction of a second I saw something human in her eyes: shame. Again I felt sorry for her—and a foolish urge to play the gentleman to her waif sprang up.

She opened the door and a drunk fell out at her feet. The

door had been the only thing holding him up and he might not get up again. I peered up the crazy-tilted stairway. There was enough moonlight coming through a hole in the roof for us to find our way.

"I will show you to your door."

"Thank you, sir."

We went up one flight and then a second. She knocked upon the door and no one answered.

"Is someone home?"

"I think so." She looked up at me, her eyes wide and calm. I turned the knob and entered . . . and a man's strong hand took me by my clothes and slammed me to the floor. My head hit something going down and I saw stars.

And then I saw Diego. He stood in the doorway of the room, his arms folded over a massive chest. His eyes were filled with hate, and I could see his fingers tighten as if he wished to strangle me.

"It was you. Not Quinn."

Kitty had fallen with me. Not thinking clearly, I tried to hold her close. He might decide to kill us both and leave no witnesses. She struggled free and I caught the look that passed between them. It lasted for an infinitesimal amount of time, but it shocked me into awareness. She had tricked me into following her here.

She stood up under his watchful eye while I gasped for breath—and kicked my head with her booted foot.

When I came to, I was stripped naked. There was a bitter taste on my lips as if some foul liquid had been spread over them. It coated my tongue as well. I tried to spit but the stuff in my mouth was too thick. A fog had entered my brain. Its stealthy enchantment made my cock achingly stiff, even though I understood that I was now in mortal danger.

Diego's eyes moved over my body, assessing my strength. If it came to that, I would fight for my life. At that moment a greater awareness dawned upon me without one word of explanation from him: he had found the letter or been given it. How else would he know that I was his wife's lover?

Our meeting in the gaming hell had come to an unexpected conclusion that had allowed me to escape, but in here he was in control. Diego unfolded his arms to put his hands on his hips and for the first time I saw the dagger in his belt.

So that was to be my fate. If he won, I would not be the first dead body in the mud of the Thames when the sun rose. From whores who defied their pimps to thieves who stole from each other, anyone who ran afoul of a criminal sense of justice might be found there when the tide receded, along with the occasional suicide. In his eyes, I was a criminal for bedding the wife he rarely saw and treated so badly. I could not argue the point. With my face bashed to a pulp, my hair torn out, without clothes to identify my remains, my body would be thrown into the paupers' pit and there would be no one to mourn me.

My devoted servants were too used to my comings and goings, and too discreet to send anyone hunting for me at once. The thought of Decimus, the butler, patiently awaiting my return and counseling the housekeeper, Mrs. Mayhew, and the servants under her to do likewise, floated through my mind and out again. There was no one who could help me but myself.

He dragged me to my feet and I summoned up the strength to face Diego squarely. His gaze dropped to my cock.

"Does danger excite you?" His voice was level but filled with menace. His eyes rose to meet mine again and we stared boldly, male animals sizing each other up before a fight, if not a fair one.

The question required no answer, but my body betrayed me. My cock would not go down—I would not die with my tail between my legs, for what it was worth.

Diego took a step forward but I stood my ground. He

grabbed my cock at exactly the moment Kitty pulled my arm behind me, nearly wrenching it from its socket. I howled with pain. The two of them got the better of me, and before I knew it, I was trussed and held prisoner, with Kitty standing guard at my side should I endeavor to slip free. My hands were bound together behind my back, and a tether held me to one of the posts. My feet were bound to each other, far enough apart to enable me to stand upright, but not kick.

Diego brought his face to mine, the better to intimidate me. He grasped my cock again, watching to see if my expression changed, as if he thought I might enjoy his caress. I did not—and still my cock stayed up. Whatever had been rubbed upon my lips was also a potent aphrodisiac.

"So you are my Xavi's lover. She likes big cocks." He stroked mine for several more seconds, then let go to unbutton his breeches. The front flap came down to reveal his own, jutting out from the dark, sweaty thatch of hair covering his groin.

His arousal was undeniable. He rolled down his foreskin and the dark head of his cock came forth, a drop of liquid at the small hole in it. He touched it to the head of mine—the drop felt scalding hot and I struggled to get away.

He would not let me. Luxuriously and slowly, he rubbed his hard rod against my own, but spared me his kiss. That he gave to Kitty, who stood on tiptoe to receive it, the vicious little bitch. He broke it off to talk to me.

"I have had you stalked for some time. I know who you are. I know that you fuck my worthless wife. Dear Xavi," he said mockingly. "She is not so innocent as you think."

I kept silent. Now I knew who had found my last letter to her. My precautions had kept Diego's spies from finding the others.

"When you walked through Soho with Anne, my men were right at your heels. You never saw them, eh?"

I had not.

"And then Fotheringay distracted you. On purpose. Paid by me. I was lying in wait for you."

He studied my face. I daresay my expression did not please him, because he slapped me viciously across the face, so hard that I saw stars again.

"And here we are," he went on calmly. "The cuckolded husband and the lover who put the horns on his head. We shall see who is stronger, eh? Two men, both angry. An even match. I too shall be naked."

Kitty stood again on tiptoe to whisper in his ear.

"Yes," he replied. "Go get it."

As to what "it" might be, I could guess: A whip or something else with which to punish my flesh to his satisfaction. She left the room and returned with a flask of wine, which puzzled me. I vowed not to swallow it. I would rather choke to death should they force it down my throat than be manhandled by Diego.

Again my body betrayed me. It wished to live, whatever humiliation I must suffer to do so. When Diego forced my head back and my mouth open, Kitty stood on the bed and tipped the flask over my mouth. Only a few drops came out, moistening my tongue. I did not spit them out, for there was nothing to spit—my mouth had gone dry. But the drugged wine must have been stronger than the liquid smeared on my mouth, for the drops had an immediate effect.

She upended the flask and filled my mouth completely. The wine spilled over my lips. I could not gag or I would have choked. Instead I swallowed with frantic haste. Diego ran his hand over the muscles in my neck, soothing me with Spanish words that I could not comprehend. The potion made a powerful sensation of warmth and erotic arousal spread through my entire body.

Consumed though I was with loathing and fear for him, I

was more intoxicated than ever and his touch was . . . comforting. His hand moved from my neck to my shoulders and chest, caressing me with skill—there was no other word for it. And it was nothing like a woman's touch, but strong and warm. A part of my mind fought against surrendering, to no avail.

He smiled slightly and let Kitty help him undress. My eyes rolled back in my head and I closed my eyelids. I did not want to watch. I had no desire to see the rest of him. Dazed, I still possessed a tiny fraction of resolve and began to explore the knots behind my back with one of my thumbs. If I could loosen one—

A mouth fastened itself over my treacherous cock, sucking and tonguing it to fresh stiffness. I prayed it was Kitty. The softness of the face that brushed against my groin told me that it was, and I opened my eyes. Diego was watching her as she bent over to fellate me.

Without saying anything, he observed the pleasure I was forced to take, noticing my shudders as I neared the release I did not want. A hallucination of writhing women on the very bed to which I was now bound assailed me.

"Stop," he commanded her.

Kitty straightened at once, my dripping cock coming out of her mouth hard as ever.

Diego went to where his clothes had been put, and withdrew his dagger. I steeled myself to endure a bloody revenge, hoping against hope to survive his controlled fury—and worked harder on the knot around my wrists.

He stepped in back of me and I stopped, surprised to feel him cut the tie to the post with the dagger. He threw it at the bed and it pierced through a pillow that was well out of my reach.

"Get down, you cur." He pushed me onto the bed, where I landed on all fours. I kept my ankles far apart, straining at the bonds that held them. One good kick backwards might do the trick—but I wanted to scream when Kitty grabbed my balls and held them tightly, just on the edge of inflicting pain.

As it was, I felt a compelling weakness seize my groin. With my balls trapped in her hand, I was vulnerable indeed. Yet the drugged wine made me register a sensation of pleasure once more.

"Kitty, take hold of his cock too. If you—" he brought his lips close to my ear, "if you do not like the touch of a man, she will do." His tone conveyed his malicious enjoyment.

I was no longer bound to the bed, but controlled all the same. Kitty oiled my cock and pumped it vigorously. Her hand tightened with every stroke. I knew that I would be made to spray cum for him—the sensations of an impending orgasm were building deep within my body—and that he would watch the spurting jets with pleasure, savoring my humiliation.

The drug in the wine gained fresh power over my mind and body, and Kitty's hands upon my cock were too skilled to resist much longer. I began to rock and moan, as if I too were enjoying my bondage and rough treatment, hoping to distract Diego while I surreptitiously worked on the knot around my wrists. Her grip upon my balls eased as the stimulation I received made them tighten and draw up to the base of my cock.

It was her skill that undid me. With a cry of mingled rage and animal lust, I reached climax.

The pulsing release felt extraordinary, and my body surged with new strength. The rush of blood through my veins helped to clear the poisonous fog at last. Somehow I loosened the knot around my wrists but I kept them together, waiting for my chance to seize his dagger and cut the longer tie that bound my ankles.

For ever after, he would have this to hold over me—unless I killed him. I put my head down, waiting for my chance. I heard him groan, and then heard the slick strokes of his oiled hand sliding over his cock. I surmised that he was bringing himself to orgasm. There was a methodical rhythm to it—fast, fast, then slow—and he was in no hurry to finish. Even so, I knew he was looking at Kitty and not me.

I spied the dagger still piercing the pillow, grabbed it, cut the tie between my feet, and rose to punch him as hard as I could with my free hand. The blow landed dead center on his upper chest, knocking the breath from his lungs and making him stumble. Kitty gave a little scream when I held the dagger to Diego's throat and edged away from us. I kept a wary eye on her—she had proven her strength several times over that night.

This time it was his arm that got wrenched behind his back and held there with all my might. I would have been happy to snap his elbow, happy to murder him in cold blood.

I jabbed the point in a fraction of inch away from the pulsing artery in the side of his neck and kept it there. A thin trickle of crimson blood came forth from the small wound. If he moved, he would effectively kill himself.

I felt him sag against me—he was heavy and it was a struggle to support his weight. But he seized the chance to pull free of my hold. With a bestial roar, he threw me down upon the carpet and the real fight began.

He had been generous with the oil, rubbing it over his groin—my thigh slipped when I tried to hold him down with it. Between our mingled sweat and the spreading oil, our naked bodies melded, but neither he nor I could gain the advantage.

Kitty watched with wide eyes. The sight of two big men, bodies slamming together, eyes on fire with fury, seemed to excite and frighten her at once. She could not escape—we were between her and the door. And I for one would have grabbed her ankle had she tried to flee and thrown her down as well.

Diego rolled upon his wrenched arm and groaned in agony. I had hurt him more than he had hurt me, not distracted by lust for a naked male body as he had been.

I grabbed his hair and smashed his face into the floor. His nose broke and a geyser of blood gushed forth.

"You killed him!" Kitty gasped.

I picked his head up by the hair. He was gagging but he was very much alive.

"No. But he might have killed me. With your help."

Diego's dark eyes were glassy and the fire in them dulled. His head grew heavy as he lost consciousness—I let it drop down with a thud. He would survive. And he would hunt me down again, I was sure of it. His malevolent pride would demand vengeance.

He had intended to kill me. I could not return the favor. Xavi would be free if I did but I would likely die on the gallows. And there is a limit to what a man will do for love.

I put on my clothes and ran for my life. My own house was not safe. I thought of Richard—he lived near the river—and was nearly spent before I found it. The windows were dark but I knocked again and again. I had to rouse him. If he could not harbor me, a friend of his might.

The parallel world of men who loved men had unwritten rules. Given that so many faces were turned against them, they protected their own. One of them would hide me.

My repeated knocks shook the door, and Richard eventually heard them. He glanced at my tattered clothes and bruised face, and let me in at once.

"Who has done this to you?"

"Don Diego. And a little bitch of his acquaintance—she led me into the trap—Kitty."

The next morning I told Richard what had happened, omitting no detail. He thought long and hard over it, looking at me with compassion before he finally spoke. "I am glad you survived. That you hurt him so badly, though, puts your future survival at even greater risk."

"He meant to kill me! What could I do but try to kill him?"

"I understand." He sighed. "At least you are safe. Above all he meant to humiliate you."

"He is good at that. And, by the way, I do not agree that he prefers women. He handled my privates with tenderness."

Richard shook his head. "I have never heard of him taking a male lover to his bed. And many of my persuasion were extremely curious about him. He was much talked about in my circles."

"If you had seen—"

"Thank God I did not." His mouth quirked in an odd smile. "But I think I understand him too. He loves power more than anything. The sex of the person whom he commands is not important."

"What do you mean?"

"He was able to arouse you. True, he had to drug you and beat you to do so, and thus dissolve your strength to resist. To experience pleasure you cannot control for the entertainment of someone you hate . . . there is no greater humiliation."

"Agh." I sunk my head into my hands. The memory of Diego's strong hands caressing me, and my body's inadvertent response to it was still painfully vibrant in my mind.

"Am I—what you are?" I burst out at last. "And do I not know it?"

Richard laughed a little. "I don't think so. But one can always hope."

"Bah! You are no help."

His voice grew soothing once more. "Every man and every woman has something of the opposite sex in their soul."

"I suppose that is so," I said grudgingly. "Given a blindfold and enough whiskey, our opposites may well put in an appearance."

Richard nodded with satisfaction. "I think you understand what I am getting at."

It took a while for me to recover from my beating and the sense of being drugged persisted (although not the interesting hallucinations). I stayed with Richard. Then Anne took me in. I shall be forever grateful to both of them.

12

Which leaves Xavi. It was many months before I saw her again. Her odd moods toward the end of our affair and her cold-hearted dismissal of me from the window of her coach baffled me. Our love was not meant to last and few do. Our dearest wishes and fondest hopes can vanish in a heartbeat.

But as Diego ceased to be a threat, I hoped to see her once more before he was recalled to Spain for his many crimes and punished there. And she granted me that much at last . . .

"Edward, I am sorry."

We were walking in Hyde Park. It seemed safer to meet outside. I longed for her still.

"You could not help what your husband did."

She twirled her parasol and would not look at me.

"I should not have lied to you."

"Everybody lies, Xavi."

"Not to the degree that I did."

I knew some of what she would say—Richard had found out much of her history and indicated there was more to come.

I guided her to a bench under a leafy tree whose branches hung down nearly to the ground on either side of it. We could speak without fear of being overheard.

She closed her parasol and leaned it against the bench.

"To begin with, there is the matter of your last letter. It was stolen."

"Ah. That explains a great deal."

"I found it among Don Diego's papers. I cried when I read it."

"Did he replace it with a forgery of some kind?"

She nodded. "It said that you had found another love—your first love, in fact. She had come back into your life and you could no longer see me. I was heartbroken."

Dear God. The letter may have been a forgery but the words were true. But telling her that would shatter her.

"So I refused to answer it. And when you came running up to my coach, I spurned you. Had I known that you were true to me . . ."

I had not been.

"I would not have been so cold," she finished. "And now it is too late." She wiped away a tear with the back of her hand.

Two gentlemen on fine bays trotted by and one turned to look at Xavi as if he knew her.

"Who is that?" she said after they had gone by.

"Lord Gordon."

"He is handsome."

She looked about distractedly. Now that we had been apart for some months, I had begun to see the instability of her temperament. Each new thing that attracted her soon became her greatest passion but nothing lasted.

"Do you want to know who—who I really am?"

"Xavi, please do not upset yourself."

She threw me a stubborn look. Her confession was her chance to make amends.

"I will begin at the beginning."

I sighed. "Very well. It is as good a place as any."

"I was born in London, not Spain. My mother was an actress."

Richard had found a picture of her. The never-quite-famous Mrs. Donnelly looked hopefully out of an old engraving of her traveling theater company. She had something of Xavi's beauty but not her fire.

"My father disappeared, you know. He left her with three children."

She gave me a watery look and looked in her reticule for a handkerchief, dabbing her eyes with it.

"Go on."

"They named me Lily. The younger ones were twins, Mary and Moira."

Who had not lived.

"I took care of them for my mother while she looked for work. But she was too old to play ingénues and there were no other roles."

In other words, Mrs. Donnelly had faded away and soon died.

"She died . . . and then the babies died. I was alone."

It had the ring of melodrama—but an interesting life often does. I knew that Xavi's confession was partly true and partly fiction. Richard dismissed her as a liar, but he did acknowledge her talent for telling stories.

Still, I vowed to listen.

"When I was fourteen, I entered a brothel."

I was silent. That might well be true.

"They kept me in a locked room on the top floor. The light came in all day from great, slanted windows—do you remember my telling you about the chapel in Spain and how I loved the light there?"

"I do, yes."

"That was a lie. In my room nothing was holy or sacred. They brought up men to look at me—they put me on a pedestal like a statue and let men look at me with nothing on. I felt like bits and pieces of me were falling off and if I looked only at the light, I would be whole once more."

It was true. I could feel my heart breaking for the girl she had once been.

"I was not touched, though. That little bit of flesh was valuable."

Men were vile beasts.

"But I began to behave so badly—I smashed all the glass to let the light in—that I was sold to the first comer."

I had an idea who that was.

"Will Fotheringay. He looked at me too. But he never saw me. Just my arse or my new-grown tits or my black hair."

The thought was infinitely sad. She had been a child inside a woman's body . . . and not in her right mind.

"But before I was sold to him I ran away."

"Where did you go?"

"I kicked about Covent Garden. Sold flowers from a basket. But they came looking. Someone had told them about a beautiful flower girl with long, black hair selling violets."

"A pretty picture."

"When people want to buy, it is."

I thought about the many times I had passed a flower-seller and not bought so much as a rosebud. Their sweet-smelling wares were not something they could eat at days' end.

"Will came in. He'd seen the glass that I had smashed out, down on the sidewalk in front of the brothel. And he saw me standing in the room, looking up at the sky. I wished I could fly away up into the clouds and never be seen again."

"I am surprised you did not kill yourself."

"It was tempting."

"Why didn't you?"

She shrugged her pretty shoulders. "I wanted to live more than I wanted to die."

"What about Will?"

"He was not so bad. But it was the same thing in a way. To be looked at and looked at makes you feel less real.

"He did those engravings of me in all those poses and sold thousands and thousands of them. I never saw the money. But there was my face and my body in the printshop windows. Anyone could buy me for a few pence. When he became famous, my price went up to a shilling. I was proud of that."

I felt that it helped her to talk. And it helped me to listen. "Go on."

"I did what every girl does once—I fell in love with a soldier. Or with his scarlet coat, I should say. I ran off again. Then he was sent to Spain and I contrived to follow him there."

By my reckoning, she would have been all of fifteen.

"A musket ball put a hole in his beautiful coat. And in him. I had to look out for myself."

She was not in the least sentimental about the memory.

"I moved up through the ranks. On my back, as they say. I had the sergeant, lieutenant, major, and then the colonel.

"He was killed last of all when the regiment was captured. They made him watch his men be shot one by one. I was put in prison. That was where Don Diego found me. One of his officers had seen me there and he came to look. And look. And look. I felt like an animal in a cage."

"But you married him."

"Yes, I married him. I was sixteen."

I looked at her curiously. "A virgin bride."

"No—did I say that?"

I only nodded.

"I was lying."

She sounded most forthright when she explained that she was lying. It was disconcerting.

"It was so easy. I told Diego my father was Spanish. I had learned the language quickly in prison. I made up the name. I had no papers to prove who I was, and no one knew me."

It could be argued that no one did now.

"Don Diego liked the idea that he could make me into a lady—and treat me like dirt."

"Why did you not run away?"

"Where would I go?"

Another question I could not answer.

"He taught me every ugly thing I had yet to learn. I lost myself again in lies. He did not know the difference and he did not care.

"When he told me of his appointment as ambassador, and I knew I would return to London, I was terrified that someone would recognize me. No one did—no one but him. When he saw his 'innocent' wife in Will's engravings he knew who I really was at last.

"But *I* no longer did. And when I saw you, I wanted to be everything to you. The self I was born with and the self I became. The only way to do that was to give you my body. And you opened my soul . . . do you understand?"

She had been so poised when I saw her in Quinn's studio. An almost empty room. Where she could look into the light and put the pieces of herself back together.

At that moment I forgave her everything.

"Yes. Yes, I do."

She picked up her parasol and stood up. Then ducked under the overhanging branches and walked away alone.

* * *

And so this romance ends in an unconventional way: I loved two women, they did not love me. And I am alone—not for long. I adore women, in all their complexity and beauty. My heart, I think, was made to love and made to be broken . . .

I would not have it any other way.

Epilogue

Back to the pile. I cannot bring myself to burn it. What will my heirs make of these love notes, erotic stories, and torn pages? The engravings of Xavi with nothing on? There is a birch twig—Anne sent that. I use it for a bookmark in my copy of *Fanny Hill.*

Among the chaos is Richard's shrewd summing-up of the affair, written in a neat hand. He pieced together histories, investigated on his own, talked to many people and visited many places. He collected a great deal of material and gave it to me. Herewith, some of his unedited notes.

Xaviera Innocencia. Born Lily Donnelly. Actress mother died young. Cared for sisters, Moira and Mary. Entered London brothel [nunnery] at fourteen. Kept in locked room at top of building. Escaped. Found in Covent Garden, returned to brothel. Sold to artist Will Fotheringay. Subject of erotic engravings done by Will Fotheringay. Ran away with soldier at 15. Camp follower during Peninsular Wars. Moved up in the ranks "on her back." Colonel's mistress. Taken prisoner. Rescued from Spanish gaol by Don Diego Mendez y Cartegna. Married at 16. Moved to London at age 23. Mistress of Lord Edward Delamar. Divorced Don Diego at age 25. Married Lord Gordon at age 26. No children.

Fotheringay engravings reprinted by the thousands. Portrait by Everett Quinn in the Royal Academy. Fotheringay engravings in private collections and museums.

Anne Leonard. Descendant of a renowned Devonshire family. Married once, widowed. A very private person. Brothel keeper and bircher extraordinaire. Mistress of Lord Delamar. A miniature exists, in a private collection.

Don Diego Mendez y Cartegna. Spain's Ambassador to the Court of St. James. A notorious brute [see records in Old Bailey]. Recalled to Spain in disgrace. Portrait in the Prado Museum.

Everett Quinn. Painter. Lunatic. Cunny man of genius and lover of too many women to count. Portrait in the Royal Academy, *The Apotheosis of Quinn,* in which he depicts himself as God and his many mistresses as angels.

Will Fotheringay. Painter and printmaker. The first to depict Xaviera Innocencia/Lily Donnelly in famous series of engravings. Rival of Quinn.

Kitty. Prostitute and opium addict. Fate unknown.

Signed: Richard Whiston, secretary to Lord Delamar.

Want more? Lord Edward first appeared in
THREE . . . available now from Aphrodisia . . .

"Come here, Fiona."

She obeyed, but still kept a little distance, unsure of herself and of him. With lightning speed, he reached out and clasped her wrist. "Lift your dress, my lady. Show me your juicy cunny. Let me look my fill. I like to look just as much as you do."

As if he knew she would not refuse, he let go of her wrist. Fiona hesitated, then bent down to pick up the hem of her dress. She wasted no time pulling her dress up high on her thighs and then to her waist, standing before him in drawers of muslin so fine it was almost sheer. Lord Delamar patted the nest of springy curls that showed through the front, and bent his head to press a kiss there. Then he parted the split in her drawers with one hand, holding it open with the other and touched a big finger to her tender flesh. "You are already wet."

He stroked her sensitive bud next, still using just his fingertip and she drew in her breath with a gasp. He had gone right to it, not fumbled or poked as so many men did, and her cunny throbbed in response.

"Sweet lady," he said softly. "Spread your hidden lips open for me. I want to have my fingers inside you and watch your face at the same time. How many fingers do you like? Two? Three?"

"Two," she whispered, sliding a hand over her cunny and doing as he asked. "Your hands are quite large."

He slid in two fingers with care and Fiona clutched her dress, swaying a little on her feet. She was tight but slick and the slow penetration felt wonderful.

"What a tempting picture you painted for me, Fiona. Pretty maids all in a row with their dresses up . . . and their most private parts fully exposed. A handsome manservant kneels to give each what she craves . . . that was a nice touch. He licks and licks . . . and they moan . . . just as you are doing now."

She had not realized that she was moaning. Edward was thrusting his fingers in and out, still keeping it slow.

His single–minded concentration upon her arousal was having the desired effect. She wanted to simply push her hot pussy into his face but even sitting down he was too tall for that. He looked at her intently and stopped thrusting, leaving his fingers inside her, using the pad of his thumb to stimulate the throbbing bud above.

With a little cry, Fiona got a better grip on her bunched–up skirts and parted the front of her drawers so quickly that she ripped the seam.

The slight sound made him look down. He slid his hand out of her cunt and pushed the muslin back with the other hand, fully revealing her cunny. He stroked her hips and sides. "So you are ready to tear your clothes off—good. I like seeing you standing so demurely in front of me—with your dress up and your drawers ripped . . . wanting sexual attention that you are not quite bold enough to ask for."

"But—" she began to protest. She had not meant to tear her drawers, which were still fastened at the waist anyway, and she certainly considered herself bold—*oh.*

Edward kneeled before her and applied his tongue to her private parts, giving her a gentle and thorough licking, treating her most sensitive flesh almost worshipfully. But he avoided her clitoris, wriggle as she might to put it in the way of his tender tongue. She clasped his head to her body and stroked his hair, abandoning herself to this exquisite intimacy.

He pulled back and wiped his mouth on his sleeve, smiling up at her. "What a feast. You are delicious, Fiona."

"Ohh . . . must you stop?" The erotic sensations began to ebb—but she wanted them never to end. "Please," she whispered. "Satisfy me."

"I think," he said softly, clasping her torn drawers at the waist, "it is time these came off." With a forceful tug, he split the center seam all the way through to the waistband and yanked her drawers down to her ankles, leaving her bare below the waist save for her white stockings and shirred garters trimmed with satin rosebuds.

"Oh!"

"Keep your dress up, Fiona. Let me look at you this way." His voice lowered to a growl. "Half–naked . . . a little embarrassed . . . and very excited. Turn around."

"I cannot—not with my damned drawers around my ankles—and my shoes have come off!"

Edward smoothed a hand over her hip and began to tease her cunny with the other. "Well, you don't need to turn around. I can see your beautiful behind in the mirror from here. Two perfect globes . . . and so white."

She looked over her shoulder. Indeed, he had positioned himself—and her—just right. With her dress up and her drawers in a tangle that she couldn't escape, her bare legs and bottom were bathed in the moonlight that filled the room and reflected off the mirror. Edward's hands slid over her hips and gripped her firmly. "Bend over. Rest on my shoulder. I want to know if I can see your cunt that way."

Swept away by excitement and the heat of the moment, she did as he asked, supported well enough by his strong shoulder and steadied by the hands that cupped her bottom. The pressure of their bodies kept her bunched dress up around her waist the way he wanted it but the lowcut bodice let her breasts pop out. She tried to pull it up again but could not quite grasp the cloth. "I am falling out of my damned dress!"

He gave her arse a friendly spank and kept her where she was. "Your clothes are falling apart. How convenient. You can play with your lovely breasts while I play with you."

"How do you know they are pretty?" she retorted. "You cannot see them if I am thrown over your shoulder."

He gave her another spank, a little harder than the first. "There are many advantages to being tall. I have been looking down your bodice most of the evening."

Fiona squirmed and he clasped her tightly around the thighs with powerful arms. She knew he was watching her in the mirror.

"Ah . . . do that again, Fiona. Your sweet pussy shows when you wriggle in that wanton way. I like it."

Keeping an inescapable grip with one arm, he fondled her there, then gave her several spanks that smarted, distributing them equally between her right and left buttocks. She rose up and twisted free—or tried to, not wanting to admit that submitting to his will excited her.

"When I am ready to let you go, I will. But first, kiss me, Fiona." He slid her down over his chest, letting her nipples brush over his shirt, and covered her mouth with his, sliding his tongue over hers, and luxuriating in the ardor of her response.

He grabbed her bottom and pulled her right against him, kissing her deeply and grinding his cock, still compressed under the supple leather of his breeches but achingly hard, into her belly.

Fiona shuddered with the pleasure of it, on fire from his

nearness, his strength, and most of all from his desire. But she struggled free.

He let her go with reluctance. "So the rules of the game change again. Why?"

Fiona let her dress fall and smoothed its crumpled folds. She did not know quite how to answer his question. In truth, she was unnerved by the strength of her unguarded response to him. "I like to take my time."

"Oho. Is that why you sat on my lap and kissed me so ardently and told me a wonderfully filthy story? Two can play at teasing, Fiona."

"What do you mean?" she asked breathlessly, feeling foolish now that they were apart. She scarcely knew what to do next now that her clothes were in such disarray and her breasts still half out of her gown. She yanked the bodice up over them.

Edward pushed a drifting lock of her hair back into place with a fingertip. "You have been trying to get me into your bed from the day we met. I knew it from the way you talked to me even then."

Fiona stepped out of her tangled drawers somehow and kicked them away. "You were unfailingly polite, I must say. Not at all what I expected from a rogue like you."

"Who told you I was a rogue?"

"Everyone knows it."

"Then what did you want from me, Fiona?"

She stopped herself from telling him the truth. *What you just did. And more.* "Never mind," she said at last.

He grinned and tipped up her chin with a finger. "I did not say your methods were ineffective. There we sat, discussing politics and the weather and the health of his Royal Majesty, et cetera, and whether I wanted sugar in my tea. It was all I could do not to take you in my arms and ravish you upon the tea cart. But I did want to know you a little better." He planted a relatively chaste kiss on her lips, just as if nothing had happened between them besides polite conversation.

She fought the impulse to slap him. "Well . . . now that you have had your tongue and fingers in me, I suppose there is little else to discover."

He shook his head. "I look forward to continuing our acquaintance."

Frustrated by his bland reply—not to mention the fact that he had not brought her to climax—and feeling somewhat dazed, Fiona said nothing but looked about for her shoes, which had come off with the tangled drawers she'd kicked aside. She bent over and patted the heap of muslin, taking out one shoe and then the other, and pulling up her dress to put them on. The drawers were a dead loss and she left them on the floor.

"I find I am most interested in what goes on inside your head, Fiona."

"Is that why you are looking at my legs? Surely white stockings do not excite you."

He smiled, placing his hands on his hips. Fiona noticed that he was still hugely erect. "Your legs are lovely."

She slid her feet into the shoes and stamped a little to get the toes to fit, still seething with frustration and the sexual heat he had awakened. "Poxy shoes. I think a heel is broken." Taking that one off, she flung it at the wall. Its mate soon followed.

Edward closed the distance between them and took her in his arms. He held her—just held her—for a long moment and made her ache with longing for him. "Ah, Fiona. You manage to look elegant, even when you are cursing and throwing shoes. Always a lady, eh?"

Hardly. At least not at the moment. She was getting nowhere, no matter what she did, and feeling more confused by the minute. Perhaps she ought to have worn stockings in whorish black and not ladylike white—oh, damn. There was no sorting out her confused feelings. Her perplexed scowl made him smile again.

"Well, here we are, my dear—halfway to heaven. But we seem to be having our first spat."

"Shut up."

He grinned and let her go. "We might begin again. Yes, I think that would be best."

"Oh, do you?" She paced a few steps away and turned her back to him, standing in front of the window. She could not remember Thomas ever making her so angry—and she certainly could not remember wanting him as much as she wanted Lord Delamar.

From behind she heard him walk closer to her. "The moonlight shines through your gown, Fiona. I can see that you are naked underneath."

"That is not news." Her tone softened nonetheless.

"Naked . . . and irresistible."

He stood behind her and caressed her shoulders, dropping a kiss upon one and moving upward to her neck. He nibbled on her earlobe and ran his tongue around the rest of it, reminding her of the very great pleasure he had given her south of her tingling ear. Damn him. The sensation weakened her resolve.

"Perhaps our game got out of hand. But I did think you were enjoying yourself."

"I was," she admitted in a small voice.

"Then you will enjoy what is to come even more. But allow me to propose a few rules, Fiona."

She turned within the circle of his arms and let her hands rest on his shirt front, unfastening his neck cloth but leaving it draped around his neck and beginning on his buttons. She folded the white linen back, admiring his smooth, strong neck and the fine dark hair upon his chest. "Very well."

He gave her a hug. Fiona rubbed herself against him like a cat, unable to resist his sensual warmth. Edward caressed her bare flesh under the light dress appreciatively. "Rule one. I may ask you to lift your dress as you just did, at any time I wish."

"All right. I have done it once, I might as well do it again."

He nodded. "Rule two. You must allow me to lick your cunny again. I enjoyed it and so did you."

"Indeed." She felt an unwilling smile curve her lips. How could she argue?

"Do you agree to rule two?"

"Yes."

He held her closer to him. "Rule three. If I desire to see you bare your breasts and play with your nipples, or if I want you to bend over and spread your cheeks and give me the best possible view of your cunny and arsehole, or if I ask anything at all, you must say yes."

"Anything at all? You will not hurt me, my lord?"

He kissed her on the nose. "Of course not. I just like looking at you. Every inch of you. And I intend to satisfy your every desire as well."

Fiona pondered his words. "That sounds reasonable." She slid her hands down his body and stopped just short of his breeches.

"Now touch me." His voice was low. He pulled his shirt out and let the loose linen billow out, holding the front of it up to allow her to do just that.

She slipped her hand inside the waistband, pulling it away from his taut, hard belly and peeked inside his breeches. There, less than an inch away, his cock stood proudly, a pearly drop upon its tip. She touched a fingertip to the tiny hole to take up the drop and bring it to her mouth. He watched her tongue tip come out and lick that one precious drop. The ridged muscles of his midsection tightened under skin that was hot to the touch, and his long, stiff cock seemed about to burst out of his breeches.

"Delicious," she said softly.

He drew in a long breath. "There will be more of that for you to taste, if that is what you like in your mouth. Much more." She slid a hand into his breeches again but he grabbed her wrist and prevented her from touching him. "You shall come first, my lady. But there is nothing soft for you to lie on in this room. Can we enter the butler's bedchamber from here?"

"Yes," she said. "This way." He let go of her wrist and intertwined his fingers with hers. Fiona took him through an empty closet with a false back that proved to be another door, slipping her feet back into her shoes along the way.

"Very clever. You must give me the name of Bertie's carpenter."

Fiona sniffed. "The last thing he fashioned for my husband was a coffin. We all wondered if it had a secret exit, you may be sure." She swung the door open into the room Lord Delamar had glimpsed through the lens in the wall and brought him in.

She glanced around. "The bed seems bigger once you are inside the room, doesn't it?"

"Big enough for Mr. Tresham and his happy harem," Edward said with a smirk. He sat down in an armchair to pull off his boots, which he thunked into a corner.

Fiona wasted no time in testing the mattress, which had been made up with a sheet and flat-stitched comforter, but no drapes hung from the canopy. She kicked off her shoes again before the last of her was on the bed but Edward made a sound of protest. "Oh no. Leave those on." He picked the shoes up from the carpet and pushed her down onto her back without further ado. "Raise your legs."

Laughing, she did, letting her dress fall around her hips, baring herself below the waist as before. She parted her legs suddenly, giving him a mischievous look as she flashed her cunny, then brought her legs together and held them straight up, toes pointed.

He clasped her ankles in one big hand, slipping on the

dainty shoes one at a time and running his other hand over her smooth stockings, toying with the garters that held them up just above the knees. Then, in one swift move, he pulled off his loosened neck cloth and used it to tie her ankles together and to the canopy rod above.

"There. Ready to be licked?"

She bent her knees a bit to test her bonds, amused by the speed of his action. "Ahh. Yes. Oh, yes." From the second his tongue had touched the heated flesh between her legs, she had wanted more, wanted to come with his mouth all over her cunny, holding his head and surrendering to his sensual expertise. The thought of abandoning herself utterly to erotic pleasure with only a silken restraint to remind her of who was now master of the game, excited her deeply.

Edward knelt by the side of the bed, pulling her hips toward him until Fiona's arse was off the bed, her back still solidly upon it, and her arms stretched out. Dragged in this way, her dress rose higher still and the bodice forced her breasts out. He rose and fastened his mouth tightly upon one nipple, sucking it deep pink and hard. He kept the sucked nipple between his finger and thumb, rolling it as he sucked the other one.

She arched her back, thrusting her breasts at him, stroking his hair as he nursed her blissfully for a minute or more. Then he stopped with a sigh, pulled his shirt over his head, and treated her to the sight of his beautifully muscular chest, traced with fine dark hair that tapered into his breeches.

Fiona reached out a hand to the cock that bulged inside, strapped back by the tightness of the leather but responding to her touch.

"May I . . . ?"

He ignored her question and went back to his position on the floor, kissing her naked thighs and bottom all over, wherever he could reach, then stroked her backside. Then he put his mouth upon her cunny, getting his tongue in with darting licks.

With her legs together and trussed up, she was much tighter. His tongue had to thrust hard to gain entrance and he used his fingers to stretch her more open, following fingers with tongue, fingers with tongue, in a deeply erotic rhythm that made her thrash as much as the silk tie would allow, bucking her arse.

"Mmmm." He stopped licking, held her steady, and began to suck her bud. Fiona moaned with pleasure. The sensation was intense—and he made it stronger when he sat back on his haunches, fondling her swollen nether lips between fingers and thumb, pressing them together, looking at her now and then and murmuring gentle encouragement.

"Come for me. Come."

She felt an incandescent desire for release, wanting him to witness her first orgasm with him and wanting to experience it with shameless abandon. Deep within her body waves of pleasure rose and rose, never cresting but only taking her higher.

Then she felt him touch her arsehole, stimulating it gently but not penetrating her there. Fiona rested, needing a moment of tender distraction from the climax that was seconds away. She knew very well that such play would make the ultimate sensation much more powerful—and she trusted him, vulnerable though she was with her arse in midair and her ankles tied.

He must love to see me like this, she thought. He was breathing hard when he kissed and tongued her cunny again, keeping his fingertip circling upon her arsehole, slick with the juices that had dripped down.

"I shall not put my finger in, my lady. But I think you enjoy gentle arse play," he whispered when he lifted his handsome head. He began to stroke her buttocks, moving his fingertips over the backs of her thighs, brushing them so softly that she began to tremble. Her need for release was almost overwhelming.

But Fiona wanted him to give it to her. Her hands were free, yet she would not use them. "I beg of you . . ." she moaned, "Now . . . I am ready . . . now."

He stood up, untying her ankles and let her legs down, rubbing them and ridding them of stiffness. The deep, massaging strokes were soothing and stimulating. He cradled each of her thighs in a strong arm as he rubbed it down, moving to her calves and feet more swiftly, intently aware of the swollen pink cunt that was spread open in front of him, awaiting his pleasure, whatever it would be.

"Please," she whispered one more time. "At least let me take you in my mouth, my lord. I must have you somehow. I must . . ."

He undid his breeches and took them off so quickly it seemed to have happened by magic. His legs were strongly muscled, his buttocks indented as if meant to be clutched by a passionate woman. And then there was his cock, jutting out nine inches or more from his taut groin and a nest of very dark curls. His foreskin was rolled back to reveal a plum–size head, tipped with a few more pearly drops of come that she wanted desperately to taste.

"Let me suck you," she begged. "Let me pleasure you as you have pleasured me."

He shook his head. "We shall pleasure each other, my love. My mouth on your cunt and your mouth on my cock. Lie back. Stay there."

He climbed onto the bed, proudly and completely naked, and turned around above her. Fiona opened her mouth to receive his member, taking as many inches as she could. But he did not thrust. He held still, letting her suck and stimulate him with her tongue, which she wrapped around his cock this way and that as she kept him in her mouth, devouring him.

"Touch my balls," he said, his voice ragged. She stroked his scrotum, feeling it tighten and draw upwards. "Ah—like that. Yes. Oh, Fiona, yes," he moaned. "Just like that. Good girl. How good it feels . . . oh!" His cock trembled and jerked in her mouth as he began to ejaculate.

Fiona clasped the shaft to keep him from ramming it in but kept the top two inches in her mouth, sucking him hard. He moaned and buried his face in her pussy, attending to her with gentlemanly ardor even as his semen filled her mouth. Discreetly, she spat out the first pulsing shots he fired and swallowed the last of it, loving the way he came, healthy, strong and hot.

Then her own orgasm took her by surprise. His vibrating moans triggered an unbelievably intense wave of sensation as he sucked her clitoris with lascivious tenderness, lapping up her juice the way she lapped up his.

They collapsed side by side, still touching each other intimately, and rested in a tangle of sweaty sheets and one very disheveled gown.

More, more, more . . . don't miss
ONE MORE TIME by Leanne Shawler.
Available now from Aphrodisia . . .

1

Abby Deane nudged the yoke, banking her plane to the left. Looking out the side window, she spotted her new home, a sprawling ancient mansion dating back to the Tudor period, added to over the ages.

Her new home. Away from the pointless distractions of men, men who were so commitment phobic, wanting only a quick shag. Thank heavens for modern invention. She owned a potpourri of devices designed to please her. Who needed a man in the twenty-first century?

Ever since she'd given up on the heartbreakers, her life seemed less off-kilter. She hoped this new job would rebalance her life. The toys'd definitely help.

With a grin, she checked her instruments and glanced ahead, squinting in the sunlight even though she wore dark sunglasses. Puffy cumulonimbus blocked her vision of the private airstrip ahead.

Circling, she slowed the Beech Bonanza into its gliding speed. She guided the plane into its descent, checking the altimeter until she broke clear of the cloud cover.

She blinked. The airstrip had vanished. She glanced to the left and the right. Had she flown over the strip? Nope, nothing.

Just below the cloud cover, she circled, searching.

What the—A runway didn't just disappear.

This one had. All she saw were mown hayfields and green fields of grazing sheep.

The engine cut out, sputtering. She checked the fuel gauges. Not even close to empty. She throttled back on the engine and gave it power again, to no avail.

Her forehead tightened. She took a deep breath. No need to panic. She knew how to make an emergency landing. She'd practiced it before.

She leveled the wings, aiming for a mown hayfield. She lowered the landing gear. At least she wasn't far from the hotel. If she managed to land in one piece, she'd walk over. If not, someone from the hotel would see her go down and come to her aid.

Checking her seat belts, Abby glided in. The plane touched down, not skewing, but bouncing over the dirt ridges and truncated hay stalks.

The plane rolled to a stop. Abby sagged in her seat. Her seat belts relaxed their grip. A bone-deep ache radiated through her, a counterpoint to her thundering heart. Without further thought, she evacuated the plane. She stood at a safe distance, but the plane rested, still and silent.

She returned to the plane, reaching for her toolbox. She touched the right-hand engine and snatched her fingers back. Cold. That wasn't right.

Abby sighed. Both engines felt like they hadn't run at all. Weird. She'd never experienced anything like this before. She'd have to contact a mechanic to repair her plane.

She unloaded her luggage, hoisting the wheeled bags over the rich black dirt to the field's edge. Through a small gap in the tall hedge surrounding the field (presumably hiding the spoils of hay from the adjacent grazing animals) Abby spotted a dirt track.

That should take me to the main road, she thought.

Two bags, one laptop, a large purse, and a long tube holding her copies of the hotel plans. She sat on the biggest bag to wait for assistance to arrive.

And waited.

Half an hour later, Abby came into sight of the hotel, her future home. Her future home with useless staff to fire. It didn't matter that her boss had agreed to keep the original household staff. Someone must have seen her plane in distress. Why hadn't anyone come to her aid?

And this drive . . . Gravel made a nice crunch under a car's tires, but dragging heavy wheeled bags over it for a quarter mile was not so much fun. The other quarter mile had been nothing but dirt.

That had to be fixed. Hotel guests may not be inclined to travel to a boutique hotel all on dirt road. She thought of flying stones scratching a BMW's paint job and shuddered.

No, that had to be rectified at once. Well, once she'd hired new staff.

She noted the shuttered windows on the house and at once forgave the staff. Keeping the windows closed preserved the restoration's freshness. That's why they didn't see her go down, and her landing had been practically silent.

Speaking of silence . . . a breeze brought the sound of baaing sheep, the rustle of leaves from the giant trees lining the drive. No sound of civilization reached her ears. Not the dull roar of the M3 highway, which was only a couple of miles off.

Abby shrugged, shifting the tube strap on her shoulder. Maybe the house blocked the sound.

She reached the grand front entrance. Two giant oaken doors, formidable and highly polished. Abby nodded in approval. The staff were doing superb work. Such attention to detail.

Leaving her luggage at the foot of the broad stone steps, she slung her purse over her shoulder. She ascended and rang the bell, an old-fashioned pulley. Another nice touch. With the hotel's official opening, those doors would stay wide open and welcoming.

She leaned backward, surveying the facade, approving of the sparkling windows and pollutant-free bricks.

A creak warned of the opening door. They polished the doors but didn't oil the hinges? Abby repressed a sigh of irritation. So much to be done.

The door opened a crack.

Some welcome. Abby huffed. "Are you going to let me in?"

A deep baritone voice answered: "Who are you?"

"Your former boss if you don't let me in," Abby snapped.

The pause from his end only maddened her further. "A woman?"

She hauled the door open, ready to give him a piece of her mind, and stopped dead. Her jaw sank and she closed her mouth with a snap.

Before her stood a gobsmackingly handsome man. She registered that much before his odd attire caught her attention. Perhaps it was the dark vee of chest hair poking out from his crumpled white shirt. Or the supertight breeches that let her know, despite the buttoned-up flap, that he was a well endowed guy. Very well endowed.

She cleared her throat. "Definitely your former boss. You're fired."

"Fired?" The man might look gorgeous but apparently he lacked in the brains department. "I do not work for you."

That gave her pause. Was this Lord David Winterton's son? She modulated her tone. "If you are not on my staff, who are you?"

He smiled, a broad smile that must have broken many a heart. Abby steeled herself. Not hers. "I'm just passing through."

Her eyes narrowed. "Trespassing? And my staff let you?"

"There's nobody here but me." He surveyed her, wholly un-inclined to leave her property. His eyelids lowering, his stern gaze turned his brown eyes into angry dark specks. "You don't look like the sort who possesses staff."

Abby's blood boiled. "You bastard." She pushed past him and into the house. Where *was* her staff?

In the middle of the large hall, she stopped, her sneakers squeaking on the marble tile floor. She frowned, surveying the space. "Something isn't right . . ."

The idiot man came up behind her. "I'm glad you're ac-knowledging that at last."

EROS ISLAND . . . where it gets *really* hot.
Here's Dawn Thompson's "The Dream Well."
Coming soon from Aphrodisia!

1

Was he the only one aboard who heard the siren's song before the galley struck the Land's End shoals? Something nudged him hard, buoying him toward shore, and Gar Trivelyan, Knight of the Realm, hauled himself up out of the creaming surf and collapsed on the strand, coughing up what seemed like gallons of seawater. Drifting mist caressed him, like hundreds of probing fingers, groping, stroking—covering him like a blanket. He struggled to his feet and staggered like a blind man into the wraithlike whiteness that all but hid the full Samhain moon from view.

He was aroused. Had he come that close to death? He'd heard such things occurred when a man was dying. Raising his codpiece, he soothed his burgeoning cock as he blundered into the mist. It seemed to be leading him inland. Until that moment, the urgency in his loins had canceled the pain in his arm. He noticed it now, for it bled profusely, running in rivulets over the hammered gold bracelet coiled like a snake just below his elbow.

Tearing a piece of homespun from the hem of his tunic, he

cinched it tightly above the wound with the aid of his teeth, and staggered on, his good arm carving circles in the air ahead of him. The mist had become a thick, meandering wall impenetrable by the eye. It was as though he'd stepped off the planet. Where had the storm gone that ran the ship aground? Why was it warm here, not bitter cold as it had been when the cruel November sea had spat him out upon these shores? Could he have crossed over into the Celtic Otherworld? He'd heard of seafarers doing just that after shipwreck in Cornish waters.

He didn't see the well until he'd run right into it, a low round affair. A gurgling spring edged with stacked stones, rising from a whitethorn grove, the trees' branches aflutter with bits of colored cloth. *A Celtic dream well?*

According to myth, if one in need of a dream fulfilled dipped a bit of cloth into the water of such a well and tied it to one of the trees that guarded it with proper tribute and incantation, the dream or wish or petition requested would be granted. He had never believed in such nonsense before, but his arm was nearly severed, and it couldn't hurt to try. There seemed no other help in the offing and he tore another strip from his tunic, dunked it in the satiny black water, and tied it to a whitethorn branch among the other bits of cloth hanging there. Then, slipping the hammered-gold bracelet from his wounded arm, he groaned and prayed, and tossed it into the well.

No sooner had he done, when the water began to roil and bubble up, spitting over the edge as the perfect form of a naked woman broke the surface, his hammered-gold snake bracelet coiled about her upper arm. She was without blemish, her skin like alabaster, her hair teasing her buttocks with a long cascade of silken waves the color of copper burnished by the sun. It was surprisingly dry for having come from the depths of the well, and none covered her pubic mound. It was hairless, her entrance beneath resembling not the sexual organ of a woman, but the column of a rare and costly orchid whose flushed lips and purple bud beckoned irresistibly in the eerie half-light. His wound forgotten, Gar could not take his eyes from it as she stepped from the well and floated toward him, rubbing her nipples to tall hardness between her thumbs and forefingers.

What sorcery was this? And what sort of fool would he be if he didn't take advantage of it? Ripping off his codpiece, he exposed his thick, hard cock to her gaze, and groaned as she took it in her hands. Sucking in his breath, he made a strangled sound as she ran her cool fingers along the blue-veined surface in a spiraling motion from its bulky root to the ridge of its mushroom tip. His mind was speaking to her then, screaming what he dared not speak aloud—not even to ask her name—for fear she'd evaporate before his very eyes, *the tip . . . touch the tip! Run those cool, soft fingers over the head of my cock and make it live, my beauty . . .*

As if she'd heard, the woman did just that, sliding the tip of her finger over the rim of his sex, moistening the sensitive head with the drops of pearly pre-come leaking from it, her forefinger lingering on the puckered opening, inviting more pearls to form.

"Your wish is granted," she murmured. "Your wound is healed."

So it was! Gar hadn't even noticed until now. That cool hand riding his hot hard shaft had canceled all thought except plunging into the petals of the exquisite orchid between her thighs until he'd filled her.

Lifting the globe of one breast, she offered her nipple. "You may have me for a little if you wish," she said. "Every year when the moon waxes full at the Samhain feast, I am allowed to rise from the well and take a lover . . . if the tribute is well to pass." She nodded toward the bracelet on her arm. " 'Tis a fine trinket, this."

It had to be a dream. He had died in the wreck, and this was his torment. He slipped his arm around her waist and drew her closer. No, this was no dream, this was real flesh he was feeling, as smooth as satin and as fragrant as the night lilies blooming in the water.

"Have I died, then?" he finally said. "Which are you, angel or demon?" Not that it mattered. He was enthralled.

The woman smiled. There was a provocative little beauty spot above the right corner of her lip. "I am neither, Gar Trivelyan," she said. "I am called Analee, handmaiden of Annis, Goddess of the Wells. This well is mine."

"How do you know my name?"

"I know much, knight of the realm," she returned. "Will you drink . . . or not?"

Gar cupped the offered breast and took the nipple in his mouth. It was hot and hard, the areola puckering taut as he laved the tawny bud with his tongue until she purred like a contented cat.

Overhead, the Samhain moon peeked down through drifting clouds like a voyeur as he nipped and sucked and drank her essence. She tasted golden, of the sun, of honey and bee pollen. Could this be happening? His mind said no, but his cock said yes as she let it go and stripped him of his tunic and breeches. He'd lost his cloak, sword, and sandals in the sea.

"Come," she said, leading him into the mist.

She led him through lush fields burgeoning with all manner of wildflowers, across streams and brooks swathed in the ghostly mist that seemed alive the way it followed them, weaving in and out among the trunks of ancient hawthorns and young saplings that seemed to sigh and sway and carry on hushed conversations with each other.

All at once, a red-and-white-striped canopy came into view; a tournament tent of the kind used by revelers at routs and feasts and festivals was nestled deep in a little clearing in the whitethorn grove, where it gave way to oak and ash. The flap was turned back, and a bed made with petal-strewn quilts of satin and down beckoned. Once inside, the goddess of the well drew Gar to her, hands flitting over his moist skin as they explored his naked body until, unable to help himself, he drove her down beneath him in the bed.

Nothing seemed real, and yet it was. Otherwordly visits were hazardous at best. Dangers lurked in wait at every turn for mortals sojourning in the parallel dimension—dangers that could trap a man forever, or devour him body and soul. Had he fallen into a trap? Was he about to lose his immortal soul? These were natural concerns. But then, in the arms of the captivating Analee, while her deft fingers were exploring his body, touching him in places no woman had ever touched him before, while her sweet essence nourished him as he suckled at those perfect breasts, nothing mattered but the moment, and the beautiful Goddess of the Well.

Straddling him, she knelt there, her hands flitting over his body, exploring rock-hard muscles that had tensed in his biceps, in his broad chest and roped torso. Inching lower, she gripped his cock in both her tiny hands, for one hand could not do it justice, and began pumping it in a spiraling motion like she had done before. Slow, deep revolutions along his shaft made him harder still, as she teased the mushroom tip just enough to drive him mad. Meanwhile, his fingers found her nipples, pinching, tweaking, until she writhed against him, grinding the parted lips of her slit into his bulging testicles, into the base of his cock as she played with it.

Gar groaned. He felt her release as she rubbed up against him, felt her juices flow, moistening his genitals, and the throbbing, shuddering palpitations of her climax. Her pleasure moans were throaty and deep, as she threw her head back until her long coppery hair rippled over her buttocks and grazed his thighs beneath her. It was more than he could bear. His cock was bursting. Profoundly grateful that she had come, he rolled her over on her back and in one motion thrust into her, parting her orchid-like nether lips, gliding on her wetness until he'd filled her.

"You said that I could have you for . . . a little," he panted, undulating gently, for to drive himself into her now would bring him to climax in a hearbeat. As it was, he'd begun to pray to forestall the inevitable; a tactic that had always given him more staying power in the past. But that was before Analee, Goddess of the Dream Well. She had bewitched him.

"For a little, yes," she purred. How beautiful she was, with her hooded eyes dilated with desire, her full lips parted to receive his kiss, her fair skin rouged with the fiery blush of sex. She was like a rare orchid, indeed, and Gar longed to open her petals one by one.

"How little is . . . 'a little'?" he asked, for that would depend upon what happened next. If she were to evaporate like the mist at any moment, he would make the most of it, but if there was time, he could address his immediate need and then love her properly. How strange that the word *love* had formed in his mind. He was a seasoned warrior, and he had bedded many, but love had nothing to do with it. He was of the firm belief that a warrior should have no truck with love. Thus far, he'd managed to dodge Cupid's darts, but that, too, was before the magical goddess of the well. Though it was plain that her advances toward him were pure lust, she had reminded him that there was such a thing as love, and that it was missing from his mundane existence.

"Until the dawn," she murmured.

Wrapping her legs around his waist, Analee wound her arms about his neck and threaded her fingers through his dark, wavy hair. He wore it long, below his ears. Her touch was like a lightning strike, the grip of those skilled fingers sending shock waves through his loins. Gritting his teeth, he shut his eyes and groaned, and she fisted her fingers tightly in the locks at the back of his neck, and arched her back, drawing him closer.

"Pleasure yourself, Gar Trivelyan," she said, her voice throaty and soft, "—even as I have done. I am yours 'till the sun chases the moon . . ."

Gar could feel her womb. There was barely room for his cock in the tight confines of her sexual seat. She felt like hot silk, her juices laving him as he pistoned into her again and again until he cried out as the petal soft lips of her vagina gripped his shaft, milking him dry of every drop.

The orgasm was like no other. He filled her to overflowing, as his heartbeat matched the pumping, throbbing, shuddering rhythm that drove his cock relentlessly inside her. The pulse beat in his sexual stream was so acute he feared it would drive his heart right through his heaving ribcage.

He collapsed into her kiss, his brow running with sweat, his cock slow to go flaccid inside her, for the petals of that exquisite orchid between her thighs gripped him still. How could he part with such ecstasy at dawn? How could he bear never to feel again what he'd felt in the arms of this goddess? There was no question that she had bewitched him. Angel or demon, he was beguiled.

Time stood still, then. Gar had no idea how much had passed before he withdrew himself and lay beside her, content but not sated. He could still feel the rhythmic contractions of her vagina, involuntary or deliberate, he couldn't tell. It didn't matter. He wanted to live inside her again and again.

"I think you have bewitched me," he said, through a heavy sigh. "One moment I was struggling to stay afloat in a freezing maelstrom of high-curling seas and flesh-tearing winds, the next I am here, with you in this warm misty place. Have I died? Have I crossed over? Or have I somehow breeched the span and entered the Celtic Otherworld?"

"Shhh," she murmured, grazing his moist brow with her lips. "Our time has just begun. We must not waste it."

Gracefully, she rose from the bed and padded to a trunk in

the corner. How lithe she was, as if she floated on air. Raising himself on one elbow, he feasted on the sight of her slender curves. He salivated over the roundness of her buttocks, over the perfect globes of her milk-white breasts, their tawny nipples standing out in bold relief against the opalescence of her skin. How the breathtaking sight of that body teased him, half veiled in the silken fall of coppery hair, like a sun-kissed halo about her.

The shock of her hairless pubic mound drew his eyes when she turned, and his cock responded to the sight, swelling to life where it rested against his corded thigh. He was hard again, and he swung his feet over the side of the bed, rose up, and approached her. But she held him at bay with an armful of what looked like cloth made of spider silk, spangled with stardust. For its sparkle was blinding.

"Put this on," she said, handing him a sheer garment, so fine he feared to force it over the contours of his muscular body. Nonetheless, he did as she bade him and found it to be quite sturdy. It fit him like a second skin, as if it had been made for him, a sheer garment the color of winter spangled with snow. ". . . And this," she added, handing him a headdress with antlers and a half-mask attached. Nodding her approval as he slipped it over his head, she swirled a billowing cape about her made of the same spangled cloth that hid none of her charms, and raised the hood.

Gar looked on enraptured as she donned a shimmering winged mask, her eyes, the color of dark water, glazed with desire burning toward him. What passion smoldered in that sultry gaze, passion he had not yet tasted. He could but stare, consumed by lust and longing, his quick hot breath puffing back against his face from inside the mask. Her mystical allure was infectious.

She held out her hand. "Come," she said, ". . . we must join the others."

2

Gar followed the goddess into the mist to an open clearing, where others gathered around bonfires. They were drinking honey mead and wine, dancing and feasting upon nuts and apples and roasted meat. Here, the mist parted to permit the moon to beam down upon the revelers. Faery lights flickered, and Wills-'o-the Wisp danced on the distant marshes. Gar had celebrated the Samhain feast many times, but never in the Celtic Otherworld, and never in a warm climate, for it was the harvest feast.

As if she'd heard, Analee said, "It is never autumn or winter here, so we make it so with costumes when we feast."

They were the only two dressed as frosty winter, all the rest wore earth colors, their costumes fashioned of leaves and moss, their headdresses wreaths of vines, studded with acorns, nuts, and succulent berries.

"I rule here," she said. "I wear the winter white at Samhain to tell the masses all will be well at the Winter Solstice. It is a sign of hope. You are garbed as the winter stag, because you are my consort . . . for a little."

Gar wished she wouldn't keep reminding him it was only *for a little*. All around him revelers had paired off, dancing around the bonfires to the music of flute and lyre. Scantily clad wood nymphs danced around him, trailing yards of spider silk spangled with some anonymous iridescence. It reminded him of the ethereal phosphorescence in the sea he'd just come from. Would he ever see the mortal world again? Or was he trapped in the Otherworld for the rest of his days? Gazing at Analee in her near nakedness, that did not seem like an unpleasant prospect.

The nymphs came nearer, almost touching him as they crowded close in their dance. How exquisite they were, one more beautiful than the next, their long hair whipping him as they passed him by. They smelled of incense—patchouli and sandalwood, angelica, and yew. It was like a drug, besotting him until his head reeled, and his body swayed to the plaintive music. All the while, the goddess looked on, her sparkling eyes riveted to him through the eyeholes in the winged half-mask she wore, her dewy lips parted.

Many men in stag antlers appeared from among the trees wearing precious little else, save leaves for loincloths, and surrounded Analee. How long had they been standing there camouflaged by the tertiary bark and branches that blended with their antlers? She spread her cape wide, inviting them to touch every angle and plane, every orifice and recess of her body as they danced around her. As they did, the nymphs began to fondle him in the same intimate manner.

"They make you ready for me," the goddess said, "just as these make me ready for you."

Scarcely able to believe his eyes, Gar watched the masked and costumed men fondle Analee's breasts. He watched them follow the curves of her body with light strokes, their hands flitting over her pubic mound, their skilled fingers riding the length of her slit, and she spread her legs apart, leaning into their caresses, writhing against the pressure of their strokes, as one by one they fondled her. They were aroused, even as he was, as the nymphs opened the crotch of his garment and exposed his cock to their caresses.

Cool, skilled hands rode his shaft and kneaded his testicles, as each in her turn rubbed up against his swollen cock, while the others groped his hard muscled chest and buttocks, and played with his taut nipples. But he could not tear his eyes from what was happening across the way, as the aroused males laved and stroked and petted Analee until she uttered throaty moans that resonated wildly in his loins.

Gar had never experienced such an arousal. Watching the revelers bring her to the brink of ecstasy, watching her alabaster skin turn pink with the sultry blush of sex attacked his loins like fiery pincers, without the nymphs' caresses.

These Otherwordly creatures lived to pleasure themselves and each other. Their carnal cravings were like the lightning, untamable, and unpredictable, like the sea that had spat him out amongst them. He had heard it was thus in their world. He was seeing it firsthand, something granted only to the chosen few. Would he remember it after? Was there even an *after*? Was death or to be lost among the fay the price for this excruciating ecstasy he had been granted *for a little*?

Someone passed him a wineskin and he drank until rivulets ran down his chin, throat, and broad chest. Where had the garment Analee had given him gone? Had they torn it from his body? He was naked and the nymphs were licking the wine from his skin; so many hungry mouths, so many groping hands. Every cell in his body, every pore was on fire, his cock bursting, aching, begging, demanding release, and yet it would not come. What sorcery was this? What torment!

One by one, the revelers began to leave Analee and pair off with the nymphs that were fondling him. Wine still glistened on his golden, battle-tanned skin as the goddess approached him. All at once, she gripped her cape, raised her arms above her head, and whirled around him closer and closer. It was plain that she meant to cocoon him in the gossamer folds and drive him down in the cool, dewy grass at the edge of the thicket. But Gar resisted, not even knowing why. Something in her strange gyrations suggested entrapment, as if he wasn't already caught in her web.

"Why do you hesitate?" she murmured. " 'Tis all part of the ritual."

"I would rather stand back and feast my eyes upon you, my lady," he returned. She shrugged and continued her strange dance, until she'd spiraled to the ground, her mantle spread out wide.

Gar dropped down beside her. The tall grass was cool around them, and fragrant with scents he had never smelled before, some otherworldly species of wildflower. It reminded him of the heather that grew on the Cornish moors, ruggedly sweet, with the barest trace of the salty mist that drifted overland from the sea. He couldn't see the flowers. All his eyes showed him was the sight of the Goddess of the Dream Well, naked in his arms, divested of her spider silk cloak. All else around them had vanished.

Where had the bonfires gone? Where were the wood nymphs and male revelers? Where were the faery lights? All that remained were the Wills-'o-the Wisp bobbing about in the distance, and the moon beaming down upon their trysting place. It had not yet reached its pinnacle. Soon it would sit high in the indigo vault above, and all too soon thereafter it would begin its descent to keep its rendezvous with the dawn. What would happen then, when his time in Analee's arms was up? He would know soon enough, but now, oh, now! Her soft flesh was underneath him, grinding against him, her slender back arched to welcome his cock. That was all that mattered.

Gar crushed her against him in a smothering embrace. Ghostly mist drifted close, reminding him that when the full moon shone down upon the feast of Sanhain, the veil between the living and the dead was at its thinnest. Which was he? That thought kept trickling back to haunt him, along with Analee's warning that he could only have her for a little while—till dawn. Time was short, and he beat those thoughts back in the rapture of her embrace, for they were both aroused beyond the point of no return.

Lying on the cool ground wet with dew, Gar could almost feel the pulse beat of the land beneath him, for indeed it had a heart, thumping to the rhythm of his own heart. Under the Samhain moon, the Otherworld had a sensual pulse. He'd felt it in the real world, too, but never as strong as now, among these creatures. Even the trees had a pulse; he could feel their roots stirring beneath him, moving in the soil beneath the tall, swaying grass. They were all celebrants in the harvest ritual—living and dead, fay and mortal conjoined under the full round November moon that seemed to shine upon both worlds.

Analee's arms were clasped about his neck as she straddled him. Raising her up with hands that spanned her narrow waist, he lowered her upon his shaft, watching it enter her inch by inch until he'd filled her, gliding on her juices. She felt like liquid silk inside, warm and welcoming. She, too, had a pulse. Right now, it beat for him. But it would not always be so. Once this little interlude was over she would lie thus with another, for that was the nature of the creature she was, this Otherworldly goddess, this sorceress of the well that had granted him ecstasy, but only until dawn. How glorious it would be if such a passion could be had among his own kind. To live in the arms of voluptuous flesh to the end of his days would be rapture, indeed. Such was the stuff of dreams, he knew, but it was a pleasant thought as he raised her up and down along the thick, veined bulk of his cock from root to rimmed tip, gazing at the glisten of her dew upon his skin, upon his shaft as he pumped in and out of her. Engorged, his penis was flushed blue, aching for release, throbbing to the beat of the astral plane palpitating in the very ground beneath him.

He could finally bear no more. Rolling her on her back, he raised her legs and thrust into her in mindless oblivion. She matched him thrust for thrust. The flower of her vulva from clitoris to vagina opening to him petal by petal until she'd captured him totally, rotating beneath him, gripping him with such sucking force his hips jerked forward as he came deep inside her, filling her with the hot rush of his seed.

All was still around them. Not even the wind sighed, though it fluttered the grass bed beneath them. It was a moment before Gar collapsed alongside her, his breast heaving as he gulped air into his lungs. They were alone, but movement among the nearby trees caught in a moonbeam called his eyes there. Someone or something had been watching them, and he strained his lust-glazed eyes, dilated in the darkness, trying to make the image come clear. A horse . . . no, a man . . . no, a *centaur!*

The pulse in the ground beneath them took on a new meter. The thudding of the creature's heavy hooves reverberated through the grassy bed they lay upon. It had an angry beat, though the beast didn't move from its position among the ash and oak trees in that quarter.

Gar raised himself upon one elbow, taking stock of the watcher in the moonlight. It was a magnificent creature, its body the dark four-legged form of a feather-footed destrier, its torso that of a muscular man, whose dark hair worn long was caught at the nape of his neck with a ribbon of vines. Their eyes met, and the creature pawed the ground. The gesture had a ring of warning to it.

"Who . . . *what* is that?" he said, nodding toward the centaur. For he truly thought the strange wine he'd drunk had had its way with him.

Analee shrugged. "'Tis only Yan," she said. "Pay him no mind. He's out of sorts."

"He looks a bit more than simply 'out of sorts,' " Gar observed. The creature looked about to charge, and they were in the open. He got to his feet and took her hand, raising her up alongside. "I think we'd best find suitable shelter elsewhere," he said. "I have no wish to be trampled. Those hooves of his look mean enough to do the job, and I have no sword to defend you."

"There is no need," Analee insisted. "I rule here, Gar Trivelyan. Yan is jealous. Eons ago, he angered the gods, and ever since on all eight sacred feast days throughout the year, he becomes the centaur. That is his punishment. When all the rest are coupling, he is denied me. He is my consort otherwise, you see, but cohabitation while he is in the body of the beast is strictly forbidden him, and so he sulks, and routs, and strikes the ground with his heavy hooves, but 'tis all bluster. He will not harm you. But he is why you can only have me till the dawn, for then his curse is eased. When he is a man again I cannot speak for your safety."

Gar eyed the centaur dubiously. "Yes, well, I still would put some distance between us, if it's all the same to you," he said, leading her away.

"No, not that way," she said, turning him toward a little lake beyond the clearing. "We shall have a sail if you fear him. Yan cannot follow there. The lake is too deep for the centaur."

"I fear no man or beast!" Gar defended. "But I have no weapon to defend you, and unless my eyes deceive me, that thing is armed!"

"I have no need of defending," Analee said. "Yan would never harm me, or you, either. He knows the rules well, though he doesn't like them much, I'll own. But that is his fault, isn't it? Come . . ."

Her words were scarcely out when the twang of an arrow whizzed through the air. It struck the ground inches from Gar's foot. Spinning around, Gar clenched both fists and started back toward the ash grove, but the goddess's quick hand arrested him.

"Pay him no mind," she said. Her voice was soothing and slow. "He will tire of the vigil. It has been thus for many ages. Believe me, he will not harm you, for then he would have to contend with me."

"No harm, eh?" Gar growled. "I just nearly lost a toe."

"No, you did not," Analee said, leading him again. "If he wanted your toe, he would have hit it. Yan is an expert marksman. He always hits his quarry. You are a seasoned sailor, Knight of the Realm, have you not ever had a warning shot fired across your bow upon the sea?"

Gar considered it, a close eye upon the centaur. The irate creature had reloaded his longbow and taken aim again. Analee saw also. Stamping her foot, she spun into a whirling cyclone, parting the tall grass and lifting dead leaves and mulch off the forest floor where the centaur stood among the trees. Puffing out her cheeks she blew a mighty wind that bent the whitethorn, furze, and bracken that hemmed the thicket. Bolting, the creature reared back on his hind legs, pawing the air amid the stinging blizzard of swirling leaves and twigs, acorns and pine needles her ire had raised, and galloped off deep into the forest.

They had reached the edge of the lake. Overhead, the moon had risen to the pinnacle. It would begin its descent now, each moment bringing it closer to the dawn. There wasn't much time left in the arms of the goddess who had granted him her favors for what reason he had yet to discover.

Yes. There were sexual creatures. It all seemed quite natural to them to pair off and enjoy the pleasures of the flesh. But then, he was a seasoned warrior and he had known his carnal moments also. Still, this was different. She had dazzled him with her magic and her beauty, and though he knew it couldn't last beyond the dawn, he had to believe there was a reason for her favors aside from the obvious. She was up to something. He would probe that issue, but not then. Not when the moon was sliding low and the beautiful Goddess of the Dream Well was standing before him naked and willing and ready to pleasure him as he had never been pleasured before.

They had reached the water's edge. It was warm, lapping at their feet and ankles—comfortable, just as everything was in the mysterious Celtic Otherworld, everything except jealous centaurs with longbows. It was bizarre moments like that when Gar was sure it was all a dream, but then he could still feel the wind the arrow made as it struck the ground so close to his foot he felt the shudder of its vibration. One did not feel such things in dreams, but they did feel such in enchantments.

Everyone knew the power of the fay. Didn't the Irish leave their front and back doors open a crack at night to give access to the wee folk that they might pass through unhindered in their night revelries? And didn't the Cornish pay tribute to the knockers in the tin mines to ensure that those little folk would lead them to the richest veins of ore? What had he bought with the tribute he'd tossed into the dream well, the coiled snake bracelet catching glints of moonlight on Analee's arm? Why was he the chosen one? What did it all mean? He longed to know, but feared to ask and break the magical spell she had cast over him.

Analee had taken his hand. A little boat resting in the lapping surf appeared at the edge of the lake. She was leading him toward it. Long and slender, in the shape of a swan, the boat bobbed gently as the calm ripples nudged it. Inside, it was made like a bed, with satin sheets and feather-down quilts. Silver bowls heaped high with grapes and plums and pomegranates set about the bow and stern made his mouth water.

"Come," she said as he handed her into it. "There is much I would show you before the dawn parts us, Gar Trivelyan, but first a moonlight sail."

3

They drifted with the current along the narrow ribbon of moon shimmer on the water as if it were an avenue. Balmy breezes fanned their naked skin, moist with the sweat of sex. There was no need of oars, or rudder. The little swan boat seemed to know the way. Cradled in the arms of the goddess, Gar had eyes for nothing else but the copper-haired, wide-eyed beauty in his arms, until another creature appeared.

Breaking the water's surface, a seal cow appeared; its limpid, human-like eyes seemed strangely familiar. It let loose a mournful wail, melancholy and sad, and lumbered alongside the boat, resting its front flippers on the side rail. Poised there, it peeked in at them, its gaze intense.

Analee vaulted upright. "What do you do here?" she scolded the creature. "Your time is not yet. Get you back to your revelry and leave me to mine, little sister."

The seal wailed again, and to Gar's great surprise, it reached to pet him with its silky flipper, its adoring eyes taking him in with much interest. The creature's touch was scintillating, its body aura charged with iridescence in the moonlight like a halo. An evocative scent of ambergris and salt drifted toward him from its pelt. It blinked and purred and shuddered in the water, making little ripples on the breast of the lake that spread out wide, like a stone makes skipping over the surface, just as her touch sent ripples of sweet sensation radiating through his loins. Instinctively, Gar reached to stroke the creature's sleek, wet head, and it closed its eyes and purred again, leaning into his caress.

Analee vaulted to her feet, nearly upsetting the boat. "Away, I said!" she commanded the seal. "This will not be borne! Get you gone!"

The seal pushed off then, spiraled down into the water with another heart-wrenching moan, and a spectacular show of tail before it disappeared beneath the trail of moon shimmer that was growing steadily wider as the moon descended.

"Why did you chase her?" Gar asked. "She was doing no harm."

Analee sank back down in the boat and reached for him. "She knows her place," she said. "Right now that is in your world. She has no business here now."

"You called her your sister," said Gar, perplexed.

"I call the wood nymphs my sisters, too," the goddess replied. "Otherworldly deities each have their place. They must remain in it. But we all have our alter egos . . ." she added, as if to herself. "And on feasts anything is possible."

The last made no sense, except that it smacked of jealousy. He ignored it. "She is an astral deity, then, that seal?" he asked.

"She is a *selkie*. When the full Samhain moon unites the autumnal currents and the streams collide, the selkies shed their skins in your world. Some mortal men will steal those skins and if they do, the seals that shed them must remain their captors. There are many wonders in our world, Gar Trivelyan. We of the astral choose with care those mortals favored to know our secrets."

"Why have you chosen me?" Gar blurted out. He had been dancing around asking that question since he met the Goddess of the Dream Well.

"Mortal men are too full of logic," she responded through a sigh that moved her naked breasts seductively. "Is it not enough that you have been chosen, knight of the realm? Must you have a reason?"

He shrugged, sinking into her arms. "There must be one," he persisted. He'd brought up the issue. There was no turning back now.

"There is," she said, playing with a lock of his hair, "but it is not for you, a mere mortal, to question the will of the gods." Her finger traced the scowl lines on his face. "Is it so important, really? Are you not pleased with the wonders you have seen here . . . with me?"

"Will I remember them when I return to my own world?" She hesitated, and his heart nearly stopped. It was the bravest question yet, for he had no idea if he would be returning.

". . . That depends," she said at last.

"Upon . . . ?"

"The gods," she said. "They have granted us this time, but it grows short, and we must not waste it . . ."

Fisting her hands in his hair, she pulled his head down until his lips met hers, but Gar had one last question, and he held back, focusing upon the provocative beauty spot above her lip, for he dared not look her in the eyes for this one.

"For all the passion here, there is no love, only lust," he said. "How is that possible?"

Again she hesitated. "The astral is a sensual plane of existence," she said. "What you mortals call love does not exist here. We of the astral view what you call by the name of *lust* as being as normal as breathing. It is a natural function that brings pleasure. We put no moral connotaions upon it. This is what divides our worlds, why one will never understand the other, and why it is best that they be kept apart. Do not look too closely at the giver, Gar Trivelyan. Simply take the gift."

"And yet there is jealousy," Gar continued, trying to ignore her caresses. "That centaur . . ."

Analee laughed. "Yes, there is jealousy," she said, "and possessiveness, but not because of love. You are an intruder here, and the enemy! Have you forgotten who it was that caused the fall that separated our worlds when time began? Man's memory is weak, but not that of we of the astral. Our recollections go back to when mankind and the fay coexisted side by side in one world—before the fall—before the Great War that rent our worlds in two."

Gar gave it thought, but there was still one more thing troubling him. "That seal before," he said. "There was love in her, I sensed it—I felt it . . ."

"The selkies are a breed apart," said Analee. "That is because once shed of their skins they take on human traits, and sometimes actually become human—*too* human."

Gar uttered a guttural chuckle. "I sense a little jealousy here, too," he observed, pulling her closer.

"Rivalry is a more accurate term," she snapped back. "Enough! Do you see that moon up there?" She waved her arm toward it then swept it down toward the shimmer it painted on the breast of the water. "The lower it sinks, the wider the swath," she said, "the wider the swath, the closer the dawn, when we must part. Take the gift, Gar Trivelyan."

Bypassing his mouth, the goddess pulled his head down, feeding him her nipple; it was hard and cool to the touch as he laved it with his tongue, making it harder still. It would not do to anger her in this melancholy mood that had come over her since the seal appeared. He was in her world now. He must play by her rules, but he couldn't free himself of the selkie's touch.

His skin still tingled from the caress of that satiny flipper, and her dark eyes with lashes that made them seem so human haunted him still.

Perhaps it was her wide-eyed innocence that had so captivated him, or the love he felt in her caress that was so conspicuous in its absence among the rest. Whatever the cause, he longed to see the little seal again if only to dispel what she had ignited in him. Meanwhile, the Goddess of the Dream Well had twined her legs around him in the plush bedding that lined the little boat. How smooth and silky soft it felt against the fever in his skin.

Analee trailed her hand in the water, then moistened his lips with it, slipping her index finger inside his mouth. Gar laved it, licking the salt from it, sucking it as her fingertip jousted with his tongue. His hand glided over her belly and thighs and slipped between, parting the petals of her sex, spreading her juices as he probed her layer upon layer until he'd slipped two fingers inside her. How warm and welcoming her body was, thrumming to the rhythm of his caress as her vulva gripped his fingers just as they had gripped his cock.

Straddling her was precarious in the narrow swan boat. Gar's tall, muscular hard-muscled body barely fit in it with her as it was, without managing coupling positions. It would have been safer were she to straddle him, but she made no overtures in that direction, reclining her back upon the feather-down quilts, her long coppery hair fanned out about her on the bolster beneath her head. She looked her in Otherworldly incarnation as if she wasn't real at all, but an illustration in a fine old tome of collected myths.

Lifting her legs, he raised her hips and entered her, watching his hot hard shaft slide inside her, gliding on the wetness of her arousal. Again and again he thrust into her as she clung to him, fisting her hands in his hair, arching her back to take him deeper still. Writhing against him, she slid her hands over her breasts, working her tawny nipples into tall, hard buds between her thumbs and forefingers just as he had done. Looking on through hooded eyes dilated with desire, Gar watched the wide areola of those perfect nipples pucker taut, watched the globes of her breasts flush and harden. His shaft plunged deeper. The sight of her thus sent waves of drenching fire through his loins, each shuddering thrust bringing him closer and closer to climax until at last he could bear no more.

Bending, coupled as they were, was difficult in the close confines of the boat, but he longed to take those nipples in his mouth, longed to lave them with his tongue until she begged for more, until he could feel the contractions of her release as he brought her to climax. Shifting position, he cupped one breast in his massive hand, lowered his anxious mouth, and suckled.

Analee let loose a guttural groan, primeval and deep. Her hips jerked forward and she lurched in his arms as he filled her, matching him thrust for thrust, gripping his cock with her vagina until, on the verge of orgasm, he shifted position and took her deeper still.

The boat began to rock to their rhythm. Faster and faster it heaved from side to side, taking in water, for it was shallow. Swamped, it keeled over when Gar scrambled to his feet attempting to steady it, pitching them both into the lake, as it spiraled down beneath the surface of the water, the swan's neck-shaped prow striking Gar a blow on the head as it sank.

Down, down, Gar plunged dazed into the still, dark water. He'd lost sight of Analee, though he groped for her as he plummeted. He had always been a strong swimmer—even injured—which is what had saved him during the shipwreck, but the glancing blow he'd taken to the head had rendered him nearly senseless, and he fought to stay conscious.

All at once a stream of phosphorescence glided toward him. He felt a sharp nudge that propelled him upward. Something silky soft leaned against him, something vaguely familiar. It raised him up until his head burst through the water and he filled his lungs with great gulps of air as it nudged him up upon the lakeshore coughing and sputtering helplessly.

Rolling on his back, he opened eyes smarting with salt to the sight of the little seal cow bending over him, her head cocked to the side, her enormous eyes sparkling down at him dazzling in the moonlight. There was a large lump on his brow, where the boat's prow grazed him as it sank. Glancing up, he could see the angry bruise surrounding it. The little seal saw it, too. Before he could raise his hand to soothe it, she laid her flipper over the lump. How soothing and cool it felt against the fire in the smarting bruise.

Stroking it, she purred like a cat and sidled closer, flopping down alongside him. How warm her body was, considering that she'd just come from the water, and how comforting as she nuzzled against his heaving chest with her sleek wet nose. Her whiskers tickled. When he brushed them away, she nuzzled his hand, and patted him with her flipper the way she had done in the boat earlier.

Gar couldn't help but smile. "You're a friendly little thing, aren't you?" he said. "I suppose I should thank you. I might have drowned if you hadn't rescued me, little friend. Well done!"

Iridescence glowed around her like a halo in the moonlight at his words just as it had before, but her purring vibrating against his skin alarmed him. It had erotic overtones about it that flagged danger, and he vaulted erect, all but toppling her over. He was aroused. Was it because he'd had another close brush with death, or had this strange selkie creature made him hard with her gentle petting?

He had to keep reminding himself that he was in the astral realm, where all creatures exuded sex as a matter of course and a natural function no more profound than drawing breath. There were no moral strictures here. Creatures went about naked, and mated in public whenever and with whomever they pleased. Having come among them, he'd been caught up in the magic— obliged to behave in like manner, for he'd been chosen by the fay, and one did not refuse that privilege or treat it lightly or without respect, else he fall to disfavor with the astral realm. No one dared risk curses of the Celtic Otherworld, least of all a seasoned warrior who depended upon all the supernatural favors he could glean on his campaigns.

Gar raised his hand to his brow to find that the lump was gone. Had she healed him? She must have done. Now, she flopped around him in the manner of a seal, and seemed to be taking his measure. There was a childlike innocence about her that made her all the more irresistible. One could not help but be endeared to such a creature. It was his natural instinct to embrace her, to stroke her head like he had done in the boat. Something made him resist the urge. Instead he sat spellbound as she waddled around him, her silky flipper petting first his arm, then his hip, then his leg. There was discovery and awe in her touch, as if she had never seen a naked man before. The tactile sensations spread by that gentle touch set his loins on fire. Every cell, every pore in his skin responded to her touch. There was no question as to the cause of his arousal now, and when her raised flipper approached his erect cock, he vaulted to his feet.

"That will do, my curious little friend," he said through a nervous laugh. He stooped and finally succumbed to stroking her head. She looked so forlorn at his rejection of her caress, he couldn't help himself. He couldn't bear the hurt in those huge limpid eyes. She seemed all eyes then, gazing up at him longingly. She was half human after all. "Hadn't you better go back as your sister said?" he urged her. "You wouldn't want to anger her, would you?"

"It is far too late for that!" said the goddess, plowing out of the lake. She approached them, arms akimbo, her long hair curiously dry for having risen from the water. "Get you back where you belong!" she charged the seal, chasing her toward the water's edge.

The seal barked a protest, her reluctance to leave evident in the way she flopped and waddled around him until Analee finally drove her back into the water with the aid of a stick that had washed up on shore. Again the creature wailed. The mournful sound pierced Gar to the core. Their eyes met for the briefest instant before the seal splashed into the water and dove beneath the surface, dodging the stick Analee hurled after her. Seconds later as if waving farewell, the creature rose up and plunged again, her broad tail rising into the air, dripping luminous pearls of water back into the lake, then disappeared.

"So!" the goddess said. "The minute my back is turned, this is what I find. Is this how you would repay my generosity, Gar Trivelyan?"

Gar shrugged. "That creature saved my life, my lady," he defended. "But for her—"

"*I* saved your life, knight of the realm," Analee reminded him, "and gave you my favors. It would do you well to remember that."

"How could I forget?" he returned, the words spoken on the cutting edge of sarcasm.

"Ummm," the goddess grumbled. "However needs must, you would do well to remember your benefactress. Our time is not yet up, Gar Trivelyan."

Gar glanced up at the moon, then toward the still breast of the water and the silvery shimmer that had swallowed the little seal. He recalled the gentle thump of her body that had guided him toward shore. It was not unlike something similar he'd felt after the shipwreck. He'd heard the siren's song then felt something nudging him toward the strand before he stumbled out of the surf. Could the strange little creature have been with him all along? Had she guided him to the Otherworld in the first place when the galley struck the Land's End shoals? So much was unclear, and yet one thing was very clear, indeed. The little seal had touched his heart, and he wondered if he would ever see her again.

4

Gar was leery of the forest, for it was dense and dark, the moon scarcely showing through the canopy of diverse branches intermingled overhead. Here, oak and ash, elm and yew coexisted with pine, the ground grizzled with hawthorn, bracken, and woodbine. They had left the willows behind beside the lake, for willow trees so loved the water and lived beside it in both worlds, so it seemed. All manner of magical tree and plant life lived here, and the trees seemed alive, as curious as the little seal as he passed among them following the Goddess of the Dream Well deeply in.

Leaves, vines, branches, and tendrils groped him as he followed a narrow footpath, acutely aware that he was being watched. The centaur, he had no doubt, though Analee didn't seem to notice, or if she did she made no mention of it. Gar was beginning to part the veil she'd cast before his eyes to mystify and confuse. He was beginning to see her intent for what it really was. He was not her guest, as she would have him believe, he was her *captive*, until the dawn. What happened then evidently depended upon what he did while under her spell.

Gar had heard of people disappearing after an encounter with the fay, never to be seen or heard from again. The Celtic Otherworld was populated with creatures, one cleverer than the next, who delighted in playing pranks upon mortals. It had been thus since the fall that separated the races and split the worlds in two. Yes, they were, indeed, a clever lot, but so was mortal man, and Gar was beginning to regret he'd ever stumbled upon the dream well and its enigmatic goddess guardian. But it was too late for those thoughts now. He would have to play her game until dawn, and hope he could outwit her and escape. He had no desire to spend eternity in the Celtic Otherworld. The trick would be to manage it without invoking her wrath. Judging from the look of her now, from the staccato spring in her step, the stiff set of her lips, and her silence as she led him deeper and deeper into the wood, it did not bode well.

"Have you dominion over these?" he asked her, gesturing toward the trees, meanwhile removing one branch that had gripped his torso familiarly as he passed it by.

"I am the Goddess of the Dream Well. There is where my dominion lies. Only the greater gods have dominion here among the ancient ones."

"But they heed you," Gar said. "I see them genuflect as you pass by."

"They show respect, yes," she said. "It is unwise to disrespect any deity. Why do you ask?"

The path they followed narrowed suddenly, or was it that he'd just begun to notice the trees on either side crowding close? He opened his mouth to speak, but too late. The goddess waved her hand, and a sturdy oak reached out its branches and tethered him by the arms to its vine-covered trunk.

"...And they do my bidding!" she concluded. Strolling back and forth before him, she pointed to the obvious. "You are aroused," she said. "The little seal's doing, while I was left beneath the lake!"

Gar popped a bitter laugh. "You cannot fault her for this," he said. "I've been aroused since I arrived here. You have seen to that. And as to leaving you, the sinking boat struck me in the head. But for that little seal, I would have drowned. She saved my life."

"*I* saved your life," she reminded him.

"Yes, you did," he returned, "and you gave me your favors until dawn. There is still some time left before that, and I can hardly do you justice tied to this tree. Turn me loose! Believe me, I perform much better as a guest than a captive."

She continued to stroll around him. "In due time," she purred.

He shrugged. "You are the one continually telling me time is short," he said. "Suit yourself."

Her eyes flashed, and she seized his cock, wrenching a groan that smacked of an odd mix of lust and surprise that startled even him. "Do you mean to say that little seal didn't cause this to harden?" she demanded. "I saw you two just now!"

"Then you saw naught but the sort of affection a man might have for his faithful dog." That wasn't entirely true, for he saw something in the little seal that struck an affectionate chord and touched his heart. Inside that sealskin, there lived an entity that could take the form of a woman, a woman who could be his for the taking if he possessed her pelt. A woman with childlike innocence possessed of a tenderness that he had never known. There was something magnetic about such a tender nature. Something once tasted no man could resist, least of all Gar Trivelyan, who had never known the like.

Secretly, he longed for the little seal's tender touch, longed for her adoring eyes and benevolent nature, for that truly was a nurturing facet of the little creature's makeup, an attribute conspicuously absent in the goddess. But it wasn't the animal. It was the creature within shining through that so enthralled him to the point that he was becoming obsessed with seeing that creature in its human form. He was haunted by the longing to see if the attributes he so admired in the seal carried over in her human incarnation.

These secrets of the heart he could not share with the goddess. It would not do to anger her. His future was still suspect. For all he knew he would never return to his own world. It was more than likely that he would remain a captive in this plane of existence ruled by libidinous lust for the rest of his life, if in fact he still had a life. It did not bode well.

Her hand tightened around his cock and he sucked in a hasty breath. There was no question that she had the touch, no argument that she possessed the power to arouse and fulfill like no other he'd ever known. Her deft fingers were picking out the distended veins in his shaft as she sidled closer, flaunting her nakedness. She'd come so close he could feel her body radiating toward him. She was on fire, so steamy hot he feared his cock would burst into flame under the friction of her touch. He could feel the blood thrumming through the pulsating veins she stroked so skillfully. She was about to finish what had started deep within his loins when the little seal nearly touched his genitals on the lakeshore. The difference was the enigmatic little selkie did not have to touch him to set his pulse racing and riddle his loins with drenching fire. If he were to come now, it would be the selkie's doing, not the hand of the goddess that stroked him so relentlessly. For it was a different hand entirely that stroked him now, playing his body like a fine musical instrument. As skilled as that hand was, there was no love in it. No. This, he would not let on to the Goddess of the Dream Well.

"I do not like tethers," he said. "Have this ancient one unhand me else I break its branches. I am well able, you know. That I remain thus is out of deference to you, but I grow tired of this game. It would be wise to let me go now."

"You change the subject easily enough," she observed. "You have not answered my question."

"I give no credence to it," he said succinctly. "What you accuse is too impossible to deserve an answer, and a moot point. What are you doing there is about to make me come. Would that not be more enjoyable if I had the use of my arms, my lady?"

"Oh, I don't know," she purred, sauntering closer still, so close her hardened nipples touched his chest and his cock leaned heavily against her slit. "There is something very provocative about bringing a bound man to climax." She began rubbing herself against his shaft, slow undulations that threatened to drive him mad. "See how it lives for me?" she murmured.

She ground the petal-like folds of her vulva harder against him, and he strained against his tether. To his dismay, he found that he could not break his bonds as he had boasted. The tree branches were possessed of superhuman strength. They were enchanted, as were the vines that roped him now, climbing his body, binding him to the trunk of the ancient tree, while she had her way with him.

"It must be nearly dawn," he said. "Can we not find a more comfortable way to couple?"

The goddess laughed. "Time means nothing here, knight of the realm," she said. "Dawn here and dawn in your world are two entirely different things."

From somewhere deep in the fuzzy labyrinth of his memory, Gar recalled hearing that time as mortals knew it did not exist in the Celtic Otherworld. A pity he hadn't remembered earlier. But he would not dwell upon that then. It was clear that Analee wasn't going to release him until she'd satisfied the lust that was inherent in her, the libidinous drive that powered all the fay. There was much he needed to know, much he needed to ask her, but not while her skilled fingers were setting fire to his moist skin, and her body was charging his loins with unstoppable lust. While she was his guest, his slave, his *captive*, he was under her spell. She had made him what she was for the duration of his stay. How long would that be? How long before the dawn? He was almost afraid to ask these questions, though what flimsy shred of humanity he still possessed in this enchanted place demanded he do so, just not yet . . .